OUT OF THE CAVE

OUT OF THE CAVE

an anthology
compiled by MacKenzie Publishing

contributions by

Chantal Boudreau, Chiara De Giorgi, Kevin M. Folliard
Heron Greenesmith, Alan Kemister, S.L. Kerns
Matthew D. Laing, Rod Martinez, Stephen Millard
Val Muller, A.W. Powers, Kathy Price, Kristin Roahrig
Tom Robson, Katherine Sanger, A.P. Sessler
E.F. Schraeder, Paul Stansbury, Jeff C. Stevenson
Randy Whittaker, Cassandra Williams

CONTENTS

FOREWORD

I have been writing scary stories for over forty years, and over those forty years I have probably sat at about four hundred tables stacked with my books, selling and signing copies for the book-buying public. If you want to grab a piece of paper and a pen and do the math for a minute, I'll be more than happy to sit here and wait.

Are you done now?

Good.

Then let's move on.

At each of those four hundred or so book-signing tables, I have had about fifty people out of the two hundred or so that came and visited one of my book signing tables on any given day of the year walk up to me and say something along the lines of "Brrr...scary stories. Those look way too scary for me," or else "Brrr...scary stories. Those look way too scary for my kids."

Bushwah, bull-puck and balderdash, says I.

Scary stories are good for kids.

In fact, I am going to clamber right out onto the highest limb of the tallest creepy old tree in the darkest Nova Scotia forest that you can find and start sawing away with my rustiest and most blood-stained handsaw bravely—on account of I believe that it just isn't healthy to be scared of being scared.

There is absolutely nothing wrong with a good scary story.

Take a moment and think about it.

You drill right down into the very heart of storytelling, and you are going to realize that stories are about people solving problems.

You take the story of Frankenstein. At the heart of it, Frankenstein is the story of a man dealing with his child. Old Doctor Frankenstein created this big old bolt-necked monster with the idea that he was building himself a brilliant future—and then all of a sudden he realized that he had created a monster.

How many parents out there have raised a child thinking to themselves that little Tommy or little Amy was going to grow up to be just like them, only better—and then, by extension, people would look at little Tommy or little Amy and think to themselves, "By golly, what a wonderful parent they must have." And then all of a sudden little Tommy or little Amy starts knocking down villagers and windmills and wandering pitch-fork-and-torch-wielding mobs and Poppa Frankenstein suddenly has to figure out how to deal with the seven-foot-tall, corpse-stitched, lightning-charged monster/ kid that he has built.

Or—if you want to get away from the booga-booga horror genre—how about the World War 2 story of Anne Frank? That, at the heart of it, is the story of a young girl attempting to learn how to cope with the idea of her family having to hide in an attic from a regime of genocidal Gestapo agents who at any moment in time might come kicking down the door of that attic and drag her family off to a concentration camp.

Can you smell the fear that is hiding in that story?

Or—how about Gary Paulsen's young adult novel *Hatchet*, that tells the story of a young boy who crash lands in the heart of the deep Northern woods and has to figure out how to survive with nothing more than a hatchet and a handful of hope. He almost starves, he faces wild animals and he learns how to overcome his fear.

Each of those stories—in their own way—is a scary story about learning how to deal with fear.

And that—more than anything else—is what a good scary story teaches you.

And that—more than anything else—is why good scary stories are important for young kids to read.

Kids of all ages CONSTANTLY live in the shadow of fear. Am I going to be good enough? Are my parents going to get divorced? Am I going to be popular enough? Will Dad lose his job? Can I pass that darned math test? Will those bullies leave me alone?

Fear—kids live in it constantly—and a good scary story teaches a kid how to deal with fear. And THAT, more than anything else, is why you ought to let your kids read all of the scary stories that they can get their hands on.

So let's do that today.

Pick up this book and buy it and give it to your kid.

Let's drag scary stories out of the darkness of the cave.

Yours in Storytelling,

Steve Vernon
June 11, 2016

PREFACE

This is MacKenzie Publishing's first anthology, and I'm pleased with the calibre of stories submitted. Unfortunately, there were many good stories I had to decline.

The stories herein are a mixture of fantasy, supernatural, and suspense, with dabs of horror tossed into the mix. Though adults would enjoy these stories, they are geared for youth as young as thirteen. My goal for this book is to instill the love of reading in teenagers. Alas, my sweet grandchildren will too soon be at that stage, and I hope they'll still be reading.

Seasoned writers know the beginning of a story or book should hook the reader. Similarly, the writing should end on a high note. I believe I have accomplished this feat. The foreword by Steve Vernon, *Nova Scotia writer, storyteller, and master of the booga-booga,* is amazing. And in the back is a special treat: one of his flash fiction stories—a mere 172 words—an excellent close to this book. (Check out Steve's profile, too, and his other great reads.)

This isn't to say the stories compiled here don't deserve merit on their own. They do—all of them!—or they wouldn't have been selected for this book. Read them, and you'll agree with me.

On the last page, check out the links. Follow MacKenzie Publishing to keep apprised of other projects and "like" the Facebook pages.

Two Eyes Open (horror for adults) will be MacKenzie Publishing's next anthology. Hmm...which famous horror writer should I approach for that foreword?

As always, any errors are mine.

Cathy MacKenzie
MacKenzie Publishing
August 1, 2016

OUT OF THE CAVE
an anthology

OUT OF THE CAVE

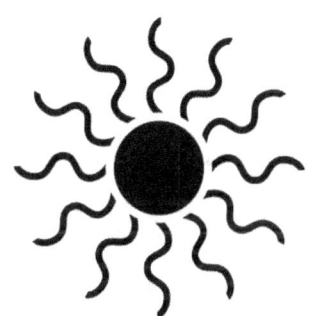

Cassandra Williams

Jamie has never known his grandfather to lie, but the boy still wonders whether trolls exist. And he is determined to find out once and for all.

Gramps insists trolls don't live in the cave by White Rock Bridge, but I don't believe him. I've never seen a troll—not that I want to. He hasn't either, so how can he say none exist? Just because you don't see something doesn't mean it isn't there.

"Trolls live in caves. Everyone knows that. And there's that *Three Billy Goats Gruff* story," I say.

Gramps laughs. "I've been in that cave many a time when I was your age. Never saw tail nor hide of no troll. And that goat story is just that—a story, a fairy tale."

"But Gramps, sometimes fairy tales are real. And couldn't the troll have come after you left?"

Gramps moved from Beaconsville when he was a teenager and returned to marry Grandma. Anything could have happened in the years he was gone—more than enough time for a troll to materialize.

But no, he shoots down that theory, too. "I hardly think trolls have come in the last fifty years."

"But trolls eat people. Maybe that's why no one has seen them. No one is left alive to tell about it." I picture stubby trolls jumping on people, tearing off their limbs, yanking flesh from bones. But are trolls that strong? From pictures I've seen, they look old like Gramps, and I don't think Gramps can do stuff like that. Plus trolls are smaller than him.

Gramps laughs again. His gnarled fingers mess my hair. "Trolls don't exist else'n I would've seen one by now. Besides, trolls turn to stone when the sun hits them. So if'n such a creature existed, you'd never see it unless you have cat eyes and saw it before it hardened."

I picture the brutes exiting dark caves, the sun hitting them and turning them to stone. "Does that mean we're safe when the sun shines? Stones don't hurt people unless we throw them."

Gramps is fed up with me. "Run off and play now."

I go to my room and plop to my bed. Those stupid trolls won't leave my mind.

My friends and I play around White Rock Bridge, but we stay clear of the cave. We've all read the tales of trolls. Isn't a cave near a bridge too coincidental? Even though I've told my friends that Gramps says trolls don't exist, they're still not brave enough to enter the cave. Not even me, and I trust Gramps. But we're still curious, always wondering.

The next day after school, Calvin, Brian, and I saunter down to the river. We don't mean to veer as close to the cave as we do, but suddenly there we are, still and solemn before it as if paying respects to a dearly beloved at a funeral. And I'm positive deadly fangs line the peripheral, the blackness a wide yawn that threatens to chew us to bits.

I eye my friends, hoping they don't see me trembling. What are we doing? Who's going to speak first?

"We going in?" Brian asks.

Calvin shakes his head. "Nope, not me. What about you, Jamie? You said your grandfather doesn't believe in trolls. You gonna prove him wrong? You gonna prove him right? Which is it?"

I wish I'd never repeated Gramps' words, but Gramps knows everything. If the old man says nothing lives in the cave and trolls don't exist, then that must be true, but it's still scary, and I don't

2

want to look like a sissy. It doesn't matter that none of my friends want to enter the cave either.

I fiddle with my hat. "Nah."

Brian's looking at me. "Double dog dare ya."

Despite my ball cap, the sun hits my face. In my nightmares, trolls hold me hostage or chase me through woods. How can I dispute their existence? Will the sun really turn them to stone? But what happens in the cave? There's no sun inside, and I won't be able to see. I hear Gramps' words: *"Trolls don't exist."*

Calvin and Brian chant and cajole and point at me. "Come on, Jamie. Be a man. Don't you believe your grandfather?"

Do I believe Gramps? *"Trolls don't exist."* I glance from one sneering face to the other and shiver despite the heat. I'll be the butt of jokes the next day at school if I don't do what they want.

How deep is the cave? Can I dart in and out before the troll notices?

I move one foot. Can I move the other? Should I turn and race home, let Ma protect me? Pa won't, but my mother will. Pa will laugh at me, call me a sissy. What will Gramps do?

I take a step. A few more and the ordeal can be over. Sweat soaks my T-shirt. I rub my arm across my clammy forehead.

"Okay." I shuffle toward the cave. Calvin and Brian cheer me on, their voices ricocheting from the cliff to my ears.

At the entrance, I stop and stare into the gaping, endless black hole. A huge shadow sweeps over me, and I'm covered in darkness as bleak as I imagine the inside of the cave will be. The troll!

I scream.

My friends scream.

And we all run, speeding as fast as we can alongside the riverbed to the relic of the rowboat, up the bank to the bending birches, and across the field to the playground. Once there, we fight for our breath. We butt fists and go home.

At school the next day, no mention is made of the day before. Calvin and Brian can't say anything, really, since they fled as I did. At the three o'clock bell, I wave goodbye to my friends and stroll to the river, toward the cave.

Last night in bed, I pondered shadows and how the sun possesses an uncanny ability to enlarge objects into odd shapes different from the original. The shadow that covered me was massive, and when the sun threw the image against the cave, I thought I saw the engorged nose and squat body of a troll. But the shadow didn't move—not once it covered me. Or didn't I stay long enough? Did our shouting lure the troll from the cave and the sun turn it to stone? If so, I'll be safe. But what if the shadow was something else? Something real?

The sun hangs to my left. Is it in the same position as the day before? We were there about four o'clock. In another half hour, the elements might align to precisely replicate yesterday's shadow.

I don't have patience, but I wait. I trust Gramps, who would never knowingly lie, but what if he's wrong? Though he said trolls don't exist, he talked about the sun changing them to stone. If trolls aren't real, why would he say that?

And then the shadow appears. I know what it is—not a troll but the sun projecting a dying, podgy pine from across the cliff, and now the cave's grim orifice isn't so scary.

I'm glad I remembered to bring a flashlight. It'll lead the way and keep me safe. But still, can I go in?

Gramps words float around me: *"There's no such thing as trolls."* I hear my father's voice, *"Be a man,"* and my mother: *"Be careful, young man."* But, of course, my parents' warnings are generalizations and have nothing to do with trolls.

What if my theory is wrong? I shudder. Clouds threatening showers stray overhead. The shadows are gone.

I look around for new rocks or boulders, but too many exist to know whether any of them have changed.

I turn on the flashlight, take a deep breath, and enter the cave. The musty, dank smell confronts me.

A few minutes into the cavern, the flashlight reveals a rough, curving wall. The ground is splattered with small, loose stones but not a speck of anything out of the ordinary.

"Gramps is right," I mutter.

While leaving the cave, an idea comes to me. I race home. In the kitchen, I shove several chalk pieces into my back pocket. From the shed, I grab Pa's rabbit trap and small shovel, and I speed back into the woods, where I set the trap. The forest is full of small animals. It won't take long.

After searching the ground for several minutes, I find my dog's grave. Rover. When I buried him a few months ago, I stuck a branch deep into the ground for a cross. I dig a couple of feet until I reach bones and haul them up. I shake off as much dirt and rotted flesh as I can and drop the bones in my knapsack. I return to the trap, where a squirming, squalling squirrel greets me.

I head back to the cave. The storm clouds have disappeared, and the sun beats down.

When I enter, the cave swallows me. I creep to the cave's end, the flashlight leading the way. Holding the light in my left hand, I scribble primitive figures and animals on the walls. I arrange the brittle bones in a pile, like logs primed for a bonfire.

The squirrel's pitiful, pleading eyes bore into mine. I thrust the serrated knife into its fur. Blood gushes across my fingers and down my shirt. I sever the head and, holding the body, drip crimson over the floor and fling guts against the walls.

I breathe deeply. Done. Perfect. I giggle. I'll be a hero when I'm the last man standing.

***

Calvin and Brian, always eager for adventures and hearing of my uneventful trek into the cave the day before, follow me back to the cave. We stare at the looming black hole.

"Did you really go in?" Calvin asks.

"Yep."

Brian shivers. "It looks dark."

"Darker than I remember," Calvin says.

"I have a flashlight." I pull it from my pocket and brandish it in the air. "Let's go."

"Ya, let's," Brian says. "I'm not scared. And your grandfather says it's safe, right?"

Calvin adds, "And you said you went in yesterday, eh Jamie?"

"Yep, I did. And that's why I went in. Because I trust Gramps. And there was nothing there."

We enter the cave. I'm in the lead, controlling the flashlight. I shuffle, waiting for the others to catch up. "Come on."

And then we're at the end. I keep the light away from the items I planted and shine it on my friends' faces. They're standing shoulder to shoulder, about to cling to each other like frightened little kids. I kinda giggle inside.

I swing the light to highlight the bonfire of bones and the cakey blood on the dusty floor and the chalk images on the pockmarked wall.

I quickly swerve the beam to Calvin and Brian again. Their mouths are wide and rounder than their eyes. They stand still for several seconds until they jump as if a busted wind-up toy was given sudden life.

Snickering, I aim the flashlight on their disappearing backsides. "Sissies." My shriek echoes. I click off the light, but by then they're gone.

I switch on the flashlight and head out. When daylight hits me, I gulp unspoiled air. The cave stinks of decay and must and mould.

Above me, storm clouds have returned, dark and menacing. And then an immense shadow as black as my father's too-small funeral suit slowly spreads over me.

I'm rooted like a tree trunk. Can I break free from limbs and leaves? I quiver. Is it a troll? More than one? I hope I look as inconsequential as a maggot on a cadaver.

Gramps' words blast in my ears: *"Trolls don't exist."* But if not a troll, what is it? I can't breathe. I want to scream, but leaves are stuck in my throat. My heart thunders up to my clogged throat. There's no escape.

It's a troll!

The hooked nose juts from the edge of the shadow, crashing upon the boulders. I inhale a great breath, and the air is sucked from me when the nose moves like it's sniffing at something it's never smelled before—me, a human—and it'll gobble me up.

As if a gunshot announces the start of a race—*on your mark, get set, go*—I'm propelled from blackness. My legs take off like those of a greyhound. And I'm gone, streaking after my friends.

PROPER METHOD

Stephen Millard

It's Jonathan Regier's fifteenth birthday, and he has two things on his mind: Autumn and her sundress. All he wants for his birthday is to see her. Unfortunately, his father has other plans. A lesson must be taught this day, and it's one Jonathan will never forget.

Jonathan Regier flung his backpack over his shoulder and headed down the stairs that led to the front door of his family's split-level farmhouse. When his feet hit the hollow tile landing, his dad called to him from the basement.

"Yes, sir?" John replied, turning around to face him.

His father stood at the bottom of the stairs, polishing the grease off a piston from a tractor engine. He'd been fixing it up all winter so that it'd be ready for planting season, a day away.

"You be back by dinner now. Your momma is makin' your favorite, and remember, we've got a surprise for you."

"Yes, sir." John turned and grabbed the door knob, pulling the door open.

"And, John," his father said, smiling with one corner of his mouth, his chewing tobacco prohibiting otherwise, "Happy Birthday."

John smiled back, with both corners of his mouth, and ran out the door and down the front steps. He scooped up his bike and hopped on, speeding off before he had both feet on the pedals. The wind rushed through his hair, which was how he gauged how fast he went.

It isn't enough, he thought as the smile broadened across his face and his legs pushed as hard as they could. But it wasn't ever going to be fast enough, not for this journey.

Although it was his fifteenth birthday, he wasn't thinking about that. He wasn't thinking about the presents or the dinner party that would be ready for him when he got back. He only thought of the way Autumn looked right before school let out. How she laughed and put her hand on his shoulder, saying, "Happy Birthday, John. What are we doing tonight?"

He thought about the summer dress she had worn that day after a winter's worth of pants and long sleeves, looking like the sun, warm with spring just to see her, had returned. Would she be wearing it again or, oh boy, maybe a special dress worn for his birthday?

John couldn't help but smile. And it wasn't a toothless, polite smile people get when they feel uncomfortable. It was a huge, overtaking jester's smile. A smile so big you had to open your mouth just to fit it all on your face. A smile that no matter the date made you feel as though it was your birthday when you wore it. And wear it he did, all the way down the dirt road and into town, past the school he'd left that afternoon, and through the small town's main street. He flew by greetings and hellos, leaving people with their hands still waving and smiles running across their faces from seeing his. All the while, his legs pushed as hard as they could.

He must've done twenty-five or thirty miles per hour the whole way to Autumn's house, and when he got there, he wasn't even tired. Sucking air like a bellows maybe, but not tired. His mind was too full of thoughts about her to even consider it.

He jumped off his bike and briskly walked it to the porch, where he propped it against the railing before climbing the steps to the front door. When he raised his fist to rap on the door, a voice gave him a start.

"John, the birthday boy." Autumn's mother sat on the porch.

John loved living in a small town, where it was as if everyone celebrated his birthday with him.

"Hello, Mrs. Winthrop."

"You lookin' for my Autumn?" she asked with a suspicious smile.

"Yes, ma'am."

"Well, she ain't here. Should be back tonight, though. Why don't you come by after dinner? I'll have some peach cobbler with your name on it."

That's odd, he thought, thinking back on his and Autumn's conversation a couple of hours previously at school.

He gestured to the front door. "Oh, she told me to come by, but that sounds lovely. Thank you, ma'am." He smiled, but it wasn't quite as big as it had been when he arrived.

She tipped her glass to him. "We'll see you soon then."

"Okay, see you soon," he said, going back down the steps.

"And tell your folks I said hello."

"Will do, ma'am."

And once again he was off, though his bottom sadly sat on the seat and his hands barely gripped the handlebars. His feet felt like marshmallows, squishing against the pedals rather than pushing them.

"I got stood up," he mumbled. "Plain and simple."

He thought back, wracking his brain to find something he had missed, and there it was. She might've been flirting with him a bit at school. But girls in high school did that all the time, didn't they? Almost as if they couldn't help it. And she was the worst of 'em. He knew that when he suddenly remembered Richie Bartlett coming over to her after he'd walked away, *right after* she asked him what they were doing that night. That jock prick probably asked why she wanted to be with a farmin' boy and teased her until she didn't want to be with him.

But she was so *sweet!* She never cared what people thought, and moreover, she punched that Richie right *in* the prick when he wouldn't leave her alone about going with him to the spring formal. *She was going with me*, he reminded himself, and his feet became a little more solid.

Then he stopped pedaling and glided down the street when a flash of realization came to him that changed everything. It was what his dad had said: *"And remember, we've got a surprise for you."*

His legs pushed even harder than they had when he had headed to Autumn's house. *They tricked me!* His mind fired. *They tricked me so I'd leave and they could set up signs and banners and blow up balloons.*

He laughed at the thought of his parents working in cahoots with Autumn and shook his head in embarrassment, flinging out all thoughts of doubt. *She didn't stand me up; she is the surprise!*

His mind celebrated all the way home, to the baffled amusement of everyone he passed for the second time within a half hour. The brakes on his tires screeched when he reached the driveway, and he flew up the steps two at a time and flung open the door, with his breath held deep in his chest.

But there were no decorations. No signs or banners or balloons. It looked exactly the same as when he had left. His newly fifteen-year-old mind was more confused than ever. But there was still hope.

He ran up the stairs and looked to his right into the living room. His mother sat on the couch, reading a magazine. She looked at him with vacuous eyes.

He opened his mouth to ask a question but then realized he didn't know what to say, and his shoulders slumped yet again with doubt.

"You need to go talk to your father," she said. Her voice sounded like she'd just recovered from being very mad. "He's out in the barn." She looked back at her magazine.

John glanced into the kitchen and saw steam rise from the pot where his favorite stew simmered. The only sound in the house was its bubbling.

"Go on," she urged.

Their eyes locked again, and then it was as if she couldn't bear it any longer. She stood, threw the magazine on the couch behind her, and rushed into the bathroom. After the door slammed shut, he heard the unmistakable sounds of her softly crying.

From where he stood, he could see the barn through the sliding glass doors at the back of the house. The barn doors were open, spilling an artificial glow into the dying natural sunlight.

He opened the sliding door and turned on the patio light. It glowed and buzzed, and he noticed a dark drop of red at the edge of the concrete slab. He walked over, examined it, and looked back to the open barn door. The grass hadn't been cut that week. He would do it the following day. With the few inches of rain from the night before last, the grass stood a good four inches. He saw an arching line as if something had been dragged through the thick grass, matting the grass to the earth, with footprints blending in every so often.

John walked directly along it. He reached the barn and peered inside as if he hadn't been told his dad had asked for him and more like John spied on him.

"John." His dad's voice boomed from inside. John entered, his feet crunching on hay, and found another red drop against the gold. "Come over here."

His father was feeding the horses. They had two of them, and John walked over and petted the one his dad wasn't feeding.

"As you know, you're going to start having more responsibilities around the farm now that you're fifteen." His dad stopped and stared at him. "I'll also pay you hourly. Five bucks to start, then up to ten if you want to stick around after high school."

John nodded, still thinking about the way his mom had looked at him before she began to cry.

"Now, I'm not gunna take it easy on you just 'cause you're my son. The work'll be the same."

"Never have, sir."

His father smiled again. "We get the best yield out of any farm in the county."

John nodded, knowing that already.

"And we plan to keep it that way." His dad paused.

Under his heavy gaze, John grew uncomfortable.

"Do you know how we do it every year?"

John shrugged.

"You speak when you're spoken to, boy." His father turned to face him, head on.

"Hard work, good seed, proper method—"

"You've got it with that last one."

His father continued staring, and John took on a look of uncomfortable confusion.

"Hard work is good and all, but the Andersons work hard. The Vickroys work hard, and shit, those damn Farrows have got five boys workin' harder than you or I ever have. But you know what they don't have?" His father moved in, talking quietly. "*Proper method*. Just like you said. In fact, that's your surprise."

"I don't understand, sir." John still wondered about Autumn.

"I just have to see if you're up for it."

They stood looking at each other for a moment. His father placed his arm around John's shoulder and led him to the back of the barn. "Do you love this farm, son?"

"Yes, sir." John was nervous.

"Would you do anything for it?"

"Yes, sir."

11

His dad stopped at a door that led to where the shed conjoined with the barn. John saw more red on the handle. His father motioned for him to open it. John didn't move.

"Daddy, why was Momma cryin'?"

His father opened the door.

The lights weren't on, but in the dimness John saw something hanging at the back of the shed.

"We have to do things. You called 'em proper method, and I think that's just about as good a way to say it as any. And we've always done it. Ever since my granddaddy owned this farm, our family has done it this way, and it's always proved to work. And you'll have to continue it after I'm gone." He turned on the lights with a loud clunk, and the room came to life.

When John saw a girl hanging from shackles at the wall, he instinctively backed up. His father halted him with a strong hand on his back.

"Daddy," John whispered.

Then his father propelled him forward, pushing him toward her. The girl's head hung forward as did her body, from chains that held her arms to the wall, making her hair flow over her down-turned face. John, his eyes huge and horrified, looked her up and down. When they got a bit closer, his dad pulled a chain that turned on another light and illuminated her body. John's heart stopped when he saw her summer dress.

"Autumn?" He couldn't stomach it. He turned to run, but his father picked him up at the waist and turned him back around.

"No, no, no," his father said, walking over to the girl, placing John inches away. "Why would I do that to you?" His voice was genuine as if he could sound caring while having a girl chained in his shed. He grabbed a handful of hair and lifted her head, his knuckles buried in the strands.

John's breath left him in a whoosh of sick relief. "Who is she?"

"Our proper method," his dad replied and reached over to the wall where a knife hung. He handed it to his son. "Do it right here." He drew an imaginary line with his finger on her neck.

"What?" John, holding the knife, gazed at the girl. Her chest rose up and down with slow breaths, her eyes closed but her mouth open slightly.

His father continued looking at him.

"She's alive."

His father nodded.

"You want me to—?" John glanced at the knife he held with two hands, one on the handle and one under the blade.

"Yes," his father replied, still holding her head up by the hair. "For the harvest."

***

After showering, John stopped shaking. His hands and forearms were a little pink but were, for the most part, clean. He dried off and with one hand wiped the steam off the mirror, captivated by his red, tearless eyes. He pondered for a moment, and a small proud smile, much like his father's, spread from one corner. He hadn't cried.

His father shouted from the other side of the bathroom door. "Autumn called. Told her you'd call back once you were out of the shower."

John didn't feel like a kid anymore. He dressed and, after calling Autumn and listening to her apologize before expressing excitement about seeing him, entered the dining room. His mother looked terrified to see him as if he'd risen from the dead, but his father had never looked more proud.

John sat at the table and, like an animal, devoured the bowl of stew prepared for his special day.

I WAIT

Chiara De Giorgi

When her mom and dad buy a beautiful house in the countryside, a teenager is not quite happy about their choice. The night before moving, her parents have a bad fight; she gets mad and leaves. She reaches the new house at nightfall, and in the darkness, she finds something that will change her fate forever.

"We've finally found it! Our dream house!"

I can still hear my mother's thrilled voice, echoing in this empty hall. But she's not here. And those words were told somewhere else.

She'll be here soon—of that I've no doubt—and her voice *shall* resound in these rooms. I don't think it will be thrilled, though—ha ha ha.

It might be useful to take a step back actually, otherwise you'll understand nothing.

This is the story of a typical troubled teenager—me—who does something unbelievably stupid just to make a point.

***

I've been on the move since birth. I've changed house, town, school, teachers, friends, volleyball team, and doctor seven times in fourteen years. Then one day I come back from school and my mother welcomes me with the above-mentioned delighted cry (the *"we've finally found it—our dream house"* one).

Since my father had health problems last year, he changed his job and now doesn't need to travel as much as he did before. Which means we can finally stop moving every two years or so to follow him around.

If I had a choice, which of course I don't, I wouldn't choose to live in this town. Anyway, I must admit this is not the worst place we've been so far, so I'm cool enough with their decision to stay here. But why do we need a new house? For once we're not changing towns, but I still have to pack my stuff and move to a new neighbourhood, new school, new volleyball team, and so on. Hurray!

"It's so lovely, you'll see!" Mother smiles. "It's a small house, with a peaked roof, and a great hall with a stone fireplace. Your bedroom is gorgeous. The walls are upholstered in white wooden panels. There's a roof window and a large normal window, and you can see the garden from there. And wait 'til you see the garden. It's huge! There's an ancient willow tree and a wooden bench beneath, which looks like it's just come out of a fairy tale. And there's a grove besides—an actual grove! Can you imagine?"

She's so enthusiastic, I want to punch her. They bought a house? A *house*? Without asking me?

"I can't wait," I say, flatly. "I'm going to wear a pretty little red-hooded cape, so I'll be lunch to the first wolf I shall meet, and my useless existence will ultimately make sense."

***

When I allow them to drive me to see this marvellous house of theirs, it's a typical autumn day: sunny and cold. The trees are half bare, and a soft mist rises from the ground. The sun is blurred, the light annoying. I smell wet leaves, fresh mushrooms, burning wood. The silence is quite overwhelming.

We leave the main road and drive up an unpaved track, cutting through a scrub of small bushes. Is this the *grove* Mother ranted about?

I hear a train whistle far away, beyond the fog. The glaring sunlight hurts my eyes. Mother keeps on chirping, and I feel a headache approaching. At long last even Father gets annoyed by her, and they start bickering. Again.

They've been quarrelling about nonsense for the past few months. Great timing, Old Ones! You've just bought a *house*! You should've kept the money for a lawyer and got yourselves a divorce instead.

I tie my scarf around my neck, put my hands in my pockets, and get away. I'm home, aren't I?

I walk behind the house, and I confess what I see takes my breath away for a moment. The grounds extend as far as I can see. Around the house, it's all green, and behind the ancient-willow-tree-with-fairy-tale-bench-underneath is the grove Mother talked about. And it's quite a large one, indeed! The path leading there is covered in leaves, red and yellow; it curves behind big trees and then disappears.

All right: I wasn't expecting anything like this. This place is crazy!

I walk down the path, and I'm all excited. I fantasize right away, foreseeing long afternoons spent exploring and my schoolmates competing to be the one who'll come spend the weekend at my place. I need *at least* a second bed in my bedroom-with-the-walls-upholstered-in-white-wooden-panels.

I chuckle while I picture myself walking here in the woods with the blond-haired guy from tenth grade. He'll have his guitar with him, and we'll reach the pond or the stream—there *must* be a pond or a stream nearby, surely—where he'll sit on a rock and play for me. Then, holding hands, we'll go back to the house, and he'll stop and kiss me once, maybe twice, and then—

Hey, now wait a minute. *That* is *not* a pond!

***

"A swamp? Really? There's a *swamp* in the grove."

Now we're all together—Mother, Father, and I—in the lovely country-style kitchen with pale blue cabinets, and I am screaming in frustration. For once—for *once*—I thought this could be real, that we were really about to live in Fairy Land. And then what? I find a *swamp*! A wretched swamp!

"You see," Father says, "this house was built inside a protected area, along a nature trail: the hill, the woods, the streams—"

"Which are *outside* our grounds," I underline, "around somebody else's house. But we get the swamp. Lucky us!"

"You know, dear, there's birds and plants around here that cannot be found anywhere else. This is a really unique spot," Mother says, her voice as sweet as honey.

I throw up my hands and roll my eyes. It's hopeless. Better to have them fight against each other. It's not fair I'm the only one who's annoyed around here.

I stomp up the stairs and reach my bedroom-with-the-walls-upholstered-in-white-wooden-panels.

So, let's see. The room isn't bad, actually. It's big enough for all my stuff to fit in nicely, and the roof window is pretty. One glance out, though, and I get angry all over again. I see the path that leads to the swamp. So much for the romantic serenades with the blond-haired guy from tenth grade. Everybody will laugh at me, as if it weren't already difficult enough to make friends in the new school. I could have them over for the party of the century, but no! All I can hope for is a creepy Halloween party, real zombies probably included.

The only good news I learn upon rejoining my parents, who now stand in front of the stone fireplace in the large hall with smooth white pillars framing the French-window, no less, is that we won't be moving here before summer, which is eight months away.

My last eight months of freedom before I become the Princess Imprisoned in the Gloomy Swamp Castle.

***

The eight months have gone by. The moving truck'll be here in a few hours.

My new bedroom waits for me, with its upholstered-in-white-wooden-panels walls and brand-new lace curtains at the window. Oh, and also some terrific speakers; I spared no expense. Father and Mother have spent so much time bickering and yelling at each other that it would have been really dumb of me not to at least take advantage of that.

Eight months haven't made me happier about the swamp, and I am still angry at them for buying a house without consulting me first.

I can't stand them anymore. Since the day my father stopped travelling, those two can't be in the same room for longer than five minutes without starting a new quarrel. I'd rather we kept moving and changing towns.

I'm really mad. My school report was awful, I couldn't make a friend to save my life, the blond-haired guy from tenth grade doesn't even know I exist, and my new house stands near a swamp.

It was probably Father throwing the glass on the floor that was the straw that broke the camel. The shattering glass; Father's voice, terse and thundering; Mother's hysteria—I thought my head was going to blow up.

They didn't even notice me leaving. I took the new house keys, jumped on a bus without paying the fare, and travelled one hour to reach the hill.

The sky is dark when I arrive. I feel slightly more relaxed after the one-hour bus journey, but I still don't want to go back. I play with the keys between my fingers for a while, and then I put them back in my pocket and walk to the grove.

The sky is clear, so blue I feel like trying to reach for it. The moon is a thin, bright crescent; the crickets chirp through the night. Are there fireflies?

I walk through the grove. The darkness makes it look different from what I remember. It's a hot summer night, but here the air is cooler and the undergrowth smells damp. The leaves are a thousand shades of green, but they look more and more the same colour in the growing darkness. The branches move and rustle in the wind. The silence in this place makes every noise sound louder than I would expect.

I haven't been here in almost eight months. Night has fallen, and I can barely distinguish the outline of the trees or the path. Did it turn right? Or left? I don't remember; I cannot see. I stop and turn around, trying to orient myself. Well done, very good. Now I'm lost. I don't even know where I came from anymore.

Anger was leaving me, but it suddenly comes back. I clench my teeth and close my eyes and run, letting my instincts guide me. My feet tangle in the wild greenery, which can't be a good sign, but I'm unable to stop.

Then I meet soft ground. It's *really* soft as if rain had just stopped. Except it hasn't.

Uh-oh. Now I cannot lift my left foot. I pull and, with a sucking noise, it finally breaks free. I should walk back, but I'm losing balance, and my foot lands heavily on the too-soft ground and then sinks again. I try to pull one foot or the other out of the mud, but the more I pull, the more I sink.

Great. I found the swamp. What should I do? Should I cry out? And who's there to hear me? The crickets? My God, this must be a nightmare! There's no human sound, no light, no nothing! Of course, I could have brought my phone, but I was in such a hurry to leave, I forgot.

I shake my legs again, but I sink even faster. I hear myself crying. I sob and scream in frustration. This can't be happening. I'm knee-deep in mud and sinking.

And that's when I see her. She's hooded, wears a cape, and holds a long silver sickle. She glides on the muddy surface of the swamp, appearing and disappearing in the foliage. She moves smoothly, calm and light, and I am transfixed. I stop crying. I wipe my nose with my fingers, which are dirty with mud, and look around. So there *are* fireflies. I smile sadly at them.

Let us overlook the next minutes. You don't really want to know how it feels to have mud reaching corners and clefts of you that you didn't even suspect were there. Nor how long you manage to stay aware while slowly sinking into a swamp.

***

The day is about to break. In case my parents haven't yet realised I'm not there, they will knock on my old bedroom's door in a short while to tell me to get up because the moving truck has arrived. They'll find the empty bed and the boxes containing my things, sealed and untouched.

Where will they start looking for me? Who will they call? How long will it take them to get to this house?

None of that matters, actually, because I am here: standing in the large hall with the stone fireplace and the smooth pillars framing the French window.

I am here, dripping mud on the cherry wood floor.

I am here, and I wait.

BECOMING CLARISSA

A.W. Powers

*Clarissa Hope is a normal high
school senior—mostly ignored,
occasionally trampled—until she
meets a guy at a carnival and receives a warning from a
fortuneteller. Things change, but there's still a chance she'll survive
the school year.*

As Clarissa Hope walked home from the Chamberlain High School
senior class autumn carnival and fundraiser, she played with the
three-inch silver cross that hung from a chain around her neck. It
was a nervous habit she'd had as long as she'd owned the chain and
cross, especially if she puzzled over something. That evening, she

thought about how her day had been the normal level of bad and then taken a turn for the strange.

Clarissa was part of the invisible caste, the group of kids too low to even abuse, and she didn't mind. But being invisible didn't mean you couldn't be trampled, as three members of the football team proved just five minutes after she entered the building that morning. The team had been screwing off as they did every day, when they ran down the hall, bouncing off lockers and people. Clarissa had frozen and taken a full frontal assault from Bart Eckstrom, who happened to be one of the biggest, best looking, most popular guys at school and the son of the football coach. He flattened her and kept going. At least she avoided the humiliation of being picked up off the floor.

As she rubbed the growing bruise on her leg and ignored her history teacher, who droned on about the settling of North America for the sixth time, in what was supposed to be a Civil War and Reconstruction class, she thought her version of hell would mean being sentenced to eternity in high school. She couldn't imagine how the characters in the *Twilight* books or the little girl in *Interview with a Vampire* had avoided throwing themselves on stakes when they realized they'd be that very same age forever.

Lunch was inedible. It wasn't described that way, but it was prepared to spoil the biggest appetite. Only a lunch from home was truly edible. But that meant preparing it before bed or getting up earlier than she could already barely manage. She tossed most of her school lunch. Too bad the school couldn't find animals with low standards to feed it to.

During fifth hour, tall and thin Mark Harrison, who had sat close to her in at least one class each year since grade school—one teacher inevitably assigned seats alphabetically—leaned close. "Are you going to the carnival tonight?"

She didn't remember him ever smelling that good. In seventh grade, during square dance in gym class, he had smelled like chicken soup, but he had never smelled like soap, fresh forest air, or an unidentifiable spice.

"I will if you will," he said.

She looked at him. Was he serious? Was he setting her up for some type of public ridicule? Being invisible did not prevent a person from developing trust issues.

"I don't know," she said.

"Please," he said. "We've know each other a long time. I should have asked you out before, but I was afraid you'd say no, so I never did." He took a deep breath. "We're getting to the end of the year. I'm running out of time."

She scanned his face, noticing his brown hair and matching brown eyes.

"We won't call it a date. You can pay for anything you want yourself. We'll just meet up and hang out."

She stared at him for a long moment. Neither broke their gaze, but he blinked rapidly and fidgeted.

"Okay," she said.

"Great. Meet me at the Scrambler at seven, okay?"

"Okay."

Clarissa had never been to a carnival. She didn't tell her mother where she was going and arrived fifteen minutes early. The crowd and noise were unsettling. She wandered the edge of the carnival, never going too far from the Scrambler and never venturing where she might run into someone she knew.

At twenty minutes after seven, Mark appeared at the Scrambler.

"Hi," Clarissa said, noticing his clean jeans and hooded sweatshirt that proclaimed support for the Green Bay Packers.

"Wow, you came. I'm sorry I'm late." He pointed at Craig Reynolds. "I was waiting for him. I hope it's okay that he's come along."

"Of course," Clarissa said. But it wasn't. She knew Craig from school. He liked to lead belching contests. His jeans and shirt were full of holes and his hair needed washing. "It's not like we're on a date or something." On the other hand, Clarissa wasn't sure if she was ready to be with just Mark.

"I'm glad it's okay," Mark said. "He shouldn't be alone. He's been drinking."

Craig wandered toward the center of the carnival. Between the rough ground and the alcohol, it wasn't a smooth wander. Mark glanced at Clarissa and sighed.

Mark and Clarissa followed Craig. Mark kept one eye on Craig and the other on Clarissa, while she kept her gaze on the ground. Not only did she not want to trip, she didn't want to step in anything disgusting. She bumped into Mark when she hopped around what might have been a cherry slush. His hand moved to her back as he caught her.

"Sorry," she said.

"It's okay," he said a little too quickly, slow to remove his hand.

Craig wandered toward the games. The booth he stopped in front of had rows of featureless dolls that were supposed to resemble lions. They were shaped like flat bowling pins, the edges surrounded with a fringe that hid how small the dolls actually were.

He handed over his dollar and received three worn, rubber-coated baseballs he was supposed to use to knock down a doll. His first two throws went through the fringes and between two dolls. The third throw bounced off the front of the shelf, came out of the play area, and hit Clarissa in the leg, just above the bruise from her morning tackle.

She folded over and grabbed her leg. Tears immediately filled her eyes.

Oblivious, Craig strolled down the row of games while the carney yelled for someone to return his ball.

Mark wrapped his arm around Clarissa. "Are you okay?"

Clarissa liked that he stayed close and silent. After a couple of minutes, she straightened up. "I think so."

"That had to hurt."

"A lot."

"You don't think it's broken, do you?"

"I don't think so, but I've never had a broken bone, so I don't know how it would feel."

"You probably wouldn't be standing if it was broken," Mark said.

"I suppose not."

"Should we keep looking around or do you want to find a place to sit?"

"We'll keep moving," Clarissa said. "You know, walk it off."

"Okay." He withdrew his arm.

They continued down the row of games. The last three were run by parents of the senior class: a kid's inflatable pool, where rubber ducks were plucked from swirling water and the winner's prize corresponded to the number on the duck's belly; a ring toss, the prize a bottle of the winner's favorite soft drink; and a fortuneteller, who would probably spout things she had read in fortune cookies.

Clarissa had heard that Bobbi Randall's mother would be working as a fortuneteller. Bobbi, the head cheerleader and most popular girl anywhere—at least according to Bobbi—had said the idea left her mortified. Clarissa knew Bobbi's mother from her one year of Girl Scouts. But when Clarissa stopped in front of the fortuneteller's booth, Bobbi's mom wasn't there. Instead, an unfamiliar woman manned the booth.

"That's a great costume," Clarissa said.

"It is," Mark said. "Looks genuine."

The fortuneteller could have come from the movies—wrinkled face and hands, gray hair poking from beneath a scarf wrapped on

24

top of her head, long dingy dress, numerous bracelets and rings. She stood next to the booth, half-covered by shadow. People mingled about.

The fortuneteller pointed at Clarissa and in a gravelly voice said, "You are not safe. Beware the dog."

"Dog?" Clarissa stared at the fortuneteller.

"Beware the dog," the fortuneteller said again.

"What dog?" Mark asked.

The fortuneteller turned and slipped into the shadows.

While Clarissa and Mark watched the fortuneteller disappear, Bobbi and her mom arrived.

"See," Bobbi said to her mother, "no one's waiting for you. You're not late."

Mrs. Randall looked like a cheerleader disguised as a hippie—blonde hair, loose scarves, and bright-colored clothing. She stepped behind a folding table and sat down. "Who wants their fortunes told?"

"Couldn't you have waited until I left?" Bobbi whined.

"Bring me a corndog and a Coke next time you come past," Mrs. Randall said. She handed over some money. "Don't worry about the change."

"I won't," Bobbi said. She started to walk away, and then she stopped and looked at Clarissa. "What are you staring at?" She followed Clarissa's gaze to Bobbi's mother. "Be the first to get your fortune read. Should be pathetic. Just like you." She shook her head, banged her shoulder into Clarissa, and disappeared into the crowd.

Mark touched her elbow. "How about we find Craig and get out of here?"

Clarissa nodded. They walked in the direction Craig had gone and found him standing near the Tilt-A-Whirl.

"Hey," Mark said. "How about we split this place? Go get something to eat?"

Craig leaned forward and puked. Vomit would have covered Clarissa if Mark hadn't pulled her out of the way. Still, some splashed on her shoes.

She spun around and covered her mouth, trying to suppress her gag reflex. Seeing her own vomit and blood was okay, but anybody else's made her puke.

Craig wiped his mouth with his sleeve and looked at Mark. "I don't feel so good."

Mark stared at Craig for a moment and then at Clarissa. His expression could only be described as that of a guilty puppy. "I'm sorry. It wasn't supposed to be like this."

Clarissa nodded. "I understand."

"No. Really," Mark said. "I may have to quit taking him places. Except somewhere to get help. This happens almost every weekend."

"It's okay. You take him and go, and I'll go home, too."

"I really am sorry. You'll be okay by yourself?"

"Of course. I got here, didn't I?"

"Can I call you later?"

"Yeah," she said.

He surprised her by leaning in for a kiss. It was a quick one to the cheek, but the sensation of his lips on her skin would be indelibly buried in her memory.

"I really wanted you to have a nice time."

"Parts have been okay."

"Talk to you soon."

He slipped his arm under Craig and straightened him up. "C'mon, buddy. Let's get you home, make you your dad's problem. It's time he learned the truth. After all, it's his booze you stole."

Mark steered Craig toward the parking lot. Clarissa waved back when Mark turned, smiled, and waved. Then she left.

No, Clarissa thought, her day hadn't been good at all.

The full moon displayed an eerie luster to the surfaces and diffused the street lights into a pale glow. The street had been covered with early evening light when she had walked to the carnival. She could see herself as not only invisible but even dissolving into the fog. Another creature of the night.

Her mind was full of questions. Would Mark call? Had he meant it when he said he should have asked her out before? What would have happened had she turned her head and met his kiss with her lips? What had he meant about running out of time?

She clutched the cross in her right hand, the chain tight around her neck.

When she was three houses from home, walking on the curb in front of the Kimball house, something crossed the street and tackled her. The impact knocked the wind from her and tossed her through an opening in the Kimball's hedge and into the darkness.

Teeth clamped on her upper shoulder. She glimpsed a huge dog and managed to punch it. The animal shifted its grip closer to her neck and bit down harder. She tried to inhale enough air into her lungs to let out a scream. Claws raked across her chest and legs. She punched again and again, alternating left and right fists, her punches landing on the dog's head, ears, muzzle, and neck. The dog growled, which reverberated through her entire body.

Clarissa heard a yelp and felt a warm spray across her face. She continued to fight. The cross she still clenched in her hand had penetrated the dog. It had gone into its ear and sank deep. Jaws and teeth pulled away from her shoulder. Blood spattered her hair and filled her mouth. The dog collapsed.

She coughed, puked, and screamed. "Help me."

Lights came on.

"I've called the police," Mr. Kimball yelled. After long seconds, she heard a door open. "I'm coming out. I've got a gun, and I'm not afraid to use it."

"Over here. Help me."

A light shined in her eyes. "Clarissa? Is that you? What happened?"

"Dog," she mumbled. "Attacked me."

The light left her face and crawled across the grass. Darkness closed in. She heard a gunshot.

The light was back in her face. "I think it was already dead," Mr. Kimball said, "but I made sure."

Lights lit up from surrounding houses. Sirens filled the air.

"Are you okay?"

"No," she whispered.

"I'm getting your mother."

The light disappeared again. Darkness returned and kept coming.

***

Clarissa woke in a strange bed. From the lights, tubing, bandages, and beeps, she guessed she was in a hospital. She wanted to move but everything hurt.

Her mom suddenly blocked her view. "Oh, my God, you're back." She stroked Clarissa's face. "I've been praying. I've been so worried."

When had her mother become religious? Her dad had left years previously, and she hadn't remembered her mother ever praying or even talking about God since then.

"How long have I been asleep?"

"More than a whole day," her mom said.

"What happened?"

"A dog attacked you. Don't you remember?" The expression that crossed her mom's face suggested she wouldn't know what to do if Clarissa were brain damaged.

"I remember," Clarissa said. "I stabbed it. Then what happened?"

"Mr. Kimball shot it. Then the police arrived and then the ambulance, and they brought you here." She usually didn't talk that fast either. "They promised me you'd be okay. But you were heavily sedated. And then you wouldn't wake up. A voice called to me and said I should I pray, and I did."

Clarissa didn't believe Mr. Kimball had killed the dog, and prayer didn't have anything to do with her being alive. Her mom was hearing voices. Obviously Clarissa wasn't the only one changed by a dog attack.

"How bad are the bites and scratches?"

"The bites were deep. They needed stitches. The scratches weren't so bad. They'll be gone in a few days."

"When can I go home?" Clarissa asked.

Her mom shook her head. "I don't know. How can you even think of leaving? The doctors don't even know you're awake yet."

"I'm fine." Clarissa twisted and inched up on her good elbow, looking for the call button. "Let's get somebody in here. I want to go home now." She found the button, pressed it a couple of times, and fell back against the pillow.

A nurse came in. "Isn't this wonderful. We've been waiting for you to wake."

"Can I go home?"

"I'm sure it's too soon. You spent the last day heavily sedated. Let's be sure you're okay first."

"I'm okay. I heal fast."

"I'll get Doctor Baker." The nurse scurried out the door.

"What happened to you?" Clarissa's mom asked.

"What do you mean? You know what happened."

"You're different."

"How could I be?"

"You've never asserted yourself like this before."

"Maybe I've changed. Maybe I'm tired of being invisible, tired of being a doormat, tired of being dog food."

A doctor entered, the nurse right behind him. "I'm Doctor Baker. Welcome back to the land of the living."

"Thank you. Can I go home?"

"Let's have a look." Dr. Baker reached for a pair of latex gloves. "I want to be sure the stitches are holding, that there isn't seepage or signs of infection."

He slipped the gown from her shoulder, which was difficult with cords and tubes attached to her arm. "After surgery and anesthesia, most people wake up groggy and need to sleep it off."

"Really, I'm fine," Clarissa said. "Maybe I'm different than most people."

"You might be." The doctor started to peel back the dressing. "You'll be happy to know there were no signs of rabies."

Clarissa laughed. "That's a relief. I hadn't even thought about that."

He removed more of the dressing until the stitches were revealed. The nurse inhaled sharply.

"I told you I heal quickly," Clarissa said, knowing the reason for the nurse's shock.

"This might be a record," Dr. Baker said, examining the area. "Most of your bites have healed well enough that I could take the stitches out." He leaned back and looked her in the eye. "But I'm not going to. I want to give them more time."

"Did the dog come here for the lab work?" Clarissa asked.

"It went to the lab, yes," the doctor said. "Seems everybody was talking about how big it was."

"Did you hear who it belonged to?" she asked.

"I don't know about that."

"Did you see it?"

"No," he said.

"I want to see it," Clarissa said. "Can you take me so we can see?"

"Clarissa," her mom said, "the doctor is too busy for that. Besides, it isn't going to help you recover to see the dog that hurt you."

Dr. Baker looked at Clarissa for a long moment. "I'll give them a call."

Clarissa figured he was humoring her.

He threw her dressings in the wastebasket and pulled her gown up to her neck. "You rest, and I'll be back later."

The doctor and nurse left the room. Clarissa's mom sat in a chair in the corner and prayed. It had already become a habit. Clarissa lay back down and stared at the ceiling.

Dr. Baker returned a few minutes later, accompanied by another doctor. "This is Doctor Ellis. He'd like to see his handiwork."

Clarissa pulled down the shoulder of her gown.

"I put those in for you last night, and I must say that is some marvelous stitching." Dr. Ellis nodded and smiled. "I don't believe you're going to have a single scar. And your rate of healing is as impressive as I've been told."

"Thank you. I'd like to go home," Clarissa said. "Unless you can take me to see the dog."

"It's been taken away already," Dr. Baker said.

"Oh. So you'll let me leave?" Clarissa asked.

"We'd rather you spent another night at the hospital," Dr. Baker said.

"I just slept for a day. I won't be able to sleep. I'll go nuts. Or I'll drive everybody else nuts. Really, it's better if you let me out."

The two doctors glanced at each other. "You'll come back right away if something feels wrong?" Dr. Ellis asked.

"Yes."

Dr. Ellis looked at Clarissa's mom, who nodded.

"Okay, go ahead and get dressed. I'll sign the papers."

Clarissa donned her jeans, but her shirt had been destroyed in the attack. The nurse handed her a fresh johnny-shirt to wear.

While her mother disappeared to the nurse's station to sign discharge papers, Clarissa sat on the bed and waited.

Suddenly, she smelled Mark. A few seconds later, he peeked in the door. "Hey, can I come in?"

"Hi," Clarissa said. "Of course. Welcome. I'm waiting to go home."

"Already? That's great. I'm glad you're going to be okay."

"Thanks. How did you know I was here?"

"I've known since last night," he said. "I tried to get in, but they said I wasn't family."

"How did you get in now?"

"If anybody asks, I'm your brother."

She giggled. "That's nice to know. Thanks for coming. I wasn't sure I'd hear from you again."

"I told you I'd call you."

"That doesn't mean anything."

"Actually, I feel bad for not being there," Mark said. "I should have left Craig at home and just been with you. Then you wouldn't have been attacked. Or I could have protected you. I feel especially bad after what the fortuneteller said."

"Yeah, that was kind of weird, but there's nothing you could have done. And I'm fine, so don't feel bad," Clarissa said. "I'm glad you're here."

"Me, too. But I can't stay."

"Just as well. My mom will freak if she finds you here. Call me later, then she can gradually get used to the idea that someone wants to talk to me."

"It's a deal." He stepped closer and bent over. She turned her head before he could reach her cheek and kissed him on the lips. Flushed, he leaned back and smiled.

"Is it okay I did that?" she asked.

"Yeah, very okay. Talk to you soon."

***

The moon shone in Clarissa's bedroom window. As she paced and wrung her fingers, she stopped, looked out the window, and smiled at the moon. The man on the moon smiled back.

She needed to be outdoors. She grabbed a sweatshirt and headed down the hall. Her mother slept in front of the TV, an analysis of world religions playing on one of the news channels.

Clarissa shook her awake. "You need to go to bed. I'm going outside to look at stars."

Her mom stirred. "Don't stay out too long. You need your rest."

"I know. I'll be fine. I'll be back in a few minutes."

When her mother ambled down the hall to the bedroom, Clarissa cut through the kitchen and out the back door. She walked to the middle of the yard and looked up. The moon was as big and as high as it was going to get for the night.

Clarissa's skin glowed in the moon's reflection. It tingled as if something wiggled beneath it. Hair erupted through her exposed skin. She frantically shed her clothes. The stitches and remaining bandages fell to the ground. Unlike in the movies, there were no screams of agony when her joints realigned and her spine lengthened. She dropped to all fours and stretched. Her claws and tail reached toward the moon, and her chin and chest bent to the ground.

She marveled—*this is what it means to feel alive.* If the fortuneteller's warning had been about the attack, it didn't help. If it was about how it felt to become the wolf, the fortuneteller had it wrong. There was nothing to beware.

Clarissa took a couple of strides, leapt over the six-foot chain link fence, and trotted across the field behind their home. As she got farther from home and from town, Clarissa picked up speed until she crossed the open field at a full run, which she normally wouldn't do. Doing that made her free and powerful. If someone saw her, they'd think she was a happy puppy.

When the field gave way to woods, Clarissa lifted her muzzle and sniffed. She slowed, turned into the wind, and followed the scent between the trees. She burst into a small clearing, and a doe with two fawns jumped to her feet. Clarissa growled and snapped her jaws but didn't stop to kill them.

Instead, her nose tracked another scent. She trotted out the other side of the clearing and through the trees until she came to the highest point overlooking the sleeping town. She sat back on her haunches beneath a tree and watched.

A car was parked to her right, with its foggy windows lowered an inch or two. She circled around and approached the car from the front.

"What do you mean you didn't get me any booze or grass?" a male voice asked from inside the car. "I'm not here for fun. We had a deal. You're supposed to be giving me this week's supplies."

"I couldn't get them." Clarissa recognized the voice as that of Bobbi Randall. "I didn't have enough money."

Bobbi was the source of the scent—Clarissa recognized her smell from the shoulder bump at the carnival.

Clarissa crept around to the passenger side, raised her head, and looked in the window to the backseat. Bobbi lay on her back, her shirt half open. Bart Eckstrom, hunched due to his size in the small car, knelt between her knees, trying to unzip her jeans. Bobbi's hands were on his, stopping him.

"You had my money. How can you not have enough for another supply?" Bart asked.

"I told you. I didn't have enough. They raised the price."

"Then give me my money back."

"I don't have it," Bobbi said. "I owed them from last time. They kept your money."

"Then you need to put out."

"No. I don't do that."

"You will tonight." Bart pulled his hand back like he was going to slap Bobbi.

Clarissa dragged her front claws across the door, which cut deep into the paint better than keys could have.

Bart looked up. Clarissa stared back and snorted, her breath fogging the window from the outside.

"What the—"

"What is it?" Bobbi pulled her shirt closed.

"A huge dog. Watching us." He yanked the door handle. It was locked. He fumbled for the lock button.

"Don't open it," Bobbi said. "Remember what's her name was attacked by a dog."

"That dog's dead," he said.

"So, don't let this one in so it can kill us."

Clarissa landed heavily on top of the car, rocking it. She growled, a long, angry howl that rose toward the moon and vibrated the car.

She heard Bobbi say, "We need to leave," and Bart reply in the affirmative.

When the engine roared, Clarissa raked her front claws across the roof, jumped off, and sprinted for the trees.

***

The next morning, Mark met Clarissa at the front door to the school. "Wow," he said. "You look different—I mean, great."

"I feel great," Clarissa said. "I went for a walk last night, figured out some stuff."

"What kind of stuff?" he asked.

She leaned and kissed him. "Like I'm going to go for things I want. I'm not going to be invisible anymore. Life can change instantly, so I'm going to make the most of it." She kissed him again, and they walked into the building, where they heard someone yelling down the hall.

"What's that all about?" Clarissa asked a student standing beside her.

"Bart's pissed off because his car got keyed. Somebody saw the scratches and asked if his date was a real dog with sharp claws."

Suddenly, two guys ran toward them, chased by Bart. Students scrambled against the walls of the hall. Instead of being knocked over as she had previously, Clarissa stepped deftly to the side, stuck out her foot, and sent Bart sprawling to the floor.

The crowd laughed and cheered. Clarissa smiled, and she and Mark walked on. Farther down the hall, Bobbi Randall held court. Clarissa stepped between a couple of the loyal hangers-on and approached Bobbi.

Bobbi glared at her. "What do you want, bitch?"

"Just want to give you some advice," Clarissa said. "Don't sell yourself so cheap. Have some standards, make them earn it. And be careful who you get in a car with. You don't want to be raped or eaten."

Bobbi's mouth hung open.

Clarissa grinned. Head held high, she walked away. Maybe, given she had an edge, the rest of high school wouldn't be so bad. Whatever happened, she was sure she could make it at least until the next full moon.

DANGER STREET

Rod Martinez

Fifteen-year-old Jonathan Torres is an only child who spends too much time in his room, playing and programming computer games. His immensely creative imagination spawns many episodes, but sometimes, as he discovers, a vivid imagination isn't always a virtue. Treading on the fine line between reality and fantasy, he loses himself in an adventure of dangerous proportions—with his wit and knowledge of the game his only weapons.

"**O**ne more sharp left turn and freedom! I will have shaken off the drug lord chasing me and escaped with a load of his cash. C'mon car, don't give up on me now!"

Sure enough, upon reaching the corner, the vehicle sputtered. It cackled and coughed like an old smoker with the flu.

"Come on," Jonathan screamed. "Come on!"

Glancing up at the rear view mirror, he saw gun barrels aiming his way. "This isn't the way to die. I'm only fifteen!"

They were closing in. Only one thing to do: abandon the car and hoof it fast and hard. Reaching behind him, Jonathan grabbed the satchel, shoved open the door, and performed his best track star imitation. In seconds, he was several feet away and witnessed his car ram into the brick convenience store. The pursuing vehicle skidded to a stop inches from him. Two tall and obviously furious men hopped out of the car.

Staring at his opponents, several thoughts entertained Jonathan. *They won't shoot me. I'm a fifteen-year-old. But then again, I did make off with their dirty money. I have my mission, though, to bring it and possibly them to the authorities, and I'm sure that doesn't ride well with them. Maybe if I run the old "only child" routine on them they'll go easy on me.*

"The gig is up, Jonathan. Mr. B. wants what's his," the taller, obvious leader of the two thugs said.

"Yeah," his accomplice barked.

"Uh...look, guys, I have a job to do, just like you. What say we all get in your car, and I take you for a little ride downtown and—"

"No, you don't, Torres. Drop the bag and walk away from it, or we'll fill you with lead."

"Yeah!" his partner belted, right on time again.

"Uh...I don't know, boys. Lead is bad for me, but I tell you what we can do—"

"Cut the funny stuff, Torres. Just give us the loot."

"Yeah."

Jonathan and the shorter thug glared at each other. Then Jonathan fixed his view back on the first thug to find a gun aimed at him. A slight sweat overcame the young lad when he finally figured there was no way out.

"Tell me something, Lurch. You're going to shoot me anyway, right?"

"That depends on how cooperative you are."

"Yeah!"

At that outburst, the taller thug turned to his accomplice and rapped him on the head with the butt of his gun. "Shut up already, will ya."

The minor distraction gave Jonathan his chance to escape. With every ounce of youthful vigor, he sprang back, pounced over the fruit table, and into the store where he froze dead in his tracks, facing a barrel again. The store owner, an aging, angry man in plaid with a noticeable nervous condition, stood on the other side of the shotgun.

"Don't bring your illegal trash in here, son. Get on out of my store. Go on, get out." He pulled back the hammer of his rifle, signifying his sincerity on the matter.

"B...b...but if I go out, they'll shoot me."

"And if you stay here, *I'll* shoot you!"

The threat proved worthless when the two irate assailants entered the store, withdrew their firearms, and aimed at the boy. The store owner's twitching finger rested on the trigger of his enormous weapon, and Jonathan knew he was in between a rock and a hard place.

"Uh...uh, guys?"

"Shut up, Torres. I told them before, just let me kill him so we can get the money, but no. Now this is it. I'm doing it my way. Say adios, you pain in the...."

The statement faded, but Jonathan sensed the danger. Usually he was the first to scoff in the face of peril, but this was real and the moment tense and nerve-wracking for everyone. Jonathan didn't have his gun. He was in the midst of what would surely explode into a crossfire of ultimate magnitude. Triggers pulled, hammers rushed with delighted anticipation to their contact point, and then—

"Jonathan, dinner's on!"

Jonathan, in his bedroom, twisted in his seat before the computer. "Aw, man, just when I was getting into it." He wiped his sweaty brow and stared back at the screen that showed the graphically animated scenario of the adventure he had just been a part of.

On his wheeled office chair, he pushed himself away from the computer. "Be right down, Mom."

"Now, young man! Put the computer on pause or something."

He clicked the save button and waited for the computer to load the program to his flash drive.

"Put the computer on pause. That's rich, Mom. You must think this works like a DVR or something." He smiled.

***

Jonathan sat at the dining room table. Across from him, his dad poured drinks.

"I tell you, Dad, once this program is completed, you'll be able to retire and chill here at home with me and Mom, raking in the big bucks. This computer game's gonna sell like hot cakes."

The older man glanced at him. "It will, will it?"

"And how far have you gotten with it today, Jonathan?" his mother asked, serving the vegetables.

"It's almost finished. I was just going through a test course. It's great. You get the feeling you're right there when you're playing."

"That, my son, is the result of being an only child," his dad said.

"Peter."

"It's true, dear. Our son's vivid imagination is due to his not having any brothers or sisters. Or a dog even."

"Yeah, Dad's right, Mom. But I like being the only child. If you guys had another kid, I'd be the oldest. No glory in that department. I'd have to babysit, change diapers, defend them in school. No, I love the spotlight, the center of attention. Ahhh, this is my domain." He beamed as he stood, his arms outstretched.

His dad glared. "Oh, brother."

His mom remained calm. "Sit down and eat your vegetables, Jonathan."

Before his parents realized it, Jonathan had cleaned his plate. Deep in conversation on current affairs and office politics, they didn't notice when he slid off his chair and under the table. Luckily, he had a bag in his pocket, and his parents hadn't noticed vegetables disappearing beneath the table. Grasping the bag of vegetables, he crawled away. Safe behind the kitchen wall separating himself from his chatting parents, he donned his spy cap and contemplated his escape.

Let's see. I can slide out the window. They can't keep Agent 001 at bay for long.

He lowered the cap over his face and initiated his plan. Just as intended, he slipped out of the house via the side window, vegetables in tow. He dropped to the ground, right into his mother's prized rose bed. A thorn caught on his shirt sleeve, nipping his arm, and he covered his mouth to shield the yelp. He yanked his arm from the prickling bush and fell back against the wall. He massaged his arm and picked up the bag next to him.

"Evening, Torres."

The familiar voice startled him. He looked up through the bush to find, to his amazement, one of the hoodlums from his computer game, standing in the flesh, several feet from him.

"Y...you. But how—"

"I don't give up, Torres. You owe me."

Jonathan knew his opponent wasn't reaching in his coat for a cigarette. He had to think—and quick—as the darkness of the evening slowly enveloped them.

"Okay, okay. I have your green, here in this bag. I was going to bring it to you. Yeah, that's what I was going to do."

"Then place it on the grass. Nice and easy like, see?" The man pulled out his massive gun to show the young lad he meant business.

Jonathan didn't need proof. He had seen the seriousness in the man's eyes. Jonathan yanked his hat lower over his face so his eyes weren't visible to his assailant and then loosened the top of the crumpled bag. "Okay, here's your stuff."

"Don't try any heroics, Torres, or your parents will end up childless. You don't want to do that to them, do you?"

The man had the gun aimed at him, following his every move. Jonathan, rubbing his sore arm, stepped through the bush toward the man.

"Give it to me."

"Okay, but remember, you asked for it." Jonathan held the bottom of the bag and hurled its contents at the man, who still pointed the gun at him.

The assailant used the gun to shield the oncoming rain of vegetables.

Jonathan smiled and screamed, "Eat your veggies."

"Jonathan Pedro Torres Junior!"

The voice startled Jonathan. He gazed around the dinner table. Vegetables were scattered over the table, in his parents' plates, and in their hair. His mother stood and brushed herself off.

His father delivered a frustrated glare. "Son—"

"But...but he was after me, for the money...had to escape—"

"Son—"

"Really, Dad, it was life or death. He threatened to make you childless parents even."

His mother sighed. "Jonathan, if you didn't want your vegetables, you could have said so. And please, take that bowl off your head."

"B...bowl?" He reached up and felt the bowl, sitting on his head like a hat. "Oh, this...heh, I can explain, see—"

"Never mind, son, never mind."

"Sweetheart, have you finished your dinner?"

"Yes, Mom, may I be excused?"

"Be our guest," his dad said, pulling a piece of broccoli out of his drink.

The young lad rushed to his bedroom.

"Darla, I think maybe we should take the boy to see a professional. This imagination thing of his is a bit overwhelming."

"Oh, Peter, he's just a child. Didn't you have imaginary friends in your adolescence?"

"No, I was busy getting beaten up by my brothers. The boy needs companionship, for Pete's sake."

"Jonathan's okay, honey. He's okay."

"If you say so."

Peter dipped his spoon into his dessert and pulled up chocolate pudding topped with whipped cream and bits of vegetables.

***

"Yeah, Amanda, come on over. You have to check it out. This game's too much. You get so into it that you lose yourself. I call it *Danger Street*. The player steals a big stash of dirty money from a big drug lord, and he stops at nothing to get it back before you get to the authorities. It's wicked, man. Come over." Jonathan cradled the phone receiver on his shoulder and rubbed his arm. "You should have been here at dinner. You would have cracked up." He listened a moment. "Okay, but hurry up. I want you to be the first to play it before I get Dad to market it. See ya."

He hung up the phone and stared at the blank computer screen for a few seconds while still massaging his arm.

"Man, what is this?" He rolled up his sleeve and saw blood. Right where he had pricked it on the rose bush. But he wasn't really out there. Was he?

As he rolled down his sleeve, he heard a rapping sound, like someone knocking on glass. "What the—?"

He glanced up and to his surprise saw his archfoe staring at him from the computer screen. The man's anger seethed through the glass.

"Come on, Torres, we have unfinished business."

"That we do, slug face."

Without a second thought, Jonathan was back at it. He turned on the computer and pressed keys. Suddenly, he experienced the sensation of being pulled into the plasma screen.

And there it was: the sleek black sedan driven by his enemy. And up in front, Jonathan's bright yellow Porsche burning rubber on the simulated streets concocted by his flying fingers and graphic imagination. The vehicles exchanged gunshots as they swerved through the digital underground of the city.

"They'll never catch me. I'll show 'em." Jonathan skidded into an alley, thinking it a through street, but instantly found himself accelerating into a dead end. Brick walls surrounded him, and he screeched to a halt, punching the dashboard when he witnessed his pursuers close in. Quickly he exited his sports car through the sunroof. He pulled his cap over his eyes, tipped up his collar, and stood in the alley.

The sedan ground to a halt. Dust and debris rose up against Jonathan and clouded the scene for a few seconds.

"He's gone!"

"What the devil."

One of the four thugs pointed to the fire escape. "There he is."

40

The assailants whipped out their guns and fired, but Jonathan had cleared to the roof before the bullets could connect. He swung over the banister to safety. "Ha! Foiled them again." He ran across the building and jumped over to the next.

Back on the fire escape, the team of enforcers were close on Jonathan's tail. They cleared the banister and were in hot pursuit of their young quarry.

"All this for $500,000! Whoever gets him first lays claim to thirty percent, but I want him alive. He's mine to kill. Just bring him to me. Get that little hemorrhoid," the leader yelled.

The thugs, their guns drawn, raced after their prey.

Jonathan had skipped down another metal staircase. He was far enough way and out of danger but decided to go back. *My car. If they go through my car, they'll find the stash in the hidden compartment behind the passenger seat and all this will have been in vain. I have to get back to the car.*

Going back up the stairs meant certain death, so he opted instead to run through the deserted building, which he did without hesitation.

"They're sure to be closing in. Hopefully they'll think I kept going," he muttered.

He hopped over storage bins and raced through hallways, slamming doors on his trek through the abandoned structure. Darkness was his constant companion, and he sprinted with the precision and confidence of a track star. Draping cobwebs broke as if a marathon runner cut through finish-line tape.

Floors above him, shadowy figures converged on the rooftop stairwell.

Enraged, the leader slammed his fist against the iron girders. "Aargh! Gone."

"What do we do, boss?"

"He can't be too far away. Ace, Mitch, you two continue the way we were going. Dave, go down these stairs and find him."

"How do I know which floor to take, boss?"

The boss man turned, rage his only sentiment. He raised his arm, swung with full force at his subordinate, and connected just below the jawline. Dave was thrown against the rusted bars of the aged stairwell, which broke under his weight. He grabbed hold of a piece of attached metal and dangled in space, while his boss glared at him.

"You just find him—or else!"

A few seconds of silent eye contact proved too much for the junior criminal. Dave dropped to the next balcony and hustled down the stairs.

The leader turned to the others, who returned a respectful glare. "What the heck are you waiting for? A sign?"

The two dashed off.

The chief enforcer stood alone on the rooftop, leaned against the rusted frame, and lit a cigarette. "I'll get you yet, Torres. You can count on it." A puff of smoke exited his mouth and rose like a storm cloud past his dark face. "Count on it!"

One more hallway to go. For some reason, Jonathan knew exactly where his car was located. The dusty, deserted building mysteriously morphed into a familiar maze, and he quickly reached his destination.

He glanced out the window. Through the dim light from the moon, he saw the sedan, and he knew the goons were on a wild goose chase on the rooftop. Without hesitation, he hopped on the terrace and landed on the fragile metal staircase. The shaking metal frame didn't bother him; he was agile. A simple slide down the bar would take him to his beloved speedster.

Jonathan landed on the wet asphalt, next to the black sedan. "Hmm, insurance." After a couple of twists, he slipped off his belt buckle, which he unfolded into a knife. He knelt and inserted the blade into one of the tires. A few seconds later, the car slumped.

"Ha ha, Agent Double-O One at his usual." Jonathan smiled. "Now to get outta here before Prince Charming and the Goon Squad return."

He sprinted to his car and was only a couple of feet away when a click behind him caught his attention. He stopped. Boots thumping on wet concrete announced another presence, and he turned to find the leader facing him.

"Heh heh. Prince Charming. I like that moniker. Maybe I'll stick with it. I give you credit, Torres. It'll be the last known thing you did in your miniature career."

"C'mon, Sourpuss, put away the gun. Let's be civil here." Jonathan knew he was vulnerable, certain his assailant was aware of that fact, too.

"Don't try anything funny, Torres. Your butt is mine this time. There's no way out. I should have figured earlier that you'd come back to the car. You didn't have the money with you on the roof. Go on. Get it out of your hiding place." The man raised his gun and aimed it at Jonathan's head.

A slight sweat formed on the usually cool youngster. This was only a computer game, after all. He hoped his antagonist was aware of that fact.

"It's here. In my car. Behind the passenger seat. I uh...think I want out of the program now."

"No, Jonathan, not that easy. You're in my world now. I'm in total control."

Jonathan stretched out his arm. The gun was mere inches away. He saw down the barrel. The man slowly pulled back the hammer.

It was all too real to Jonathan. "Okay, abort program...escape...control F12...delete—"

"Ha ha ha. No, Jonathan, we play this game to the end now. The money is in the car, you say?"

"Yeah, I'll get it for you."

"No, stay there. I don't need you anymore. I've won the game, but just in case you're lying, I want to make sure." The thug grunted. An evil smile covered his face just before cigarette smoke exited his nostrils. "You're an unessential computer character like the rest of us. I suppose you can say your character will 'byte the dust.' Ha ha ha!"

Sick humor, indeed, but Jonathan wasn't laughing. This was too real.

With the gun still aimed at Jonathan's face, the man walked over to him. He pushed the boy aside, and with his free hand, reached in behind the seat and removed the briefcase. He dropped it on the ground between them. "Open it."

"Huh?"

"Hard of hearing? Open it. Now!"

Jonathan bent down, snapped the catches, pulled up the top, and took out a stack of fifties neatly wrapped in a bundle.

"Yeah, okay, walk away."

"Uh, wait—"

"Walk away. Now!"

The gun forced Jonathan to obey. He moved and leaned against the car.

"Okay, say goodbye, Torres."

Jonathan shuddered and shivered. "Please, please—"

"No, Torres, you've been a pain in the butt ever since you stole our money. This is it. Say hello to the end!"

"No...no...."

"Ha ha ha."

***

The doorbell rang. Darla Torres opened the door to find Jonathan's best friend, Amanda Gomez.

"Amanda, hi."

"Hello, Mrs. Torres. Is Jonathan here? He asked me to come over and check out the new computer game he's programming."

"Sure, Amanda. He's up in his room. He's been ignoring my calls. I was just about to go up there."

The two went upstairs.

The door to Jonathan's room was ajar, and his mother pushed it open. "Jonathan, Amanda's here."

Laughter came from the computer.

Darla approached her son, who sat before the computer. "Jonathan. Jona—oh, oh nooo! Jonathan!"

Blood seeped from a bullet hole in the boy's chest. Amanda pulled a crisp fifty-dollar bill from his hand.

THE GRIP

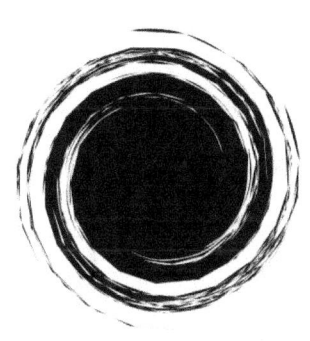

Val Muller

An afternoon of babysitting turns spooky when Megan takes young Olivia to the abandoned cabin at the edge of the woods at Galahad Estates. It was supposed to be a fun afternoon hike until Olivia, small enough to fit through the cabin's window, squeezes into the cabin and through the hole in the floor—the hole leading into a dark abyss. And when she climbs back out, the darkness surrounding her seems contagious.

"I'm leaving you ten dollars for gas money, Megan. I thought you could take Oli to McDonald's and then to Galahad Estates. She's been talking about hiking there for days now."

Megan smiled at Mrs. Olsen. The sun streamed in through the kitchen window, and Megan averted her face.

"And here's twenty dollars for McDonald's. Please treat yourself, too. I won't be back until after nine o'clock. Oli will probably already be asleep. Oh, and frozen pizza for dinner."

"Sure thing." Megan pocketed the money and looped the Olsen's spare key around her keychain just as Olivia bounded down the stairs.

"All set," Olivia announced. She spun around, allowing Megan to inspect her outfit: cargo shorts, a white T-shirt, and a fuchsia hoodie.

"A little warm for a hoodie?" Megan asked.

Olivia shrugged. "Can never be too prepared for a hike."

Mrs. Olsen bit her lip. "That's what her father always said." She sighed and looked up at the girls. "I know you'll have a lot of fun today. Be back later." She leaned in for a kiss.

Olivia obliged but scowled.

"I have to work, you know. That's how you can afford all your hoodies and hiking gear and McDonald's and—"

"Didn't have to work so much when you and Dad were together."

Mrs. Olsen started to speak and then stopped herself, turned, and left.

Olivia pouted. She stood still, staring out the window as her mother pulled out of the garage and drove down the street. The sun disappeared behind a cloud, and Oli, her eyes fiery, turned to Megan and said, "Let's go."

***

Megan sat across from Olivia, picking at her fries while the little girl pried off the plastic on the toy that came with her meal.

"What'd you get?" Megan couldn't help but smile at the little girl's indelible spirit. She could barely remember what it was like to be that age, when a toy in a meal equaled happiness.

Olivia's face cracked into a smile. "Haunted Helen."

Megan raised an eyebrow. "Haunted Helen?"

"You know, from that monster show. The one who likes to date werewolves and goblins."

Megan shook her head. Kids' television sure had changed in the previous decade or so. "Why is she called Haunted Helen?"

"Because she's a ghost."

"Ah." Megan slurped the rest of her milkshake. "You sure are excited about a bunch of dead people."

"Dead teenagers," Olivia corrected her. "They go to high school."

"In the underworld?"

"Uh huh."

Megan shook her head. "Look at you. Dressed in a pretty pink hoodie and matching pink sandals but liking everything macabre."

"It's fuchsia, not pink. And what's macabre, anyway?" Olivia asked.

"That's macabre." Megan held out her hand for the toy.

Olivia handed it over.

"Finish your chicken nuggets. Then we're going for your hike."

Olivia's smile grew again. "I can't believe we're really going to Galahad Estates. Mom only takes me there once in a while. She's busy all the time. I hate it. Dad and I always used to go."

Megan glanced down at the pale but beautiful chunk of plastic in her hand. The perfect teenage ghost. "Go easy on your mom. She works hard to provide for you. Grown-ups aren't lucky like kids are. They don't get the summers off."

Olivia sighed.

"Finish your nuggets."

"Meh. I should've got a burger this time."

"Well, you got nuggets." Megan looked down at the ghost girl again. "How about I tell you a ghost story about Galahad Estates while you finish?"

Olivia's eyes lit up. "Okay."

"Have you ever been on the trails there?"

"A little."

"The one with the haunted cabin?"

Olivia shook her head.

"There's a haunted cabin on the property. It's near the edge of a clearing in the woods. There used to be a rope swing hanging there that my sister and I swung on to take a break from walking, and we always looked at the cabin as we swung. Its roof is partly caved in, and the whole thing is covered in moss. Most of the windows have been broken. If you peek inside on a really bright day—or if you use a flashlight—you can see that people have been inside the cabin over the years. There's some graffiti and empty bottles."

Olivia giggled. "Beer bottles?"

Megan smirked. "You're too little to know about any of that."

"I'm not little, and I'm not stupid."

"Okay, okay. But don't even think about drinking. You're only ten."

"Yeah, yeah."

"Anyway, if you look really carefully, you'll notice there's a hole in the floor of the cabin. It leads into a deep, dark place."

"Have you ever been there?"

"No. My sister and I could never go inside the cabin. Our parents were always with us and never let us get inside."

Olivia raised an eyebrow.

"That's a devilish look. Don't get any ideas."

"But Mom won't be there. It would be the perfect chance to sneak in and see what's in that hole. What do you think is down there?"

Megan smiled. "My sister and I always joked that it was an entrance to Hell, a doorway used by witches and drug addicts. We always argued over whether it would be very hot or very cold."

"But you never found out?"

Megan shook her head. "And I'm never going to, either."

"Why not? We can find out now. Please?"

"No."

"At least can we look in the window?"

Megan frowned. "Are you going to finish that last nugget?"

Olivia obliged. "So can we?" she asked through a mouthful of food.

"Okay. Got a flashlight?"

Olivia shook her head. "At home."

"We're not driving all the way back home."

"How about we use the change from lunch to buy a flashlight?"

Megan cringed. She was planning on pocketing the change.

"Did you hear me? I said we can buy a flashlight."

"From where?"

Olivia pointed out the window to a pharmacy.

"I'm sure they don't have very good flashlights there."

"Then we can use your phone as a light."

Megan checked her battery. "No way."

Olivia pouted. "What, then? Please, please, please can we get a flashlight?"

"Oh, all right. We'll go to the pharmacy." Megan counted her change from lunch. Then she swept the wrappers from the table onto the tray, dumped it into the trash, and followed a skipping Olivia out the door.

***

It had been several years since Megan visited Galahad Estates, and the cabin looked even smaller than she remembered. And while the old tire swing hanging in front of it seemed inviting in the filtered sunlight through the forest of pines, the house at the edge of the forest seemed much more sinister. Something about its aura looked oppressive, as if it sought to steal light from the clearing in front of it.

Behind it, the thick forest of pines rose, the smell of elderberry or another musky plant clinging to the air. Megan shivered, tugging down her T-shirt and rubbing the goosebumps on her arm.

"Hey, Oli, want me to push you on the tire swing?"

But Olivia already had one foot in the forest. "Nah, let's check out the cabin. Who used to live here?"

Megan shrugged. Though she and her sister had frequently visited the park, they'd never taken the time to find out about the wealthy family who had once lived there. Who would have lived in such a cabin? A servant, perhaps? A gardener?

"Maybe it was a witch," Oli said as if answering Megan's thoughts.

"No. Witches in New England lived here much earlier than this estate was built." Megan stopped. What was she talking about? Witches in New England? Had she lost her mind? "Besides, there's no such thing as—"

But Olivia had already disappeared behind the house.

"Careful, Oli. There might be broken glass back there."

"You mean from beer bottles?" her tiny voice asked, muffled from behind the moss-covered cabin and rows of pine trees. "There's a window back here busted open pretty wide. Let's see if we can get the flashlight through here."

Megan crept around the side of the shed. The sunlight vanished behind the house, and even though the cabin stood at the edge of the forest, it hid in darkness as if it were right in the middle. She knew before she handed over the flashlight that it would do little to cut through such blackness.

"I can't see." Olivia craned her neck through the glassless window. "This flashlight is terrible."

"What do you expect for ninety-nine cents?" Megan had skimped on her lunch to pocket the extra change. She wasn't going to spend all her savings on a flashlight.

"Tell ya what. Why don't I take a picture of you in front of the cabin?" Megan said.

Oli's eyes lit up, and Megan smiled at her ability to distract. She stepped back from the cabin and aimed her phone while Oli posed. "Looks good. Now smile!"

But as soon as Megan snapped the picture, Oli hurried again to the cabin's broken back window.

"Maybe if I lower the flashlight to the floor." Olivia climbed deeper through the window and her torso disappeared into the cabin. Only her legs hung out into the forest. Her feet lifted off the ground when she transferred her weight to the windowsill.

Megan dashed to grab her legs. "Careful there."

"I'm okay."

Megan grabbed tighter.

Olivia kicked. "I *said* I'm okay." She kicked again, and Megan shied away.

"Okay, already. But don't get cut on any stray glass from that broken window. Your mom will kill me."

"Nah. She'd never notice. She's never home, remember?" Olivia pulled her head out of the window long enough to glance back at Megan. "Besides, it looks like you're the one who got cut."

Megan followed the girl's eye line to her arm, which was indeed cut and bleeding. A dark red trickle had left a streak the entire length of her forearm. "What the—"

She trudged back toward the clearing to examine the wound in the sunlight. It was a long scratch, and she couldn't believe she hadn't felt whatever had cut her. She wrapped her arm in the bottom of her T-shirt. "Thanks for noticing, Oli," she shouted. "Who knows how long this would have—"

She looked up. "Oli?"

Though she couldn't see Olivia from her vantage point, something about the situation felt wrong. The girl was too silent, the place too empty.

"Oli?"

Megan raced to the cabin's back window to find a legless window bereft of light or life or sound.

"Oli?"

Megan took up Olivia's former position, sticking her head through the broken window and craning her neck to see in the dark. The cheap flashlight lay on the floor, its bulb producing the most pathetic ring of light.

"Oli?" Megan's voice did not echo as she thought it would. Rather, the cabin swallowed the sound into its decrepit walls like weathered wood absorbed paint. She may as well have been screaming into a pillow. She tried calling for the girl again, but her voice disappeared into the darkness.

As her eyes adjusted, she examined the inside of the cabin. Never as a child had she been allowed to get so close to the strange place. Inside was the ancient frame of a bed—a wooden one, too, from an era when things were made to last. It was covered in all manner of graffiti and markings that she could not quite make out. In the corner, on a small table, was an ancient can. It looked unopened though maybe it was topped with dust.

What a tiny house. If it had ever been for servants, how simple a life they must have led. Megan's parents' bathroom was larger than the entire place.

She shook off the thought. It didn't matter. What mattered was that the little girl in her charge was missing, and the day wasn't getting any younger. Besides, if Oli had gotten lost, there'd be something more serious than the darkness to worry about.

In the corner of the cabin, a torn and tarnished mattress sat insidiously. It looked more modern than the bedframe and of more obvious, unwholesome purposes.

"Oli, are you over there?"

The girl still didn't answer.

And that's when Megan saw it. It looked as frightening as it had when she was a kid. The hole in the floor. The doorway to Hell.

"Olivia?" Megan's voice seemed even more impotent. She pushed herself back out of the window. The opening was small enough for Olivia to fit through, but Megan certainly couldn't. How did teenagers get in to drink and party? There had to be a bigger opening somewhere.

Back in the daylight, Megan could breathe again. She crept around to the cabin's front door. It was locked tight. How was she supposed to get in? Sweat gathered at the middle of her back, making her spine warm and wet. How could Olivia have fit through the window, and how far could she have gotten through that terrible hole to Hell?

No, think rationally. Of course it wasn't a hole to Hell. It probably led to the basement. Worst case, some drunk or stoned teenagers were down there sleeping off a night of partying. If someone menacing were down there, she would have heard them. And if Olivia were in trouble, Megan would have heard her, too.

Right?

But all that entered Megan's mind was the look on Mrs. Olsen's face when she arrived home to find her daughter missing. What would Mrs. Olsen do? Would she call the police? Would Megan be held responsible? Was it a crime to be in charge of a ten-year-old who went missing? Could Megan go to jail?

"Olivia?" Megan screamed.

"Are you all right, miss?"

Megan spun around to see two hikers. She blushed. "Oh, I—I'm fine. You didn't happen to see a little girl, did you?"

The hikers exchanged glances. "No. Is someone missing?"

Megan shook her head. "No. Just my, uh, sister. We're playing hide and seek. She's too good at the game."

The hikers laughed. "I'm sure you'll find her soon."

Megan watched them enter the clearing. The sun glowed against their skin and clothes, burning her eyes. She turned back to the shaded wood and allowed her pupils to readjust.

"Olivia?"

She hurried back to the cabin, trudging past the moss, and nearly tripped. She rubbed against it, adding green and brown stains to her already red-stained shirt.

"Olivia?"

At the window, she closed her eyes to enlarge her pupils. She stuck her head through the opening again and craned her neck to look toward the opening in the floor. Something made her heart leap. In the darkness it didn't look quite as bright, but she was sure of it. It was a pink hoodie, caught on the opening of the hole, but in the darkness it looked almost crimson.

"Olivia?"

Something clawed in the darkness. Probably a rat. But no, it was getting louder, and it sounded more and more—human.

"Olivia?"

Then, in the darkness, two pale arms emerged from the hole. And a white T-shirt. And a curious little head with matted brown hair.

"Olivia!"

The girl scurried out of the hole without a word, only her panting breaking the silence. She grabbed her sweatshirt and hopped up toward the window. Megan helped her squeeze through. Outside, Olivia stumbled to the ground and then scurried backward like a crab until her back hit one of the solid pines. She kept the cabin in her sights, and as Megan approached, her eyes looked wild and paranoid.

The eyes of a trapped animal.

"Olivia, you okay?"

The girl would not speak. Megan's lunch stirred heavily in her gut. The look on Olivia's face was perhaps more frightening than the prospect of her having gone missing.

"Olivia, what happened? What was down there? Were there people? Teenagers maybe?"

The girl shook her head. Then she shook it harder. And harder still until she trembled and finally screamed incoherent syllables. Glorified baby gaggle.

"Shh! Olivia, what's wrong? Hush, now, you're going to make a scene."

But the girl continued to pant and tremble and scream.

"Olivia, they were just teenagers, I'm sure."

"No," she screamed. She clawed the air.

Megan tried to grasp her arms, but Olivia was too fast.

"They may have looked pretty bad. Sometimes when people drink, they—"

"They weren't teenagers, and they weren't drinking beer." Olivia's voice reflected the edge of panic.

"What were they doing?"

"It wasn't doing anything," Olivia said.

"It?"

"It was just waiting."

"It?"

Olivia nodded.

"Waiting for what?"

"For me."

Megan almost laughed. The situation was ridiculous. And Olivia acted so serious that it barely seemed real. But the crazed look in the girl's eyes lingered, and Megan shivered.

"Tell ya what. Let's go home. Maybe we can stop for some ice cream on the way. Then we go back and get you a shower so your mom doesn't wonder how you managed to get so dirty. I'll even throw your clothes in the laundry." She looked down at her shirt. "And maybe mine, too."

Olivia took in the words slowly, her face melting like ice in the spring. Finally, the hint of a smile emerged. "Okay, that sounds good. Except one thing."

"What's that?"

"The Grip."

"The Grip?"

"I have it now, and I want to get rid of it."

"What's the Grip?" Megan instinctively stepped backward.

"It's what it was waiting to give me. What it gave me when it touched me."

"Oli, you're starting to creep me out. Let's just get home, okay?"

"But I don't want the Grip anymore. Please. Help me."

"I think your imagination ran away with you. Maybe Haunted Helen wasn't such a good idea after all."

"This has nothing to do with Haunted Helen. This is for real. I. Don't. Want. The. Grip." She was working up to a fit again, her breathing fast and irregular.

Megan saw hikers coming from the sunny field and didn't want another scene. "Okay, how do we get rid of the Grip?"

"It's like cooties," Olivia said. "I have to give it to someone."

Megan shrugged. "Okay, give it to me."

Olivia motioned toward the approaching hikers. "Better if I give it to them."

"Why?"

"You won't like the Grip, either."

What the hell was the girl talking about? She was ten years old, old enough to know better. She was acting like a baby. Best to humor her and be done with this. "I'll be okay, Oli. I'm older than you. And I'm very brave."

"You have to be braver than brave to have the Grip."

"I am," Megan said, eyeing the hikers. "Give it to me."

Olivia shrugged. Then she reached out her index finger like a claw.

Megan stepped closer.

"Hold out your arm," Olivia ordered.

Megan did.

Then Olivia pierced the still-damp cut on Megan's arm with her clawed finger.

"Ouch!" Megan cried. Tears welled. What a sick little kid. "All right, you better now? Let's just get the hell out of here."

Olivia giggled. "You said a swear word." She looked years younger than she had a moment previously.

Megan scoffed. "I guess you're feeling better, Miss Psycho. Now let's go. And not a word of this to your mother."

Olivia nodded. "Just one thing."

"What's that?"

"It was very, very hot. I thought you'd want to know."

***

Megan twisted on the couch, watching Oli drift to sleep. French fries followed by frozen pizza must have taken their toll on Megan; her insides pulsed with pressure. Behind her, shadows flickered on the walls with the television's changing light, and she shivered.

"Oli, time for bed," she said.

Olivia's eyes popped open. "Hey, can I see the picture first? The one you took of me at the cabin?"

Megan grasped her stomach as she reached for her phone. She opened the camera app and scrolled to the picture. Her guts froze. Oli was in front of the cabin, but behind her stood a shrouded figure with its arm around her. A shadow. It had to be a trick of the lighting.

Megan's ribcage tightened.

54

"Megan?" Oli craned her neck toward the phone. "Your face just went white. You look like Haunted Helen—like you seen a ghost."

Megan searched her mind for words, any words.

"Megan, what's wrong?"

Finally, her brain fired up again. "Nothing, Oli. It's just—I must have done something wrong. The picture didn't take."

Oli frowned. "Sucks."

After Oli went to bed, Megan sat on the couch, glancing down the hallway that led to the bedrooms. She had seen a nightlight in the bathroom, a light-sensor type that flickered in response to the changing light from the television, and each time it flashed, Megan startled.

And then a shadow moved behind the television screen. In the corner of her eye, a figure dashed across the room.

Megan, they're just shadows. Get a grip.

Then she trembled. The Grip. Maybe she already had it. What had Olivia meant? What was the Grip, exactly? What a dumb question. The Grip was a piece of a child's imagination, nothing more. Megan flipped to another channel—a romantic comedy. She let herself get lost in the cheesiness of it until a small white flash scurried across the floor.

A mouse?

She craned her neck down the hall.

Nothing.

She picked up her phone. She didn't want to look at the picture again, but she had to know. She opened the picture. The shadow was there, and it looked even darker than previously. Her body trembled and jolted as if she'd fallen down a flight of stairs. She swiped the photo and attached it to a text message. Who could she send it to? Which of her friends would take an objective look at the picture and offer advice? What about her mom? Or maybe she was crazy. It was just a trick of the light. This was stupid. She deleted the unsent text message and then deleted the picture.

That's what she got for eating too much junk food—waking nightmares.

She tried to settle back into the movie, but the skittering started again—behind her—in the hallway. She hated mice, so she muted the television and strained her ears for more signs of scratching or tiny scampering feet.

Nothing.

She got up to investigate. Something small and white hid in the shadows. It didn't startle at her approach. She crept closer.

Haunted Helen.

Hadn't Olivia brought the toy to bed with her? Megan was sure of it. Olivia had set Helen on the nightstand to watch over the room. How did Helen end up in the hallway? Megan picked up the toy, and that's when she heard it. The distinct creek of the bathroom door.

"Oli?" Her voice sounded weak in the empty house. "Olivia?" she asked, louder.

No response.

She continued down the hall. The bathroom light shone through the bottom of the closed door. "Oli, you okay in there?"

Mrs. Olsen would not be happy if Olivia were sick. She hated having to take time off work to take her to the doctor.

"Oli?" Megan put her ear to the door, straining to hear. It was that same scratching from earlier. But it was too strong to be a mouse. And there were—whispers. Megan's arm throbbed where she'd cut it. Though she'd poured rubbing alcohol on it that evening, perhaps it had already become infected. She'd have to ask for hazard pay—especially after spending her extra change on that cheap, stupid flashlight.

"Oli, do you want me to call your mom?" Megan asked through the closed door.

More scratches.

"Oli, you're scaring me. Can I come in?"

The whispers grew louder and more frantic.

"Oli?" She held up her hand. "Look, I found Haunted Helen. You must have dropped her...."

A chill ran from the toy in Megan's hand, up the injured arm to her shoulder, and down her spine. She wanted to leave, to get far away from the bathroom, but she felt stuck to the spot, as if she'd collapse if she tried to move. She felt like she was held in a huge fist, only the fist gripped her from the inside, pushing against her ribcage and trying to get out.

"Oli?" she asked through tears. "Please, come out."

The grip loosened slightly, enough to allow her a thought. *Check Olivia's bed.*

Megan shuffled down the hallway, not wanting to see what would be there but needing to at the same time. Olivia's door was ajar, and Megan pushed it open. The hair on her arms rose when she heard Oli's sleepy breathing. But, nonetheless, she continued to the bed to check.

She moved to the side, allowing light from the hallway to spill into the room. It was bright enough to reveal Haunted Helen, still alert at her post, where Oli had left her. She looked at her own hand, now empty, and gasped at its betrayal.

And in the bed, snoring softly, was Olivia.

Who, then, was in the bathroom?

Or *what*?

A rattling of keys and clanking of the front door restarted Megan's heart, and she dashed back into the hallway to see Mrs. Olsen placing her keys and phone on the entryway table.

The older woman's eyes bulged when Megan approached. "Oh my, aren't you animated! And where's Oli? I thought surely she'd convince you to let her stay up past her bedtime."

Megan didn't even pretend to smile. "She passed out. The hike was pretty tiring." She turned to the hallway and then glanced back to see if Mrs. Olsen noticed.

"You sure everything's okay? Should I go check on Olivia?"

"No, everything's fine. I, um, I just checked on her." She turned to look at the bathroom door. It was still closed, and light still shone from beneath. *Get a grip, Megan.* "It's just been a long day, and I'd like to get home."

"Okay, give me a minute. You've been here since...let's see, that's...."

Megan tried to breathe while Mrs. Olsen counted out the day's payment. Something in the bathroom scratched at the door. Louder and louder until it became a clawing. Each scratch left a line of pain on the inside of Megan's ribcage, and she fought the nauseating realization that the pain would be indelible. Clawed onto her soul.

Mrs. Olsen continued counting the money, oblivious to the clawing or to Megan's plight.

"Actually, Mrs. Olsen, don't worry about the money for now. I'd just like to get home. The McDonald's and gas money is enough."

"Don't be silly. I was a teenager once, too." Mrs. Olsen held out several bills.

Normally, Megan would have been calculating her hourly rate and rounding to the nearest quarter-hour to make sure she'd been compensated fairly, but all she cared about was getting out of the house before whatever was in the bathroom came out.

She caught a whiff of elderberry and mud, and she remembered the crazed look in Olivia's eyes and the way the girl's claw-like finger seared into her flesh as she "transferred" the Grip. The pressure against her ribcage became so intense she could barely contain her scream. Instead, she reached out her hand, being careful to curl her pointer finger just as tightly as Olivia had done. Then she reached toward Mrs. Olsen's awaiting hand and grabbed the money, clawing the front of the woman's hand in the process.

"Ouch! I mean, really, Megan. I believe you've drawn blood! What's gotten into you?"

Megan smiled. The pressure on her ribcage deflated instantly, like a balloon. Her lungs had room to function again, and the sweat cooled instantly. The noises from the bathroom quieted, and the light from under the door extinguished. Refreshed, Megan breathed in the cool air.

"Sorry, Mrs. Olsen. I guess I'm just a little too enthusiastic to get home." She looked at the tiny dots of blood pooling at the site of the scratch. "You'd better put something on that cut, Mrs. Olsen. You wouldn't want it to get infected."

The woman shook her head in disbelief, looking down at the wound. "All right." She looked back at Megan. "I'm sure you didn't mean to be so rough."

"I'll let myself out."

When Megan got to the front door, she turned back to see Mrs. Olsen standing in front of the bathroom door, knocking quietly.

"Olivia? Is that you in there? And what are you whispering? Honey, please let me in. I need to get some rubbing alcohol before this gets infected."

Megan didn't stay any longer but hurried home to search for a new summer job. Her babysitting days were over. Something scratchy sounded on the sidewalk behind her, and she turned to be sure. But only emptiness and moonlight pooled on the grass. The darkness released its grip on her, but she rushed home anyway and left her lights on all night long.

DOWN THE MYRTLE TREE

 ## A.P. Sessler

Connor has never been outside on his own at night until tonight—Halloween. While the evening crosses the threshold into All Saints' Day, he and best friend Brad are determined to find out what the big deal is, but someone—or something—might find them before the night is over.

The digital alarm clock read 1:20 a.m. Connor's parents were fast asleep in the neighboring room, which Connor knew because the *Late Show* had been turned off in the middle of the monologue almost an hour previously. He knew that because the Bridell home had thin walls, and an occasional sleeping snort from his father also confirmed the coast was clear.

Connor took his clothes from beneath the bed and, in the dark, put them on. He slowly slid open his bedroom window and climbed onto the small section of pitched roof. Once his tennis shoes found their grip on the shingles, he eased down until the large tree branch came into reach. He hung from it and found the foothold in the trunk he had used several times previously, but this was his first going down without first going up. And it was night.

Halloween night.

Branch by branch, foothold by foothold, he descended the peeling crepe myrtle onto the night-damp grass of the lawn. He made his way through the narrow passage between the house and his neighbor's tall wood fence to the front yard. He nervously glanced over his shoulder at the black rectangle of his parents' bedroom window, afraid a light would explode at any moment, but it didn't.

It was then he realized their unusual psychic sense to catch him in any mischievous act was completely dormant while asleep. He turned to face the street where, in the middle, stood Brad Turner, his best friend, holding the plastic bag of candy he had gathered earlier.

Connor didn't say a word until they met. "How long have you been here?"

"Like five minutes," Brad whispered, looking at his watch.

"Just standing in the road?"

"Yeah."

"What if you got hit by a car?"

"I guess no one drives this late at night."

Connor looked up and down the street. "Okay."

"Let's get moving before your parents wake up," Brad said and led the way.

The two walked down the middle of the two-way street, Connor turning his head on occasion to look for cars. "This is awesome!"

"Why haven't we done this before?" Brad asked, reaching into the bag dangling by its handles from his wrist.

"There's a first time for everything."

Brad unwrapped a chocolate football, placed it in his mouth, and took another from the bag. "You want one?"

"Heck, yeah," Connor said and held out a hand.

"Here you go."

Connor took the piece of candy and peeled off the foil wrapper. "Dang it, I can't see." He walked into the light of the next streetlamp. His fingers fumbled to remove every piece of foil, which he let fall to the street. He popped the football in his mouth and rolled it about with his tongue. "These are so good," he said, his mouth full.

"I know."

"You ever wondered what makes Halloween so fun?"

"It's the candy," Brad said as he shook the bag.

"But you can get candy anytime."

"Not free candy."

"Yeah, but that's not it."

"Wearing costumes?"

"That's fun and all. But remember the time we had Halloween at the community center?"

Brad nodded. "That was lame."

"Exactly."

"I don't know. Going door to door?"

"We did that for fundraisers in broad daylight and that was even more lame."

"I give up."

"It's the only night we get to wander the streets at night. That's why it's so cool—the dark. Playing a game of Horse until eight o'clock? Driving home from Grandma's at night. That thirty seconds you spend outside between the car and your house. That's where the magic happens."

That was the most Connor could articulate. He couldn't define the true mysteries of night. He made no mention of its cool, crisp air, how it tickled and tingled the nerves; its sterile cleanliness—that refreshingly invigorating air void of smog and noise. Or how within its misty depths, beneath the surface where no light reached, lay the things of old—things of fable and fairy tale.

A light appeared from behind.

"Car," Brad said.

The boys took to the sidewalk and hid behind a holly bush. Beneath the canopy of maples that lined the block, they waited for the vehicle to pass. The blinding white eyes of the car rose and fell with each dip in the road until the car slowed to a stop.

The door opened, and out stepped a silhouetted figure, its head a twisted mass of snake-like things. It walked to the front of the car, where its shadow spread across the street like a giant victim.

"Who is that?" Connor whispered.

"Bradley Turner! You are in so much trouble, young man," the woman shouted.

"Busted," Brad said.

"Do you think she saw me?" Connor asked.

"Just stay here unless she says something."

Instead of a head of writhing snakes, the Medusa's crown was lined with pink plastic curlers, but her unblinking gaze had nearly the same effect as a Gorgon's stare. Bradley stood stone-cold frozen.

"You get over here right this minute!" she said. "Did you think I wouldn't hear you making all that noise?"

Brad sprung to life from behind the bush and went to his mother, his head humbly bowed and back bent.

Connor watched the two get in the car, shut the doors, and drive past him. He suspected she had spotted him, but he sat still behind the bush until the car turned into a driveway across the street, did a U-turn, and drove down the street past his house to theirs.

"Dang it. What do I do now?" Connor mumbled.

"Stay with me," a voice said from behind.

Connor leaped forward with a yelp, turning midair to face a girl. A striped knit tuque and scarf hid the majority of her hair, which was the color of fall's last leaves. She looked familiar, like an old locker combination.

"You scared the crap out of me," he grumbled as he dusted himself off.

"Halloween tradition. Who are you?" The girl offered a hand to help him up.

Her hand was cold when he took it in his own. "Connor Bridell. Aren't you the new girl?" He stood and released the cold hand.

"It's Amy Drake. And I've been here two years. I'm in the eighth grade now."

"You showed up at homeroom in seventh grade, then you were gone. How come you stopped coming to school?"

"I got real sick. I couldn't be around too many people or I'd get sicker, so Mom and Dad pulled me out."

"Then how'd you get to the next grade?"

"Homeschool."

He wore a satisfied smirk and then his expression dulled. He looked away, fighting the desire to ask, but curiosity clawed at him until he caved. "What did you have?"

"An autoimmune disorder."

"Are you better?"

"I'm out here, ain't I?"

"Yeah," he said, putting on that same smirk.

"Sorry your friend got dragged off."

"And it was the first time either of us snuck out at night."

"Fun, isn't it?"

"It was till he got caught," Connor said, kicking at the crack in the sidewalk. "Guess I should just go home."

"You're already out. Come with me instead."

He smiled at her and wished he had the nerve to tell her it was a far better alternative. "Where do we go?"

"Anywhere we want." She smiled back, walking away from his house.

"This isn't your first time?" he asked as he walked beside her.

"Nope."

"Cool."

"It is, isn't it?" she said as a brisk breeze blew down the street, rustling the maple leaves above them. A handful drifted around them.

He stopped and reached out until one landed in his palm. He twiddled the red leaf in his fingers and then handed it to her.

She stuck it in the folded brim of her tuque.

"You look like a Canadian," he said.

"Take-off," she said.

They laughed.

When the night silence settled, they soaked it in like sweet music for a moment.

"Guess we shouldn't stand here all night," she said and continued walking.

"So when you're out here, where do you normally go?"

"Braid Cemetery."

"Why there?"

"It's Halloween. You're not supposed to hang out at the post office or someplace boring." She took a right at the next street. He followed her lead.

"You ever see anything?" he asked.

"Like what?"

Connor didn't want to answer.

"Like what?" she repeated.

"You know." He paused until he had the courage to say it. "Weird stuff."

"You mean like zombies and witches?"

He nodded.

She laughed. "Not yet. Just people like you."

"What's that mean?" he asked, his face contorted.

"Curious people. That's all." She mirrored his expression.

His guard lowered. "Oh. Okay."

They came to Braid Cemetery. A streetlamp illuminated the iron bars of its gate.

"So this is your favorite hangout?" He gazed up at the dark, gnarled trees that lined the property's perimeter.

"You'd prefer the playground?"

"Okay. But we better see some zombies."

She laughed as she crossed the threshold, tramping leaves underfoot. "Nerd."

Slowly and unsure, Connor followed her into the moonlit graveyard, carefully watching where each foot landed while she kept her same, steady pace.

When she was well ahead of him, she stopped. "You're dragging behind."

"It's dark. I don't want to step on anyone's grave."

"Guess you should be careful of that," she said, her head cocked slightly.

"Why?"

"You know what happens on Halloween, right?"

He shrugged, thinking of the conversation he and Brad had earlier and that somehow his answer would be insufficient.

"It's All Hallow's Eve. The night when the veil of spirits is thin. The spirits of the dead roam the earth from nightfall till sunrise," she said. "Stepping on someone's grave might make 'em really mad."

He looked around at the graveyard. "I guess ghosts aren't real, either."

"Sure they are. When the veil of spirits is thin, it becomes like a two-way mirror."

"What's that mean?"

"They can see out, but you can't see in, and sometimes it's the other way around. Sometimes it's so thin you can see each other."

He laughed. "Whatever. I just wanna see a zombie."

"Tell me you didn't really expect to see monsters on Halloween."

"I don't know."

"Aren't you...like, fourteen?"

"Yeah, so?" Something stirred in the brush. He jumped, bumping into her. "What was that?"

"Your manhood," she teased.

"Sorry. I don't spend all my free time in graveyards like you do."

Her expression went blank, followed by the furrowed brow of offense. She turned away and marched ahead. The *squish-squish* of damp grass grew soft as she disappeared in a shadow beneath the canopy of a giant oak.

"Hey!" he yelled. "What's wrong?"

She didn't answer.

"Did I say something?" He received no answer. "Dang it. Wait up!"

He marched after her, fearfully flinching at every chirp and croak around him. With each step the canopy grew nearer, and with it the fear of what lay in its shadow. "Amy?"

He stopped short of the shadow. He reached his hand into the dark and stepped beneath the canopy. The darkness was thick. Its coolness tickled his hands and face.

"Amy?" he called again and took another step. He bumped into something. It stood erect but gave way to his momentum. "Oh, man!" he blurted but swallowed his pride and reached out for the shape in front of him. "Amy?"

"Wimp."

"What are you doing here in the dark?"

"Same as you," she said.

Her breath swept his cheek. It grew cool. "Is it okay for you to be this close?"

"Why wouldn't it be?"

"I thought you'd get sick."

"I'll be fine."

"Should we keep walking?"

"There's no rush," she said. The mist of her breath settled on his lips.

He swallowed and reached into the black for some part of her. He found her sleeved right arm and followed it down to the cold hand. "I'm sorry if I made you mad."

She said nothing but took his hand in hers. His hand warmed hers like a slow-burning ember. Her body grew close to his, breasts brushing against his chest and then pulling away. Hand in hand, his arm extending, she pulled him to the edge of the shadow, near the center of the cemetery.

"So what do you think of your first night out?" she asked.

He stepped closer to her and squeezed her hand. "It's all right." He wanted to say more but didn't want to sound soft. She would look down on childish expressions.

"Are you mad there aren't any monsters roaming the streets?" she asked.

"I am slightly disappointed," he admitted.

"You can kiss me if you want."

He flinched and swallowed before speaking. "What about your dis—won't you get sick?"

"You worry too much."

"But what if—"

"You don't have anything that could hurt me."

"How do you know?"

"Shh," she whispered.

Though they were both in the dark, he closed his eyes and leaned forward. Her breath and then the moist lips, first top and then bottom, pressed against his. He opened his eyes.

She giggled into his mouth. Her breath felt like night air. She pulled him out of the shadow into the moonlight and smiled at him.

"That kinda makes up for not seeing any monsters," he said.

"You can say you saw a ghost," she said.

His head jerked side to side in search of the phantom. "Where?"

"Over there!" she pointed.

He let go of her hand and followed the direction of her pointed finger, only to find a trio of headstones.

"Here? There's nothing here." He turned to face her. But she was gone. "Amy?"

He returned to the shadow of the canopy, thrusting hands in every direction and height. "Where are you?"

No answer.

He left the shadow and looked where she had pointed: the three headstones. Dread fell upon him, pulling him irresistibly forward. He wanted to stop, to turn back, but he couldn't. In a moment he found himself standing at the foot of three graves, where a long, horizontal stone lay. It read:

A THREEFOLD CORD IS NOT QUICKLY BROKEN
Ecclesiastes 4:12

He gazed at the first headstone and read each from left to right, as the sickening dread stirred in his gut:

ARNOLD DRAKE
1975 -

AMY DRAKE
2002-2015

CINDY DRAKE
1979 -

In the center plot, the red maple leaf he had caught for Amy lay pressed gently into the moist earth. His heart beat rapidly. He turned to flee. From where he stood to the tall iron gate of Braid Cemetery, the entire graveyard was full of moving shadows and forms, from barely visible to corporeal.

His legs froze when Amy's words played in his mind. *"When the veil of spirits is thin, it becomes like a two-way mirror.... They can see out, but you can't see in.... Sometimes it's so thin you can see each other."*

He screamed until his legs broke free from their icy grip, and he fled, dodging solid forms that stood in his path. His arms flailed, thrashing, passing through the phantoms, fanning them away like smoke, their faces breaking apart the way a reflection does when stirring the water's surface.

"Come back!" some cried.

"Don't leave!" others said.

"Please stay!" more pleaded.

He ran screaming until he passed beneath the gate of Braid Cemetery and onto the empty street. He kept running, fearful of every sound or movement, until he reached the small grassy yard of his two-storey home where he climbed the peeling crepe myrtle onto the roof, went through his bedroom window, and slammed it shut.

He leaped into the solace of his bed and buried himself beneath the blankets, praying the man-made veil would be dense enough to obscure his presence from the things of night.

TAKERS

Paul Stansbury

Sometimes there's more than meets the eye. A young girl learns a vital lesson from her grandmother. It's the lesson of a lifetime.

Old Gramma Zola was the grandchild of a Shawnee medicine man. That's what she told me. And I never knew her to lie. Besides, she was so old she didn't have to lie. No one older than her lived to contradict what she said, so she could say anything without getting in trouble. My gramma on my momma's side was long dead when I was born, but Gramma's mother, Old Gramma Zola, was still living.

It was because Old Gramma Zola was the grandchild of a medicine man that she had the sight. And that's why I got it. Old Gramma was born around 1850. Nobody was sure about the exact date. Her daddy was thrown from his horse and died when she was about five. Her mama died of consumption a year or two after that. Then she had been taken in by a farmer and his wife to do hard chores. When she was fifteen, the farmer arranged for her to marry a widder-man. She said he got a pretty good price for her, and that is pretty much the story of her life. That and the fact she lived to be 103.

Old Gramma Zola was real old when I was born. Thin as a rail. I remember she spent her time mostly on the back porch in her rocking chair or in her bed listening to the radio. The back room was fixed up as her bedroom. She took her meals at the kitchen table even on Sundays when the big table was used. Always wore a faded bib apron. She had long, thick grey hair. I helped her wash it once a week. After it was dry, I would braid it into a thick cord that she draped over her left shoulder. Bright black eyes—Shawnee eyes, I suspect—looked out from deep within her wrinkled face. As I approach my ninety-sixth year on this earth, I see her face in mine when I look in the mirror.

When activities of the day had stopped and everybody readied for bed, Old Gramma smoked her pipe. She only used it when the Takers were about. She clamped it between her teeth, puffing blue smoke out from the side of her mouth. I'd plump up her pillows, and she'd pull up the covers. She kept a fan from the Robertson Funeral Home on her night stand. It had a painting of Jesus with lambs on one side and the address of the funeral home on the other. It was my job to fan her, sending the smoke drifting across the room. When it was time for me to go to bed, I would turn on the GE fan, which sat on her dresser.

On a spring night when I was thirteen, Old Gramma called for her pipe. "Takers is about tonight," she said.

"That's an old wives' tale," Momma said. "Don't be filling the chile's head with such nonsense. She don't need to be hearin' all that jus' cause you want to smoke your old pipe. She'll be havin' nightmares again."

"Ain't no tale. Your momma didn't pay it no heed and she got took before her time. Best you start believin' and the chile, too. Well, I guess I'll go to bed so's not to upset you no more," Old Gramma said in a huff. "Can the chile come sit with me whilst I go to sleep?"

"If you promise not to fill her head with ghost stories."

"They ain't ghosts, they's Takers. There's a difference."

"I don't know, and I don't care. You been talkin' 'bout nonsense all my life an' I'm tired of it. No more talkin' 'bout Takers or you can go to bed by yourself."

"All right," Old Gramma snipped. "You won't hear no more from me tonight. Come on, chile."

Momma looked at me. "And you be in your bed before the clock strikes ten—or else. And don't forget to wash your face and brush your teeth."

I followed Old Gramma to the back room and turned down her covers and plumped up the pillows while she washed and changed into her nightgown. She sat on the side of the bed, and I helped swing up her legs. She poked and prodded the pillows until she sat comfortably and then pointed to the lowboy, where her pipe, matches, tobacco, and the Robertson Funeral fan were.

I poured tobacco into the pipe and tamped it tight with my thumb before handing it to her. Clamping the stem between her teeth, she took a match and struck it along the side of the box. She waited until the flame died down before touching it to the tobacco and taking a deep draw.

"Don't like that match smell in my baccy," she said, smoke tumbling out of her mouth. "Get the fan, chile."

"Right here," I said, pulling the fan from behind my back.

"That's a good girl. Let me have that," she said, holding out her hand for the fan, "while you go see if your momma's light is out."

I left her on the bed and made my way down the hall that led to our bedrooms. I crept toward Momma's room, careful to avoid the squeaking spots. Then I got down on my hands and knees and peeked into the space under her door. I didn't see a light. I listened a bit but didn't hear anything either, so I headed back to Old Gramma's room. She sat where I had left her, pipe smoke drifting around her head while she rhythmically moved the fan back and forth.

"Light's out," I said.

"Here, chile." She handed over the fan. "They ain't ghosts or devils or anythin' like that. They's Takers, wandering about 'til they finds someone to take away."

"You told Momma you wasn't gonna talk 'bout them no more tonight."

"Said she wouldn't hear no more from me tonight. Now that she's gone to bed and mos' likely asleep, I figure she can't hear us having a little chat."

"Ain't that lying?"

"Well, you could call it that, but I don't. Said she wouldn't hear me and she won't, so's I don't hardly think that's lying."

I thought about it for a minute. Since I had questioned whether she was lying, it'd be all right. "How d'ya know if Takers is here?"

"You see's 'em," she said.

"But you said they was Takers about tonight. I didn't see none."

She pulled the pipe from her mouth. "That's 'cause you wasn't lookin'. You can't see 'em just by havin' your eyes open. You gots to be lookin'." She pointed the stem toward the door and blew a stream of smoke in that direction. "They's one right now."

My heart pounded so hard I thought it was going to bust out of my chest.

"See for yourself."

I turned my head and looked but didn't see anything. "Don't play tricks like that."

"Weren't no trick. You think they'll let you see 'em that easy?" she said. "No, you gots to look in the shadders and the nooks and crannies to see 'em. You gots to look out of the corner of your eye to see 'em. They comes in through the keyhole or slides out from behind the chifforobe. They floats up from between the floorboards and down outta the cracks in the ceiling.' An' they's just there for a second. Ain't goin' to stand around while you gawks at 'em. No, you gots to be ready. Jus' let your eyes ease out an' you'll see 'em. That's when you'll see their wisps like the last breaths of morning fog hanging on the hillsides. That's what they looks like. Little bits of fog or tiny shreds of clouds that fall down toward the ground. Gone as soon as you see them. Keep movin' that fan, chile. They don't like that. Fans and smoke—no, they don't truck with that at all."

"How's that?" I asked.

"Why, chile, use your brain," she chortled. "A fan jus' blows 'em away like you would shoo a fly offen a pie with your hand. They ain't nothin' but vapors. That's why they don't like smoke. It confuses 'em."

"How they take you then?"

She spoke in a hush. "When you goes to sleep and everthin' gets calm. That's when they gets you. They come right up to your face and rides your breath inside. That's when they takes you."

I watched her lips move, hanging on every word, when I thought I saw something in the shadows by the lowboy. I must have twitched because she immediately said, "Ha! You jus' seen one—your first— but not your last. They knows you now. Don't worry none, though. It ain't you they wants tonight. Just the same, from here on out, you gots to be on the lookout. Now keep that fan goin'."

I looked around the room but didn't see anything. Neither of us said a word for some time. I jumped at every creak and groan.

"Steady, chile," she said, "they don't make noise. It's jus' this old house coolin' off and settlin' in for the night."

After a while, I got up the courage to ask, "Ain't that jus' dyin?"

"What's that, chile?"

"When they take you."

She furrowed her brow. "No, chile, dyin' is somethin' altogether different. When you dies, you goes to plead your case with God, and he sets out what you gonna do from then on. But iffin the Takers gets you, it's a whole 'nother matter. They takes you away where nobody can find you. But they leaves your body for your kin to find. That's all you need to know."

"If you goes to God when you die, where do you go when the Takers get you?"

Old Gramma squeezed up her face real tight as if she sucked on a lemon, and then said, "Well, chile, I guess you gots to know sometime. They takes you to the shadder place where nothin's the way it's supposed to be. You feels the air, but you can't breathe. You eats food, but you stays hungry. You drinks water, but your mouth stays dry. The sun shines, but you is cold. You hear the sound of voices but don't know what they's sayin'." Her voice creaked. "You sees things, but you don't know what they is. You calls out in misery, but you don't make no sound. You is thinkin' hard, but you don't understand nothin'. And you know why? I'll tell you. It's 'cause the Takers live in the shadder place and they is powerful jealous of what we got. So they come out of the shadders and the nooks and the crannies an' sucks everthin' that makes you a person right outta you. That takes a powerful long time, an' all the while you gets paler and paler until you is nothin' but a wisp and you starts wandering in the shadders lookin' for someone to take 'cause you misses it so. That's where they took my baby Susie. That's where they'll take you iffin you ain't on your guard."

That was the first and only time I saw Old Gramma cry. She didn't bawl or anything, just a tear at the corner of her eye. I didn't ask any more questions because I wasn't sure I wanted any more answers. I had enough to think on, and it weighed awful heavy on my mind. I kept fanning while she smoked her pipe.

After a while, she handed me the pipe. "Here, chile, fill this up for me."

When I had done that, she said, "Best be gettin' on to bed now before the clock chimes."

"But can't I stay a bit longer? Don't you need me to fan away the Takers?"

"Iffin you don't get to bed before your momma told you to, that would be jus' like tellin' a lie, an' I don't put up with lyin'. You hear?"

"Yes, Ma'am," I said.

"So that's settled. 'Sides, got my GE fan to do the fannin' whilst I rests my eyes. Now jus' you turn it on and give Old Gramma a kiss before you go."

I cut on the fan. She leaned over, and I kissed her cheek.

"That's my good chile. Sleep tight an' don't forget what I told you."

I left her sitting in the bed, puffing on her pipe while the GE fan hummed on the nightstand.

The next morning, I got out of bed and went down to the kitchen. No lights were on; no coffee brewed. Momma and Old Gramma usually sat at the table sipping coffee in the morning. I went to the backroom to see if Old Gramma was still asleep. Her room was empty, too. Then I went to see if Momma was in her room. I pushed open the door and saw Old Gramma sobbing, holding Momma's hand.

She looked around at me. "She's done gone, chile. She's done gone."

I rushed over to the bed, and Old Gramma caught me in her arms. Her chest heaved as she stroked my head with her hand. Over her shoulder, I saw Momma, her face pale and still, eyes open a slit. I buried my head in Old Gramma's shoulder and cried.

She held me for the longest time until I stopped shuddering and the tears slowed. She pulled a hanky from her pocket and dabbed around my eyes. "Chile, think you can go nex' door and fetch Missus Ellis? Tell her I needs her over here. Can you do that?"

I nodded.

"That's a good chile. Now go on."

I went over and got Missus Ellis. She saw right away something was wrong. She called for the funeral home to come get Momma and helped Old Gramma with the arrangements.

No one could ever say exactly how Momma died except it was most likely from natural causes. At the funeral, the preacher said a lot of things about her going to her reward and being up in Heaven and looking down on us. I knew different, but Old Gramma told me not to say anything, so I kept my mouth shut.

The Great Depression had just begun, and we had to give up the house and move in with Aunt Verda. Old Gramma died some years after that. Aunt Verda came and got me at the bomb factory one day. She said Old Gramma had been sitting on the back porch, fanning herself, and just slumped over. I was pretty sure she made it to Heaven.

***

That was a very long time ago. Nowadays, the thing about the Bell Meade Retirement Home is they won't let me smoke, but they don't care if I run the ceiling fan all night. And they say they have a backup generator in case the power goes out. Still, I keep that old Robertson Funeral Home fan on the nightstand.

Just in case.

THE LEGEND OF POUTINE

Randy Whittaker

*A tongue-in-cheek look at the origins of the
greatest thing to come from Quebec, Canada,
next to the Montreal Canadiens.*

Pierre sat on the edge of the St. Lawrence River and watched the
current race toward Lower Canada. The sun was about to set, and
mosquitoes were coming out in droves, eagerly seeking their prey.
He stooped down and grabbed some of the rich, black dirt and
smeared it on his face—a trick the Natives had taught him to stop, or
at least minimize, the bloodthirsty barbarians.

The fire raged beside him, smoke curling up into the clear, crisp
air. He stood and looked around. He had no wonderment of his
surroundings. To him, this was home, a place he was much more
comfortable in than his home in New France.

His father had never understood his son's desire to trade and
explore. Although Pierre tried to explain to him the call of the wild,
his father never got it. Pierre was a high-spirited individual who

answered the call because in his heart it was what he was destined to do. He felt older and wiser than his seventeen years.

As he stood there, the mosquitoes buzzing around his mud-caked face, the bushes behind him rattled. He grabbed his rifle, turned, and brought the weapon to his shoulder in one quick motion.

He chuckled. "Oh, it's you. I thought maybe a bear was coming for me."

Daniel, his partner, smiled and hoisted the rabbits he had trapped. "We eat good tonight, my friend."

While the rabbits cooked over the open fire, Pierre opened the tin of tobacco and rolled a cigarette. When he finished, Daniel grabbed the tin and did the same.

"You know, Daniel, with these furs we have on this trip, I think we may be able to make a nice little sum for ourselves this time."

Daniel lit his cigarette from the fire, and his face took on a devilish aura. "I know, Pierre. The Natives have been very good to us this year. We need this. I could use a good bottle of whiskey for a change instead of this rot gut." He swallowed the last of his drink. "Well, I think that's it for me. Good night." He stood and went to the sleeping area next to the fire.

Pierre stared into the heavens. The clear night sky was brilliant with countless stars looking back at him. He tipped back the last of his drink and headed for his spot near the fire. As he lay on the ground, he had the sense someone or something watched him. He peered into the darkness, only seeing the millions of fireflies looking for love. He shook the uneasiness from his tired brain and closed his eyes.

That night, his dreams were filled with images far beyond what he had ever dreamed of previously. An oozing, warm comfort he had never experienced wrapped around his body. A viscous liquid surrounded him in a thick, pleasing sensation. His stomach felt full like he had eaten a huge meal, and the satisfaction made him smile in his sleep.

He opened his eyes and looked over at the red embers, which pulsated with a life force all their own. He stretched, got up, and noticed Daniel's spot was empty. He looked down the river and saw him walking back to camp with several fish on his line.

"We'll have these before we head out. We have to make the bend in the river today, so we probably won't be stopping much."

They ate the fish in silence, each man alone in his thoughts. Pierre often thought of his parents back in Montreal. His father, a wealthy business owner from the Old World, had given Pierre every advantage. The best life with the best education money could buy.

The plan was for Pierre to follow in his father's footsteps and carry on with the family business. Pierre, however, had other ideas.

"What do you mean you're going out into the woods? There are savages out there that will eat your heart," his father had screamed.

Pierre had met many natives in his travels and found them to be of a helpful, spiritual nature. The Iroquois were to be avoided, but the Hurons were great trading partners. Their spirituality affected all aspects of their lives. Pierre smiled as he thought of their story of the man beast known as Pou'Tawn, a large creature said to inhabit the dense forests along the banks of the St. Lawrence.

The legend stated the creature would rip a man apart and use the fat and bones to make its meal. The Natives knew someone had died when the air was filled with the rich, heavy aroma of the fat cooking on the fire. It was said the beast was huge with an enormous stomach covered in gray thick fur. Pierre had never seen one, but he knew enough of the Native life and beliefs that it would be unwise to discount their stories.

He and Daniel paddled their birch bark canoe in silence as the oars slid in and out of the water, a rhythmic dance they had been doing for years. Their hard, sinewy bodies were used to the arduous task. They would often row all day, neither complaining of the strenuous nature of their calling.

As he paddled, Pierre could not shake the uneasy feeling they were being followed. Several times he looked back over his shoulder, disrupting the rhythm.

"*Tabernac*, Pierre! What is the problem back there?" Daniel scolded.

Pierre apologized and continued his job. He looked into the forest sliding by, and his uneasiness grew. As they pulled the canoe to shore, Pierre thought he caught movement out of the corner of his eye. His hands immediately went to his rifle.

"What? What do you see?" Daniel asked as he, too, instinctively grabbed his weapon.

There were many animals in the forest that would make a quick meal out of a human, and both men knew that. Years of living in nature's world had taught them to always err on the side of caution.

"I don't know." Pierre slowly approached the edge of the trees. With his gun in front of him, he peered into the swaying forest but heard nothing except leaves blown by the approaching cooler air of the night. "I must be tired," he said, relaxing.

Daniel looked at Pierre with a cocked eye. "Are you sure you're all right?"

Pierre glanced at him, aware of Daniel's concerns. Daniel had witnessed men go crazy from years of isolation, crushing winters, and unrelenting stress of the *courier de bois* lifestyle. "Don't worry, Daniel. I am fine. Come on, let's get a fire going. I'm starving."

Pierre lay by the fire, listening to the cracking and popping of the burning branches. Daniel's snoring was the only other sound breaking the nighttime silence.

As Pierre drifted off, he heard a large crack of a branch from behind him. He spun around onto his stomach and held his breath.

He squinted, desperately trying to see into the pitch black of the night. Was that movement against a tree? His heart raced; his gun was out of reach. Still as a stone, he remained in the dust and continued to stare into the abyss. His breath came in short, quick gasps.

Was that a large figure standing next to a tree? He blinked. The apparition dropped to all fours, turned, and fled into the woods.

Pierre closed his eyes, fear making his heart pulsate. He opened his eyes and peered into the darkness.

The trees swayed gently in the breeze, and nothing but blackness met his gaze. His heart continued to race, and he was unable to move. He looked over at Daniel, and the loud snores told him he was still sound asleep.

Pierre was finally able to find the courage to stand. He grabbed his rifle and stepped into the night. He approached the area where he thought he had seen the creature. He advanced to the tree where it had been standing, and his breath, for the second time that night, was gone. On the bark was a large tuft of coarse gray hair.

When Daniel woke, Pierre said nothing of the encounter. Daniel already thought his partner might be losing his senses, and Pierre did not want to do anything to encourage those thoughts.

As they pushed the canoe back into the water, Pierre stared back at the tree. He breathed a sigh of relief when nothing but forest met his gaze.

While they paddled, Pierre's mind kept returning to the image of the creature he had seen: a large, almost wolf-like creature standing on two legs. He shuddered.

They paddled farther than they had planned that day, and by the time they stopped, the sun was already setting.

"I'll take a quick look around for some game," Daniel said.

Pierre was about to issue a warning but thought better of it. "All right. I'll get the fire started."

He watched Daniel walk into the ever-darkening forest as he gathered up firewood.

When the flame sputtered to life, Pierre's blood ran cold. From the forest, his friend's screams shattered the night air.

Pierre quickly grabbed his rifle and headed into the darkening world. His heart beat so hard he thought it would push through his chest. Daniel screamed a second time, and Pierre raced into the forest, his eyes adjusting to the darkness.

As he ran, branches sliced across his face, leaving bloody welts. He stumbled through the ever-thickening underbrush for what seemed like forever. Just as he was about to turn back, he found a cave.

His chest heaved and sweat rolled into his eyes despite the cool temperature. He raised his rifle to the ready and slowly crept into the lair.

As he inched his way in, he smelled smoke and the heavy, rich aroma of cooking. Heading deeper into the cave, dampness chilled him to his bones. His arms shook, and darkness wrapped around him like a blanket. He turned a corner and saw shadows from a fire dance on the opposite wall. The fire crackled, and the sweet aroma made him salivate despite his fear.

Pierre's heart thumped in his chest as the cave beckoned him in deeper. When he poked his head around the corner, his heart jumped into his throat. Beside the fire, splayed open like a canoe, was what remained of Daniel, his innards thrown on the dusty ground, thick blood pooling and mixing with the dirt.

Vomit raced up into his throat, and he puked on his shoes. As he wiped his mouth, he looked around the lair. On the fire was a kettle and beside that a plate with food on it. He inched closer to see what had been cooking. When he looked into the kettle, bile rose up again. He choked it down and stared into the bubbling thick mass.

Bones, devoid of meat or tendon, bobbed around in the liquid like large pieces of potatoes. Immediately Pierre knew they were Daniel's. The fat globules coagulated, and Pierre was reminded of his mother's fresh goat cheese. The entire mess mingled with a thick brown liquid. He looked over at the plate, and the steaming pile of food told him that who—or what—had done this to his friend had just left. He quickly retreated to the entrance of the cave and ran back to his canoe.

Pierre knew paddling at night was fraught with danger, but the thought of staying a minute longer in the area was not a consideration. The image of Daniel's torn, open body made his decision easy.

He pushed the canoe into the water and paddled as if his life depended on it. When he glanced over his shoulder, his body froze.

Standing on the shore was the largest creature Pierre had ever seen. He watched as it came out of the forest like an apparition. The creature stood at least seven feet tall with an enormous stomach. Its entire body was covered in a thick gray fur. Pierre swallowed hard and dug his paddle deep into the black water.

***

"This is a fascinating account of your life," the young woman said.

Pierre looked at her and smiled. "Yes, it is. And the strange part is that it's all true."

He had been invited to the Great Exhibition in London, and he looked around the Great Hall and sighed. He often had pangs of guilt for leaving his friend's body in the cave but knew he would have become the creature's dinner himself had he stayed any longer. The tales of his encounter and escape from the Great Beast had thrilled audiences, especially the meal that had been concocted.

As he sat there, his nostrils filled with a somewhat familiar yet disturbing aroma.

His aging, arthritic body creaked when he stood. He groaned and headed for the kitchen. As he opened the doors, his mind raced back to that fateful night when he found his friend. The aroma overwhelmed his senses.

The chef ran to greet him. "Pierre Royer, what a great honor, sir, to meet you. I have read your story countless times. In fact, it inspired me to create a dish in honor of your friend." He smiled from ear to ear and pointed to a plate on the counter.

Pierre's nostrils were still assaulted by the distinctive aroma of fat and sweetness, and he approached the plate with much trepidation.

"I took inspiration from your description of the boiling cauldron on the fire when you discovered your friend," the chef said with much glee in his voice. "I call it poutine, after the Great Beast himself."

Pierre looked at the plate of potatoes, cheese, and gravy, and his shoes were soon covered in vomit.

THE MONSTER OF BEINN LEITIR

Kristin Roahrig

Annaliese, orphaned during one of Scotland's many wars, is taken by the man-eating dark faire of the woods and, in order to survive, will make decisions that affect the surrounding countryside for years to come.

$\mathbf{F}$ar overhead a raven cawed, its voice the only sound Annaliese heard while traveling worn paths that no one besides her had used for many days. Ordinarily, those roads of the forest would have a steady stream of travelers: people on foot, the rich riding fine horses, and merchants pulling carts of wares. Gypsy caravans would be set up along the roads, the vendors camping near the edges and selling brilliant-colored cloth that couldn't easily be found in the area.

Annaliese once would have enjoyed the road, seeing the different people and wishing she could afford the trinkets the merchants carried. That once was not even that long ago, only a few days—days that no longer mattered, for she was truly alone in a world that changed with no conscience or remorse. The people who should be traveling those roads were gone, hiding or more likely killed by bands of soldiers that swarmed through the country, fighting a war Annaliese little understood. Understood only as one of many conflicts the great in the land had undertaken against each other.

Once again, she wished to retrace her steps and hide in her home in the valley beside the mountains called Beinn Leitir. Surrounded by those highlands, snow could still be seen on them despite the warm weather. Winters were harsh and summers short. It was only midway through the warm season, but Annaliese already faintly smelled the snows and ice that would soon return. She once had felt safe in her home from those elements, but that was no longer possible, for nothing remained. Smoke from the fires set to her village had lasted longer than it took the soldiers to kill her people. Ash from the flames had burned in her lungs for days afterward, creating a bitter taste. Who guessed a small place could make such a large amount of smoke.

The only reason she survived was because her parents had hidden her in their root cellar, and by some unknown grace, she had been overlooked. But Annaliese wasn't so certain if living was a blessing. Almost no food was to be found, and at times, she ate sticks and grass.

And the unnatural silence unnerved her. When night came, she was unable to sleep. The silence was too loud. The only time she saw another was when the bands of soldiers came through the area. The single thing about the silence that helped her was the ability to hear horses and men's voices so she could hide. Once she didn't hear the voices until it was almost too late.

Annaliese saw an orange flag and recognized the standard as the group who had destroyed her village. If she hadn't seen the standard, she would have been found and probably raped before they killed her.

After the near miss, Annaliese left the path, going into forests that hadn't been felled and keeping to the direction where the mountains stood. In the woods, no path of any sort existed, and she shifted among brushes and fallen trees. The closer she neared to the mountains, the darker the forests grew.

The sun fell in slender streaks between the large trees, but the light didn't warm her. The few strands were more like knotted claws trying to enclose her in their grips. Occasionally, she found food and heard animals.

When she was thirsty, she would go to a small lochan for water. Before the destruction of her village, she had never taken water from that lake. Not for fear of drowning, for the waters weren't deep; they barely rose above her waist. It was because of the name of the lochan, Lochan nan Corp, "the little loch of the dead." The name had once caused her to stay away until it became the only place to find a drink.

She stared into the waters, watching the currents move slowly, almost rhythmically, in a circle. Other times, the waters jerked, yanked by an unforeseen force.

She never saw living creatures. If she weren't half-starved, she would have thought that odd. But Annaliese was too hungry and tired to give it any thought. Despite that, even though she felt spied upon, she never heard nor saw anyone though the feeling of watching eyes stayed—eyes that studied her every move, causing a soft voice within her to speak, whispering to her that something was there, tracking her.

One evening when Annaliese was drifting off to sleep, she heard a rustle similar to leaves brushing against each other. Opening her eyes, she saw a slender woman with angular features standing in front of her. Pale, nearly white skin offset her dark eyes and hair. Her dress, although beautiful, was in rags and made of a fabric Annaliese had never seen previously. The woman smiled, showing sharp yellowed teeth with strips of meat stuck between them.

The ways of the land were never easy to understand. Large areas could be unexplored for years, never seen by a human eye. Annaliese had heard strange creatures lived in the mountains. People claimed to have found wolves as large as bears and monsters they saw as shadows. Others claimed to have seen winged beings, sometimes called faires, which were said to be benign, but more often than not, they were as like to eat your heart out as look at you. And she had heard of the Baobhan Sith, which resembled women and preyed on hunters and drank their blood. There were also the faire who stole children and made that child one of them.

Annaliese had never been certain whether to believe such stories or not, yet before her stood a woman, certain to be one of the creatures Annaliese had heard tales about.

"Are you lost child?" the dark faire asked.

"I'm not sure," Annaliese said.

"I think you are, but even if you're not, you have no one. You are all alone without family." The faire said the words briskly.

What magic enabled the faire to see into her past? The words that pointed out her dead family made Annaliese's eyes wet. Without realizing it, she was crying.

"How did you guess my family are gone?" Annaliese asked.

"Because the wars have killed many, and there is no one here with you, foolish child."

No magic. Only a reasonable guess; nothing more. Annaliese wasn't certain if the dark faire would provide protection or harm.

"Who are you?" Annaliese asked.

"Who? I'm a faire."

"What's your name?"

The dark faire cocked her head, her expression both curious and annoyed. "We don't have names."

"You must be called something."

"I am not."

"Are you a Baobhan Sith?"

"I've been called such by men."

Annaliese couldn't decide if the woman was a faire, a Baobhan Sith, or both. She'd rather think of her as a faire; she felt a little less fear at that belief.

"What do you want from me?" Annaliese asked.

"It depends," the faire said.

"Depends on what?"

"If you survive."

"Survive? I don't understand."

The faire's grin widened before she bent toward Annaliese. When the faire raised her hand, Annaliese noticed for the first time the faire's long and sharp fingernails. The nails pierced Annaliese's skin, cutting her hard on each side of her neck. A sensation that caused buoyancy and sickened her at the same time flooded through her body, and she felt herself drowning while a liquid filled her throat, causing her to gag.

Impassively, the faire watched her. Wanting to run, Annaliese tried stepping back but instead fell, absorbed completely in the liquid. She remained on the rough ground, not caring that small rocks bruised her skin. She closed her eyes, hoping to have her first true sleep since her family's death, but voices soon interrupted.

"Why did you bring her?" a voice whined.

"You complained the other day you wanted a playmate."

"Can I eat her?"

"No."

Annaliese opened her eyes to find herself in a large, foul-smelling cave. Above her loomed the dark faire who had bitten her and a young girl about Annaliese's age. The girl was human, but that was where the similarity between the two girls ended. She was shorter than Annaliese, with rounded curves, reddish hair, and sharpened teeth. Her angular face reminded Annaliese of the dark faire.

The faire rose and walked to the edge of the cave, staring out at the night sky.

Twisting around, the girl looked at Annaliese and sneered. "The thing is finally awake."

Annaliese shifted, noticing the liquid in her throat was gone. Each side of her neck ached. Raising both hands, she felt wounds that stung at her touch.

"Those wounds will heal," the faire said without turning.

Annaliese quickly lowered her hands.

"There is food left in the corner," the faire said.

Annaliese looked around and found a rabbit, which looked as if it had been dead for days, and a hand she was certain had come from a human. She turned away, trying to keep from heaving. "Is there anything else to eat?"

"No, there are too many dead, so blood is scarce. We eat meat when there's little else."

"I don't eat your food. I'm not like you," Annaliese said.

"You will be. You'll change slowly until you become as I am," the faire said.

"No, it's not possible."

"Look at the other girl. She has changed much already. My venom is in you. Those it doesn't kill, change. It's unavoidable. Come here." Still not turning, the faire held out her hand, indicating Annaliese should join her.

Obediently, Annaliese walked to the edge of the cave. They were on the side of a cliff. The drop was miles down, and she saw no end. The valley, nestled against the highlands of Beinn Leitir, spanned in every direction. Afraid of heights, Annaliese wanted to step back from the ledge, but the faire wouldn't let her. Nothing hindered them from the sky. The stars were the closest she had ever been to them, and Annaliese felt she could reach out and easily cup one flame in her palm.

"This is your place. Accept it," the faire said.

Annaliese's throat once again tightened, and she tried to stifle it. She'd only cried that one time since her village had been burned and all killed, and she didn't want to cry twice in one day.

The other girl in the cave sighed loudly, saying, "She's not going to be sniveling all the time, is she? I won't share my food with a sniveler."

The faire said nothing. Instead, she stared intently at the night, sniffing the air. Wings as dark as her hair spread out around her. Annaliese hadn't noticed them previously. The faire flew away.

For a second time, Annaliese forced herself to not cry. She faced the girl and watched her for a long moment. Despite what the girl had said about eating her, Annaliese asked, "What is your name?"

"I don't have one."

"You must. Everyone has a name. Every person that is," Annaliese corrected, remembering what the faire had said.

"If you feel you must call me something, I used to go by Garia."

"What will happen to me?" Annaliese asked.

"You've been bitten. You will either die from the poison or you won't. She already explained it to you. Are you witless as well as a sniveler?"

"Will I die?"

"So far, you appear to be living."

"So I'm safe?"

Garia grinned, letting her sharpened teeth show slightly. "Until I kill you."

***

The dark faire delivered food to the cave. She smelled of human blood but brought only fresh meat from animals—or so she said. Annaliese was certain some was human. She wanted to refuse the food, but she was too hungry so she ate it—all except the meat she thought might be human.

Along with the food, the dark faire brought female children, who would die before the next sunrise, to the cave. The faire's eyes saddened when she talked of Annaliese's little sister who had been lost. Annaliese wanted to tell her she didn't have a sister and that the girls the faire brought had never been her sisters.

Garia ate the corpses and taunted Annaliese while doing so. Annaliese hid her revulsion and anger. She hated Garia, who took food from her and hit her and bit her for no reason other than for enjoyment. Many times Garia ate the animal meat and mockingly offered a child's corpse.

Despite her hunger, Annaliese had kept herself from eating human flesh. She believed if she ate it that she would become one of the dark faire. She considered escaping, but the cave where they lived was located higher than she ever thought possible. Except for the fact that the height hindered her escape, she enjoyed the view.

Once she had been scared of heights, but they no longer daunted her.

Losing her fear of heights wasn't the only change happening to Annaliese. Her teeth sharpened, and her body became angular in shape, much like the faire and Garia. She was beginning to forget; memories of her home and parents were harder to recall. And she shied away from the sun, preferring an overcast sky.

She wanted to ask the faire about the changes, but she was almost never at the cave.

There was only Garia.

"What is happening to me?" Annaliese asked.

"You're becoming as we are," Garia said, sitting at the edge of the cave opening. She had grown wings that were dark with shades of blue highlighting the feathers. Somehow, though, despite the variance of colors, they looked dull compared to the dark faire's. Unlike the faire, Garia never tried to hide them and let them spread out.

Annaliese grew wings, as well. They were small, a varnished red, and her shoulders ached from the pain of them growing from her body.

"Why should I lose my memories?" Annaliese asked.

"Why do you want to keep them? Those are memories of a girl. A girl who was nothing."

"I don't want to forget," Annaliese said.

"You're a strange one."

Some days the faire took Annaliese and Garia into the forests. Annaliese's wings had grown larger and continued to feel as awkward as ever. Her flights were more often falls, her body hitting hard branches of the trees until she landed in the dimness of the forest. No matter how bright the sun from the mountain height where she lived, the forest was always in perpetual twilight, never truly morning nor evening.

The faire used those times to teach them to fly and hunt. Once they found two hunters. One was too young for the wars and the other too old. Fascinated, Annaliese watched while the faire moved imperceptibly to the men, charming them with only a smile before raising a nail to slash their skin and drink the trickling blood. She let Garia have a sip.

"That tastes better. Why do we have to settle for meat?" Garia asked.

"I told you the wars have made small bands of these men scarce. We cannot take on an army. We can only get what we can." For the first time, the faire's tone betrayed irritation.

On one of those expeditions, the faire found a baby swaddled in rags, abandoned under an enormous ancient tree. Annaliese grabbed the baby, propelled by two instincts: the first from when she was human and cared for those in need and the second, which she hadn't realized until then, the instinct to take the infant as her own and if that failed, to eat the infant.

She imagined how the fresh meat would taste before realizing they were her thoughts and not words suggested by Garia or the faire. Confused, Annaliese held out the baby.

"Stop playing and eat it," Garia snapped, stepping closer to Annaliese. "I'm hungry. Hand it over."

Annaliese shook her head and continued to hold the baby at arm's length.

Garia's mouth curved until the sharpened teeth were easy to see. "Hand it over, or I'll have you for dinner," and she snatched the infant while Annaliese stood mute, unable to stop her.

Garia tore the baby's throat with her teeth, an act so quick Annaliese nearly missed it.

"You need to control your hunger. That baby could have been one of us," the faire softly chided. Her tone held a trace of sorrow Annaliese had never heard previously.

"It would have died. The rest of them do—except that one." Garia indicated Annaliese.

"I always need to have at least two children," the faire said.

"Why two?" Annaliese asked.

"It is our way to survive. We need to have at least two children if not more. And I'm one of the blessed to have two that have survived so long. Remember, it is not just blood and meat that keeps us alive. It is those we change into one of our own. Without them, our race would wither away until none existed.

"Take better care to control your hunger," the faire said to Garia. Turning back to Annaliese, she added, "And you need to learn to accept your hunger."

***

Light from the setting sun was nearly diminished, leaving only a faint glow along the edge of the mountains. Many seasons had passed, and the sun's place in the sky had shifted.

Having just woken up, Annaliese settled back against the cave's wall, waiting for it to grow dark. She didn't enjoy the light, not as she once had. Flurries blew into the cave.

The faire flew in, landing beside Annaliese. Folding her dark wings close, she inspected them, pulling out bugs and twigs. After flinging them out the opening of the cave, she said, "Stand, we're going to hunt."

"I am?" Annaliese asked.

"Yes, you can fly. It's time to hunt."

Annaliese glanced toward Garia, who reclined in the corner, asleep. Annaliese flexed her wings, their shape continuing to feel unnatural and clumsy.

"It's time for you to learn," the faire insisted and, without waiting, flew out of the cave, leaving Annaliese no choice but to follow.

The faire had never raised a hand to Annaliese as her parents sometimes had. Yet Annaliese continued to secretly fear the creature in a way she never had her mother or father, although she would never think to disobey her.

The two flew for a good while before finding prey. The faire found it first, a rabbit. Annaliese saw the animal, too, even though the flurries had thickened. They set off after the rabbit. With one bite of her teeth that had slowly sharpened, Annaliese snapped the thin bones of the animal's neck, killing it instantly. She was surprised at the ease of it.

That was the first kill, for the rabbit wouldn't be enough to feed the three of them.

The hunt continued without trouble. Annaliese enjoyed being in the air, the breeze from her wings brushing her fingers. Then burning wood disturbed her enjoyment. The smell was one she had smelled previously, when the village she lived in had been burned.

The faire angled herself so her flight took her toward the fire. Annaliese followed, seeing a pale wisp of smoke rising above the treetops. The smoke was paler than the night sky. From the air, she saw shifting forms of the smoke. The smell of burned wood and flesh increased, nearly choking her.

She hesitated when the faire landed in the middle of what was once a village. Annaliese did not want to stand in a place so similar to her old home, but a sharp glance from the faire forced her to set down beside her.

The band of soldiers that had decimated the village was long gone. Annaliese recognized their work, even if it had been a great long while since she been in that world of people who lived in wooden houses not high in the sky.

The faire moved quietly forward, with Annaliese following, not stopping until she reached a house whose roof had fallen in. It hadn't burned down or been destroyed as had most of the other buildings, but flames had left scorch marks.

Reaching for the door, Annaliese opened it. In the shadows, she saw a boy with fair hair, about a year younger than she. At the sight of him, the hunger that had gnawed within her during the hunt sharpened and turned painful. The hunger dulled her senses until she could focus only on him. When she moved toward the boy, a small protest murmured in the back of her mind. Forcing her fingers into claws, she tore a thin strip across the boy's throat. She bent down, smelling the dirty meat still fresh and alive. Through the odor, another smell leaked through—his blood.

The faire grabbed her hand before she completely ripped the boy's throat. "Careful." Her tone sounded pleased.

Annaliese withdrew her hand from the boy, her dulled senses clearing. What had she almost done?

Stepping around her, the faire walked up to the boy, folding her wings behind her so they couldn't be seen. She clasped her hands in front of her, the long nails overlapping.

"No, please," Annaliese said.

"No? I'm afraid you have little choice. You did just attack him. Watch and learn."

Annaliese wanted to cry out or do something to stop her. Instead, she watched the faire soothingly speak to the boy, treating him as she had once treated her. The boy tried to struggle but couldn't. Annaliese stood, watching the faire take in his blood. Rising, the faire grabbed Annaliese's arm in a tight grip, forcing her to bend over the boy's throat.

"Drink it," she said.

Annaliese tried to refuse. Opening her mouth to say no, she instead found her mouth on his throat, drinking in the venom that tasted of metal and dirt. And something else, far finer than anything she had ever drunk.

"Best pick him up and add him to the other meat. We should then have enough to eat for a while."

"I can't touch him," Annaliese said.

Picking up the boy, the faire threw him at Annaliese, who jumped aside.

"We can't be picky about our food. We must eat what we can find," the faire said.

"I can't. I can't touch them."

The faire looked at her a good long while. Her eyes betrayed no emotion or thoughts.

What was the faire thinking? She had never stared at her in such a way before. The air smelled of a cold storm. The flurries gathered, becoming a steady snowfall. Finally the faire spoke, her voice so low Annaliese had to strain to understand her words.

"My child, you are not like this boy anymore and haven't been for a long time. You must accept yourself and what you've become. You must, otherwise you'll never thrive."

Annaliese pondered those words for days afterward. Garia kept trying to antagonize Annaliese, but for once her efforts came to nothing. Annaliese spent the next days alone, watching them pass until one evening when she crept close to the edge, glancing over Garia's shoulder into the dark vastness that had no end.

"Get back," Garia snarled.

"I have a right to be here."

"You're in my space. If you think of refusing to become what we are, you can just go far, far away. Let me have all the food."

Annaliese stepped back, trying to ignore the meat that lay nearby—the rabbit and a human arm, the only piece left of the boy that Garia hadn't devoured. Annaliese reached for the rabbit, but Garia snatched it before Annaliese could touch it. At the theft of the food, a simmering anger filled Annaliese.

She spied a rock, with a natural sharpened edge, by her foot. She gripped her fingers around it, ignoring the sharp edge that cut into her skin. Walking up behind Garia until she was close enough to smell her breath, she smashed the rock into Garia's skull. The bone crunched, and blood seeped down her back. The blow stung Garia momentarily, and Annaliese pushed the body forward, letting it tumble over the edge.

Annaliese didn't bother to watch Garia's body hit bottom. Instead, she entered the cave and ate the rabbit. The taste of flesh increased her hunger, and she turned to the meat. Her blind, instinctive rage continued to fill her. She grabbed the boy's arm and bit into it.

Nights later, the dark faire returned. Her eyes searched the cave and didn't stop until they rested on Annaliese. "What happened?"

"She took my meat, so I killed her."

The faire sat. Annaliese stayed still, quietly studying the faire to see her reaction to Garia's death.

"Now you understand why there must always be at least two children. The stronger will kill the weaker sibling. That is how we survive and grow more powerful. I survived by killing my sisters. Truth be told, I thought you would be the one killed. But no, you have come into your own, no longer a child. I see there is nothing more to teach you." The faire stared out into the night, never looking back at Annaliese.

***

The leaves stirred, brushing against Annaliese's face as she flew over the forests, searching for prey or lost children. The people who lived in the valley by the highlands of Beinn Leitir remained hidden in their homes, for some had already seen a shadow fly in the sky—the shadow many called simply the Monster of Beinn Leitir. Children were kept near the hearth fire, with no need for tales of terror to keep them close at hand. They knew well enough that a monster existed in the valley.

Not too concerned, Annaliese glided effortlessly for a while. The past few nights she had drunk well, having found a small raiding party of three men. She had caught plenty of children in her time but had never been able to take a child and make it her own. They had always died. One had lived through most of the night but was dead by the following evening.

Still full from the previous day's kill, she returned to the cave, folding her wings with the reddish tinge behind her, and sat on the ledge. She did this at times when she was no longer hungry.

The dark faire she killed long ago had said memories of another life faded until they no longer existed. Perhaps it had been different for the faire—or whatever she had been called—or maybe she had simply lied.

Annaliese watched the sun rise. Her eyes had become used to dark forests, so the light nearly blinded her. But still she sat, remembering what she once was.

BEARING WITNESS

Alan Kemister

A teenager takes a stolen car on a joyride to the beach. Seconds after he abandons the car, it explodes, killing four bystanders. From that night, he is tormented by demons who blame him for the deaths. He struggles to escape the demons but cannot shake responsibility for the deaths of an innocent woman and her three small children.

I was seventeen in July 2000 when I stole a totally awesome black BMW Z8 sports car. It was Friday afternoon, and an idiot had left his wheels with the engine running outside a store.

I parked at the beach and threw the keys into the dunes. A woman driving a wicked red convertible pulled in beside the Bimmer. As I walked toward the beach, she fussed with three kids and their beach paraphernalia.

Moments later, a massive explosion flattened me. When I sat up, I saw a pile of burning wreckage where the Bimmer had been. The convertible teetered on its side, leaning against another vehicle. The bloody remains of the young woman and her three kids were scattered far and wide.

I stood, shrugged my shoulders, and strode away. How could I have known someone rigged the car with a bomb? Tough luck for the woman and her rugrats, but it was the luck of the draw. You win some, you lose some, and she just lost big time.

Something, or someone, visited me that night, but I couldn't see a damn thing when the deep, mechanical voice assaulted me. "You murdered four people and walked away without concern for your victims."

"What should I have done? The explosion wasn't my doing, and with guts everywhere, what hope was there?"

"One child was alive when paramedics arrived. If you'd returned, you might have saved her. But no, you abandoned the scene without accepting responsibility for what you did."

I reached for the bedside lamp. A jolt of electricity threw me into the corner but produced no light.

"Sit there and listen," the voice boomed.

Silence pervaded the room after the voice explained my fate. I pondered his words. Did he lurk nearby? According to the voice, my teenage stupidity and a cavalier disregard for human life doomed me to observe 1,000 incidents of teens confronting life and death situations. The lives of innocent victims would depend on the choices the teens made during events they were partly or wholly responsible for. Unable to influence the events, I would be there to bear witness.

After that, my life—to the extent I still had one—focused on those life and death events. They didn't occur in a predictable manner, and I didn't know how much time had passed. I was no longer a carefree teen but an adult of indeterminate age with numerous health problems. I'd had a particularly difficult battle with testicular cancer that left me a useless, castrated eunuch. If that wasn't bad enough, an old injury deteriorated, leaving me crippled. I wore a knee brace and shuffled about with the help of an old man's four-footed cane.

My mental state was my greatest concern. I'd witnessed 796 incidents that imperilled lives. Only eight had positive outcomes. The others ended in slaughter—sometimes a single person, other times thousands. Witnessing the carnage produced by teens behaving as I had that day in the beach parking lot destroyed me. I'd tried to off myself five times, but the person, persons, or things controlling my life wouldn't let me die.

In an attempt to maintain a tiny vestige of sanity, I documented the eight positive incidents. I titled the first story, "Dina's Sinkhole." With these stories to sustain me, I might survive until I'd borne witness to my thousandth incident. Then they would free me from this servitude and let me die in peace.

***

Life was totally unfair. Dina's friends went home at 10:15 or 10:30 on school nights, but she had to be home by ten. She didn't go out every night. Most weeks she only went out on Thursdays, when she attended events at the community centre. The activities ended at 9:30 p.m., and everyone hung around talking and flirting. But to make it home by her stupid curfew, Dina had to leave by 9:45, and that didn't give her time for anything.

And leaving early meant she had to go home alone, which wasn't even safe. If she stayed until 10:30, Dina argued to her mother, she could walk with Brenda and Sally and everything would be cool. But no, she had to be home at ten.

As usual, Dina loitered, not leaving the centre until 9:50. She hurried along the shortcut through Tanner's Wood, which wasn't easy because rain that had fallen in torrents earlier in the evening had turned the path into a quagmire.

The rain had stopped, and the few breaks in the clouds helped, but it was still dark. She could barely make out the path and looked ahead at the gap between the trees on either side to keep from getting lost. She was running when, like a foolish character in an old-fashioned cartoon, she stepped into space and plummeted into a massive hole. A second later, with a sickening jolt, she landed on her left ankle and collapsed on her knees in half a metre of freezing water.

It was March, and the snow had only recently melted. The ice-cold water soaking through her jeans made movement almost impossible. It was black, and she couldn't see the walls of the pit she'd fallen into. The edge she'd plummeted over must be close, but she didn't know which way to turn. When she looked to the charcoal grey sky, the jet-black edging three or four metres above her gave her an idea of direction.

Dina struggled to her feet and stumbled ahead, hoping to find dry land. When she found the wall of her prison, but no respite from the water, Dina panicked as she struggled to climb. Her fingers and legs were so cold they'd become numb. Hypothermia, with loss of control and maybe even consciousness, was a real concern. Her left ankle hurt so much that every step was excruciating, and every time she winced with pain, she feared she would fall.

97

She tried to remember what she knew about hypothermia while she searched for dry ground along the wall. Thirty minutes, she thought. Someone could die after thirty minutes in icy water. She was only soaked to her waist, so she should last longer than that, but the time until she stopped being physically and mentally alert and capable of rescuing herself would be much shorter.

Trying to pick up her pace was a big mistake. She caught her bad ankle on something and down she went, face first in the water. The shock was extreme. She may have been cold previously, but that was nothing compared to the mind- and muscle-numbing pain of complete immersion in the freezing water.

Dina banged the top of her head on an overhanging tree root as she struggled to her feet. She fell backward into the water and didn't move.

Back at the community centre, David Banks shut off the last computer and glanced around the room, looking for anything he'd missed. He nodded to Eddie, his fellow volunteer in the Simple Computing for Seniors course. Eddie switched off the lights, and the two headed for Tanner's Wood and the fifteen-minute walk to their neighbourhood. The digital clock over the door read 10:02 p.m.

Eddie was not one of David's real friends. His mean and vindictive comments turned off everyone, including David. But having company for the trek through the dark and foreboding woods was worth a few nasty cracks. He would have preferred to walk home with one of the girls hanging around the centre, but he was too much of a computer nerd for them. They preferred the hunks on the rugby team or the ne'er-do-wells loitering by the video arcade.

Before they entered the woods, Eddie yanged about David's clothes, which was an old complaint and not one David needed after a trying evening with two old biddies who couldn't understand something as simple as e-mail. Eddie droned on, making fun of David wearing a mid-winter parka when everyone else wore hoodies. But while the others shivered, the parka kept David warm. There shouldn't be an argument, but he would never convince Eddie of that.

"Oh, just screw off and let me wear whatever I want," David said with more vehemence than usual. He didn't want to admit it, but his lack of success with girls was getting to him.

Girls came to him for help with their homework but turned him down if he suggested anything else, and he couldn't understand why. He was sixteen and decent looking, nearly six feet tall and strong and fit. Sure, he didn't have the killer abs of the guys who pumped iron, but he wasn't wimpy. And he got along with everyone, not like Eddie, the obnoxious jerk.

"You'll never find a girl if you refuse to dress like everyone else," Eddie said as he stormed ahead.

Suddenly, David saw a strange black shape across the path in front of Eddie. "Stop!"

Eddie pulled up short. "Shit! It's a bloody great hole."

"What should we do?" David asked as he rushed to the edge.

"The town's work crews will solve it tomorrow."

Typical, David thought. Eddie was a self-centred bastard. "But what if someone comes along and falls in? What if someone has already fallen in? We should check that out and set up temporary barricades."

Eddie had pushed his way into the undergrowth, away from the blocked path. "Suit yourself, but I'm going home."

"So you won't stay and help?"

"Nope. I'm outta here."

"Can you at least stop at my place and tell my father what's happened?"

"Whatever," Eddie replied over his shoulder as he jogged away.

David dumped his backpack and crept to the edge of the abyss. "Anyone down there," he yelled.

No one answered, but he thought he heard sounds. Probably an animal he'd disturbed, but he decided to investigate. He returned to his backpack and rummaged for his flashlight. The small device had an LED rather than an incandescent bulb, so it cast a strong but narrowly focussed beam of light.

He crawled to the edge of the sinkhole and slithered on his stomach until he had his head over the opening. He switched on the light and shined it into the darkness. David saw nothing at first, but as he gained better understanding of the problem, he determined the walls were more or less vertical with no dangerous undercutting. They were three or four metres high, and the bottom of the pit was covered with water. When he scanned his light across the surface of the water, he glimpsed a girl clinging to tree roots on the far side of the pit.

"Hey," he yelled as he focused the beam on her face.

Her eyelids quivered, and she opened her eyes. She moved, but barely.

"Come on, you can do it. Stand up and help me get you out of there."

He hurried around the pit until he was above her. "Whoa. This is dicey. I'm not sure I can reach you. Look straight up into the tree roots. You should be able to see me."

She tried to stand but stumbled and fell back into the water.

"Careful," he called. "Are you too frozen to move?"

The girl managed to get close to vertical with one hand on a root. He struggled to reach through the maze of tree roots, but their hands were still a metre apart.

"Over here."

She made a giant effort and stumbled forward with both arms extended. He grabbed one of them as she fell once again into the water. She twisted when she landed, but the one hand he gripped prevented her from submerging completely.

"I've got you. If you can stand up one last time, I should be able to brace myself in these roots and pull you out."

She got her second hand into his, and David managed to yank her to an upright position at the edge of the root mass. He crouched in front of her, her head at the level of his knees.

"Ready," he whispered. "I have my feet well-planted and a good grip on your arms. If I stand and lean backward, I should be able to pull you up here with me."

She nodded, and he grunted as he struggled to lift her. At one point, he thought they would topple and both end up in the water, but he managed to drag her through the roots and into the undergrowth beside the muddy forest path. He tugged off her coat and pulled her sweater over her head before wrapping his mid-thigh length, down-filled winter parka around her. The dry warmth of the coat enveloped her, and she drifted into semi-consciousness.

David was shocked by how close to death the unidentified young woman must have been. She hadn't uttered a word and had no control over her movements when he hauled her through the tree roots onto solid ground. Her hands and face, a pasty white, were tinged blue in several places. Her eyes opened and closed while she nodded off into unconsciousness.

She hadn't even resisted when he removed her wet clothing. He had thought about pulling off her jeans but wet jeans might be warmer than bare legs exposed to the elements.

Who was she? He'd lost his flashlight when he pulled her from the water, and in the dim light, he couldn't make a guess. She was probably heading to his neighbourhood since that path was rarely used, especially on a Thursday evening. He was mentally ticking off possibilities when she stirred, which reminded him he hadn't completed his task. His backpack contained a towel and a tuque. He would dry her hair and cover her head. Then he could determine how to warm her legs.

"Don't go anywhere," he said. "I'm fetching my pack and something for your head. It's on the other side of your swimming pool."

By the time he returned a few minutes later, he'd figured out she was Dina Matthews, a relative newcomer to their neighbourhood, who lived a few blocks from him. He remembered helping her with math once.

He dried her hair and stretched his tuque over her head.

"What should we do?" he asked, not even sure she was awake enough to hear him. "I don't suppose you're up to walking, and it'll be hard to carry you if you can't hold on."

He paused, hoping she'd respond, but she said nothing.

"Eddie was with me when we found the sinkhole, and he said he'd send my dad back to erect a barricade."

Mention of Eddie's name elicited a response, a sort of snort.

"Not impressed with Eddie? He's definitely a jerk, but I think he'll do what he said."

More reaction. She might have been trying to shake her head but still hadn't said anything.

"You may be right. Should we try to walk out?"

Dina didn't respond. In fact, she'd gone back to sleep. David tried to remember how they'd described the fireman's carry in first aid.

When he tried to lift her, he heard a car. Seconds later, headlights came into view, and David relaxed.

David's father took charge, instructing him to strip off their clothes and snuggle together on the backseat of the SUV. Mr. Banks jacked up the heat in the car and smiled when he noticed his son hadn't removed his briefs. He wrapped the emergency blanket around them and piled David's parka on top.

"You get her as warm as you can. If that idiot friend of yours had told me you'd rescued someone with hypothermia, we'd have an ambulance here by now. And if he'd come back with me, we could have barricades up in no time. But don't worry. An ambulance is on the way as well as patrolmen to look after the scene."

"I could help with the barricades," David suggested.

His father shook his head. "Your job is to get that girl warm. She appears to be on the borderline between moderate and severe hypothermia, so this is no joke. I'll turn the car and head toward the road. We'll flag down the ambulance when we see it."

Mr. Banks jumped in the front seat. Within seconds, he had turned the car and the portable red light flashed. Most of the time,

David would rather not have a police detective for a father, but at that moment, his dad the policeman was perfect.

"Do we know her name? Has anyone informed her parents?" his dad asked as he accelerated down the narrow forest path.

"She's Dina Matthews. I didn't have my phone or I would have called you ages ago. Her phone and stuff are probably at the bottom of the pit."

Detective Banks stopped at the edge of the woods. The ambulance, with sirens blaring and lights flashing, was only one hundred metres away.

***

For days, I struggled with retelling the story about Dina and the sinkhole. I never paid attention in school, so the whole process was incredibly difficult. After three days, I had a reasonable draft— hardly polished prose, but hell, I was a complete beginner. After reading what I had written, I was happy with the result.

I slept through the nights I worked on the story, but the night after I finished it, the voice returned, and I was once again thrust into the role of witnessing events I could not influence. I leaned heavily on my cane while I hobbled toward my next encounter.

Two teenage boys sat hunched over computer terminals in an attic room that must have been one of their bedrooms.

"Yes, we've done it! The missile is launched. Man, this is great. I'm right inside their command centre. Look, I can even launch drones that will protect our missile. They're like Kamikaze planes that sacrifice themselves by intercepting missiles launched to destroy ours."

"You sure? I'm into their missile tracking system and can't see it."

"That's because I'm too smart for them. The idiots at the Turkish base who monitor the area aren't even aware it's been launched."

"But the launch site is manned. They must know."

"I'm sure they do, but by the time they realize the launch order came from hackers, it'll be halfway to the Kremlin."

"And to destroy it, they must take control back from us."

"Yeah, really, and they only have fifteen minutes."

The door to the room flew open, and soldiers in body armour rushed in and cut down the two hackers with a hail of bullets from automatic weapons. A storm trooper threw off her helmet, pushed the body of one teen to the floor, and attacked his computer terminal. She hammered away at the keyboard for several minutes.

"Got it," she exclaimed. "We're in control. Do you copy me? Nine minutes and fifty-four seconds to impact. Transferring control to Central Command."

When I awoke, I turned on the twenty-four-hour news channel. No mention of a rogue attack on Moscow. Had it been averted at the last moment, or had there never been a real threat? The local news didn't mention a swat team raid on a residence or the death of two teens.

Later that day, I started recording the second of my good-news stories, and over the following weeks, I witnessed more horrors. My efforts relating the heroics of the few teens who prevailed, saving themselves and one or more others, only gave brief respites from the misery of watching one tragedy after another.

Finally, after untold days and nights, I'd witnessed my one thousandth incident. Free from my servitude, I acquired a gun and returned to the beach where the horrors began.

***

"What have we got?" Detective John Spence asked Constable Megan Smith as he strode toward floodlights lighting a hollow in the dunes.

"Crime scene specialists are busy with the scene, but it looks like a suicide. High school student apparently put a small calibre pistol in his mouth and pulled the trigger."

"Then why call me out in the middle of the night?"

"We're not twenty metres from the place where the BMW blew up three days ago killing that woman and her children. Witnesses said they saw a teenage boy leaving the scene. Our victim fits the description. Seemed like the sort of unlikely coincidence that would attract your interest."

"Right, let's see what the medical officer and our crime scene colleagues can tell us."

Dawn was breaking when the detectives uncovered the critical piece of information.

"His prints match those on the key fob discovered in the dunes after the explosion," Megan announced.

"The key for the Bimmer?"

"That's right. Almost certain our suicide hijacked the BMW and took it for a joyride. Got to the beach, threw the keys in the dunes, and thought his little adventure was over."

"Then the Bimmer exploded, killing four people, and his lark turned into a nightmare."

"He couldn't live with it. He came back to the crime scene and killed himself."

"That doesn't solve the bigger problem of who planted the bomb and why, but it should tie up one loose end. Before we close the book, we should visit his folks to determine if he's been depressed or displayed other behaviour that suggests he contemplated suicide. It's also possible he has an alibi for Friday afternoon."

"There might even be a suicide note."

"I doubt it, but a search of his room may tell us something."

"Looks pretty clear cut," Megan said after the visit. "We already knew he drove the BMW to the beach. No suicide note but plenty of entries in his computer that attest to his mental state. And we learned where he acquired the gun."

"And his parents confirmed that he hardly left his room from Friday evening until yesterday morning. Suggests he brooded over his actions for two and a half days."

"What else do we need?"

"Nothing, really. But I don't understand why he was clutching a cane. His folks said he was healthy with no mobility issues."

THE GRAVEDIGGER

Tom Robson

The only problem living next to the graveyard is the custodian, Bart Bonds. But a young boy has no idea how much of a problem Bart will become.

Everybody liked him. Everybody except me, that is. And I'm still not sure why I didn't. But I was right. Now that everyone knows about that night's happenings and what followed, Bart Bonds' name has slipped way down the popularity list.

Bart was the kind of man who would help anybody. He'd cut grass for someone who'd broken their ankle in an accident. He'd plough the driveway for a sick neighbor during a January snowstorm. He'd keep an eye on your house if you were down south in the winter months. He'd do those things and not expect any payment. He was also a reliable and available Mr. Fix-It in any electrical, plumbing, or house repair emergency. Odd jobs were how he earned money.

Among those jobs were groundskeeper and gravedigger at the local cemetery in our village of Fletcher's Falls. If you saw or heard his mini backhoe working in the churchyard, you would know the obituary of a local individual would appear in the next day's paper. Funeral to follow.

The back garden of our house sloped down to the cemetery, so quite often I saw Bart mowing grass, trimming hedges, or tidying neglected burial plots. He even repaired and resurrected tipped-over gravestones when those dumb kids knocked them down. Bart presented himself as an all-round good guy, but he never liked me hanging out in the graveyard.

The first time he chased me out was when he found me cleaning moss and dirt off one of the older tombstones. I was trying to trace my family history. That particular marker was my great-grandfather's, and I wanted to see what useful information was carved into the stone.

Bart didn't want to hear my explanation and made it clear he didn't like fifteen-year-olds hanging out in "his" cemetery. That didn't stop me, but after that, I always checked to make sure he wasn't around when I prowled the grounds.

Toward the end of September, while adding to our family tree on my computer, I realized I was missing a vital piece of information. I suspected the missing birthplace might be on great-grandmother Crowell's grave marker. Though it was evening and the light fading, I walked down our garden to the gap in the hedge that led to the cemetery. I had heard Bart's mini backhoe stop a few minutes previously, so I figured he had left. Despite that, I checked to make sure before I stepped through the gap.

And I noticed something not quite right.

Bart had been digging the grave for the next day's burial of old Mr. Jones, who used to run the corner store before Sobeys took over. I saw mounds of earth that had been removed from the hole, and then, in the fading light and rising fog of the cool evening, I saw Bart. He carried a large bundle over his shoulder. I couldn't be sure, but the bundle seemed to be wrapped in garbage bags. While he staggered with his load toward the newly dug grave, he stumbled over a pile of fresh earth. To avoid a fall, he dumped the bundle, which slid down the mound.

He straightened and meandered behind the other mound of earth. He returned with a short ladder and disappeared down the hole. Seconds later, he emerged without the bundle, pulled up the ladder, and started the backhoe, which was still parked close by. He dumped a few buckets of dirt into the hole and used the bucket to tamp down the earth. Whatever the bundle consisted of was well and truly buried.

By that time, it was too dark to read gravestones. Besides, Bart was still tidying up the piles of dirt and hiding them beneath blankets of plastic grass. I was becoming cold and damp, so I hurried home. I could do my graveyard research the next day after school.

It wasn't until I was in bed, tossing and turning, unable to sleep, that I thought about the buried bundle. What was Bart up to? What had he put in the bottom of Mr. Jones' grave? The next morning, the coffin and a lot more earth would lay on top of that mystery.

I was probably overtired and not thinking too clearly when I decided midnight, on that foggy fall night, was a good time to find answers to my questions. I convinced myself it was then or never.

Quietly, I dressed and sneaked out of the basement where I slept, stopping only to grab a flashlight. Outside, the fog reflected most of its light, but I knew where I was headed. Despite that, it took me a while to find the fresh gravesite. I almost fell into the hole when I tripped over the artificial turf that disguised mounds of earth.

I needed the ladder to climb down the hole to uncover the mysterious bundle, but Bart must have put away the ladder, for it wasn't where it had been the previous day.

In the far corner of the graveyard sat an old, abandoned house used as storage for the cemetery. Bart kept tools and mower and goodness knows what else there. At the back was a parking space for his mini backhoe. The ladder had to be in the storage house.

I found the gravel road and followed it to the house. Through the fog, I thought I glimpsed a light in an upstairs window, but I didn't think the house had power. As I neared, the light no longer shone. Maybe it had been a reflection of a street light in the upstairs window of the storey-and-a-half relic.

I hoped the ladder would be stored outside, not locked inside. At the far side, my flashlight picked out the short aluminum ladder leaning against the house. When I reached it, I heard a thump from inside the house.

I hesitated. Then a shuffling noise came from the upstairs, where I thought I'd seen the light. I stepped back around the corner and looked up at the dirt-encrusted window. I didn't see a light, but that shuffling noise started again. I strained and thought I heard a muffled voice. Was it the imagination of my tired mind? No! There it was—again.

Right then I should have hurried home to wake my parents. They would have called the police to investigate. But over-tired fifteen-year-olds don't do what they are supposed to do. They also believe they don't need help with anything. I was so into the mysterious happenings and believed I could solve the puzzle without adult help. Something—or someone—was definitely in the cobwebbed attic of the old house.

Another thump.

More shuffling.

Indistinct, muffled shouts.

I had to get inside. But the doors were locked, front and back. I walked around the house, checking windows. A small basement window wasn't fastened, so I opened it. I wasn't sure I could squeeze through, but I did, and a workbench beneath the window broke my fall. After I crashed on it, I heard a series of thumps from above.

My flashlight revealed an untidy workspace where various tools were stored. Then my light found the steps leading up to a door on the main level. Should I yell that help was on its way? But what if Bart was somewhere in the creepy, old house?

Maybe he waited for me on the other side of the door to the main level. Perhaps he had hid in the attic, guarding whatever or whoever was there. Perhaps he'd been the one who had turned off the light. If he was there, he surely had heard my noisy entrance through the window.

The sounds from the attic continued. Wouldn't Bart have quieted the noises if he was in the house?

In case he waited for me, I snatched an old table leg that lay amongst the rubbish on the floor. I climbed the stairs to the door, praying it was unlocked while hoping Bart wasn't there to see my flashlight shining beneath the door.

Slowly, and oh, so quietly, I tried the doorknob, which turned easily. Before I opened the door, I hesitated. I had never in all my life been this scared.

I pushed the door hard, hoping to knock over Bart—if he hid behind it. But it slammed open against the wall. No one was there.

More thumping and muffled voices came from upstairs. I switched on a light. Nothing happened, so I shined the flashlight around. Closed doors led off the hallway. At the end, another flight of stairs headed to the top floor. Still terrified, I decided against checking what was behind the closed doors. I hurried to the stairs and quickly ascended, hoping my sneakered feet were not too noisy. The stairs creaked, but it didn't matter. If Bart was here, he would already know someone had invaded his sanctuary.

The door at the top was locked.

Frantic thumping and a yelling, indistinct voice came from behind the door.

I don't weigh much, and I'm not exactly muscular, but every kilo and last morsel of energy was in the shoulder that hit the locked door. It wasn't as secure as I had thought, and I crashed through, finishing in a heap on the floor next to something that kicked and made strange noises.

I'd managed to hold onto the flashlight, which shone on a pair of huge, terrified eyes from above a gag-covered mouth. It was a boy, perhaps younger than I. His hands were tied behind his back, and his legs were roped together from knee to ankle. The gagged sounds urged me to set him free.

The gag easily slid from his mouth and down his chin. After he thanked me, he said we had to be quick so we could get away before "he" came back. I worked on the knots around his wrists. They were stubborn, but once free, the boy shook his hands to get the feeling back.

He tried to help remove the green plastic rope from around his legs, but we got in one another's way. Eventually, he was free, but it took him a few minutes before he could stand.

I could tell he was scared. During his nervous gabbling, he said his name was Michael. He also said we had to look for his friend Chris. The man had taken Chris from the attic before it had gotten dark.

I asked about "the man," and Michael's description fit Bart Bonds to a T. Bart had offered the two boys a lift from the bus stop in town to Bedville, where they lived. The last thing Michael remembered before he woke and found himself tied up in the attic was drinking pop the man had given both of them in his truck.

"Ready?" I asked Michael.

But before he had a chance to reply, we heard the lock open on the front door.

"Shh!" I whispered.

Stupid me. Bart must have been able to see this place from his house and had seen my flashlight shining through the windows.

I turned out the light, whispering to Michael to return where he'd been. "Lie down and put the gag over your mouth again."

I felt around and grabbed the table leg I'd put down while I worked on the knots. Quietly, I closed the damaged attic door as much as I could and stood behind it, table leg on my shoulder, ready to swing it like a baseball bat.

Footsteps came down the hallway, from the front door to the foot of the stairs. Slowly they climbed. On the top step, outside the door, the person stopped. I knew it was Bart. Did he notice the damage? Did he realize the door was unlocked? Did he remember locking it before he left? Did he wonder if something awaited him on the other side of the door?

An explosion of movement occurred when the door flew open and he barged into the room. I swung at the crouched figure. My intention had been to strike the large target of Bart's belly. I figured I had one shot, and then we'd run while the older man had no breath left.

Instead, the table leg glanced off his hand held in front of his face though with enough force to hit him on the head. It was too dark to see exactly where I had struck him.

He screamed and went down.

I didn't need to tell Michael to get up and run. I took the stairs three at a time, and Michael and I almost fell over one another.

Bart had left the front door unlocked.

"Follow me!" I yelled and headed down the path to the main gate of the cemetery. The fog was thick, but it was the quickest way out to the road. I scrambled over the iron gate. Michael fell off but picked himself up.

It was way after midnight, but the dim lights of a car came at us out of the fog. Both of us waved frantically, but the car vanished back into the misty night.

I knew my best bet was to get us home before Bart found us. While I was deciding the best way to get back up the hill, I heard a truck start from the direction of Bart's house.

"What do we do?" Michael asked.

At least I knew where we were and where I wanted to go. Michael must have been totally confused. "To my place. Quickest way is back through the graveyard."

"What about Chris? We have to find him."

I hesitated. "I think I know where he might be, but we need my dad and maybe the police to check it out. Come on, let's go!"

I scrambled back over the gate, into the graveyard. Michael climbed a little more carefully this time.

"Stick close," I said. And he did.

A vehicle came down the hill. Without warning, lights on top of the truck's cab swung in the direction of the cemetery. The truck stopped while the lights searched for us. Thank goodness for the fog that swallowed the beams. We crouched behind tombstones until the lights turned off and the truck moved down to the main road. It turned toward the village centre, kerb crawling, its lights searching ditches and driveways.

We headed up the sloping cemetery, stumbling among grave markers. I wished I hadn't left the flashlight in the attic. The fog added to my confused sense of direction. It took some time, but I eventually got us to the gap in the hedge at the bottom of our yard.

My parents had no idea what was happening when I pounded the front door and woke them up. My older brother and my kid sister woke, too, before my dad calmed me down enough to ask about the boy I'd brought home at two o'clock in the morning and what we'd been up to. I told my garbled tale of kidnapping and the good guy Bart Bonds being a bad guy.

I wasn't too far into my story—frequently interrupted by Michael's version of events—when Dad told Mom to call 9-1-1.

The police arrived fifteen minutes later, just after the ambulance.

"We don't need an ambulance, Mom!" I said.

"Probably not," Dad responded. "But if you connected, like you claim you did, with that table leg, Bart Bonds may need help from the paramedics. If it was Bart Bonds."

"What do you mean 'if'?"

"Did you see who you hit?"

"No. It was too dark. But it had to be him," I insisted.

The policeman intervened. "Another police car's gone to pick up Mr. Bonds. As caretaker of the graveyard, he has to let us into that house where Michael was held. If he was on the receiving end of that homerun swing with the table leg, we'll know."

And so it continued, with Michael and me giving statements to the police, but not before Michael's parents were contacted and a police car dispatched to bring them to Fletcher's Falls.

Bart wasn't at home when the police went for him. But, of course, I knew that. He was off in his truck, trying to find us.

Once Michael's parents arrived at our house, they and their son were whisked away so Michael could be checked out at the hospital.

Mr. Jones wasn't buried the next day. His gravesite was a crime scene. I ran on adrenaline while I watched, from a distance, the white-plastic-clothed police remove earth from the hole and bring up the wrapped bundle. Much later, after I'd slept, I was told that it was the body of Michael's buddy Chris.

Two days later, in a small town in a neighbouring province, the police arrested Bart in a hospital emergency room. Apparently, he wanted his broken pinky finger straightened and set, but the doctor was more concerned about his damaged jaw. The doctor was also suspicious, and after reporting the injuries to the police, he delayed Bart's departure until they arrived.

Back in our province, Bart was charged with murder and kidnapping. Before he came to trial, a long investigation revealed that, over the years, a number of children in Fletcher's Falls and in neighbouring communities had disappeared. Forensics linked some of those children to evidence found in the attic of the old house where Michael and Chris had been kept.

A smart detective matched the dates of those disappearances to funerals and burials in our cemetery. Bart's popularity declined even more when permission was given to open up seven graves, where remains of missing children were found beneath six of the coffins.

Bart Bonds, Mr. Nice Guy who'd help out anybody, was in fact, a serial killer.

Michael and I met often during the investigation and trial. He and his parents thanked me every time for saving him.

It's nice to know that occasionally when fifteen-year-olds do wrong, it turns out to be right after all.

IN TENTS

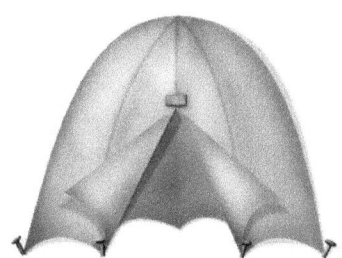

Heron Greenesmith

Two teenagers agree that something weird and awful changed their lives one night. But what? Nothing is right and everything is wrong in this story about two siblings who want a night under the stars.

The only thing J and I agree on is this: something weird and awful changed our lives that night. The way J tells it, some sort of tornado, a "time tornado" he calls it, tore through our back field, pulled up our tent, and deposited it, rainfly and all, stakes taut in the ground, twenty feet from where we had set it up.

I don't remember a "time tornado." I remember a sickening, wrenching feeling in my gut that woke me up regretting not cooking the steak longer and had me reaching for the zipper to get at least my head out of the tent before I threw up.

But I didn't throw up. No, I remember that clearly.

We had pitched the tent under the little group of pine trees at the end of the driveway because the forecast had said it might rain. It hadn't rained, though. What I remember thinking before I even stuck my head through the tent door was that the quality of light had changed. No longer the looming pines between us and the staring full moon. Strong, clear light filled the tent, and when I finally jammed my head through the zipper, gasping for air that would never really be there again, the moon beamed at me without any piney filter.

I was confused. I forgot to be sick. The tent unzipped the rest of the way, and we were standing next to it, babbling and blubbering before I could find the pine trees. All the way down the field they were, though J still maintains his twenty-foot story. But in my memory of that night's events, we stumbled out of the tent nearly an acre away from the edge of the pines, smack in the middle of our back field.

We also disagree on what happened next though you'll understand why I maintain a staunch position on this point. In J's story, right here is where I faint. Clean pass out. He says I pointed at the pine trees, looked back at the tent, and keeled over. Of course, that's not what I remember at all. I'll admit to a blank space in my memory, but you can hardly fault me that.

While I was *allegedly* out, J admits to being very scared, and I will charitably back him up on that. But I wouldn't use the word scared. What I remember is feeling displaced, unhomed, wronged, but not yet knowing why. Scared yes, but deeper than simple fear. I was terrified and couldn't have told you why. Something had fundamentally changed, and we didn't know what. It felt like coming home to an empty house at a time of day when it should have been full of light and noise and knowing something must have gone terribly wrong to take everyone so suddenly away. An accident, a tragedy, a death. It felt like that dream you have where you're so busy running or saving someone or doing something really important that it's not until you wake with a gasp that you realize it was a nightmare. You just hadn't seen the monster right behind you.

Those first few minutes in the field were sickening and disorienting.

Finally we found each other's arms and staggered toward the house, agreeing on one thing: we didn't want to be outside any longer. Camping had been J's idea though, of course, he says it was mine. Either way, I think we both wanted some time with the other, away from Mom's clinginess while I readied for senior year at high school and J to junior high. You'd think we were going away to college the way she had carried on instead of school minutes away. Perhaps she was endeared by us wanting to spend the night sleeping so close to each other. She got that look on her face, the crumpled chin and shining eyes of sentiment. We mumbled things about marinating meat and let her hug us too long.

The forecast had said slight chance of rain, so we set up under the pine trees and threw the rainfly over the tent just in case. I would have liked to look at the moon rising through the pines.

It was overkill, but we built a fire, really doing it right. We marinated the steak and let it rest momentarily on the coals before inhaling it along with stale potato chips. Then we lounged around the fire, throwing pinecones at each other and laughing until we choked. Mosquitos drove us into the tent, and we farted at each other until we fell asleep. Then whatever happened, happened.

While I was passed out or whatever, J says he crouched over me, scared of who knows what. Says it was the longest minute of his life because he didn't know what had happened, and suddenly I was gone. Says he almost cried a few times, might have lain next to me to pat my face and whisper my name. I am honestly grateful he shared those things. I feel the loneliness creeping now, the mortification at the idea of not sharing this with anyone, of having to navigate this alone. J saved my life, and I saved his, and we save each other every day. Thinking of my body on the ground, alone, makes my skin crawl. He was there. He made sure I woke up.

I did wake up. Or sit up. Or whatever. And he was crouched over me, saying, "Oh, thank God thank God thank God thank God."

Under other circumstances, I would have laughed at his face, that wide, down-turned mouth, but something made me reach out and touch him, bring him closer. We hunkered on the ground, in the middle of the field, for some time.

Then we were standing and walking toward the house, hanging onto each other and holding up each other at the same time. We shook and cried a lot, staggering through the glaring moon-lit field toward the pine trees that were supposed to have protected us and to the back door of our house, where white shingles glowed quietly. J tripped on the long cement step and steadied himself with a thud against the house. Our feet weren't working. My mouth was so dry.

"What *was* that?" J said. Didn't say it. Whispered it. Whined it.

I shuddered and almost told him to hush. I was afraid to turn around to look back at our tent in the center of the gleaming field. What if it was back under the pines? What if it wasn't there at all? What if we weren't here?

"What was *that*?" J said again. He, too, stared at the house. Not looking at the field or the pine trees or the tent.

I shuddered again. I felt a pressure between my shoulder blades and at the back of my neck where little hairs react to cold and breeze and others' attention. I closed my eyes as if I needed to physically stop myself from turning around to look.

"What was that?" J said again.

Then the door opened and Mom stood before us, lit only by the pearly gleam of her bathrobe, clutching a turned-off flashlight. Her feet were bare and bony, toes long and nails ragged, nails painted only at the tips from neglected self-pedicures. The hem of her bathrobe was uneven. She had the bathrobe tied tightly around her waist, one side pulled higher than the other. Her hands around the flashlight were bony, too, her skin more translucent than I remembered.

Once again, J and I disagree on the details. He says Mom reached out and touched our shoulders, brought us inside the kitchen, turned on the light over the sink, sat us down at the table, and only then looked at our faces.

But she looked at me while we were still outside. I know because I was looking at her and saw the worst thing I could see. I saw in my mother's eyes the same confusion and shock I knew was plain on my face. Her eyes widened and her mouth gaped, tensing at the corners into a wide, terrible O.

She did reach out to touch our shoulders, and she did bring us into the kitchen. She did sit us at the table and turn on the light over the sink. J was right. But he was focused on his feet, stumbling around the counter and chairs, while Mom and I stared over his bowed head.

Sitting wasn't better. J trembled, and I think he still mouthed *oh God oh God oh God*. I reached out to touch him and saw that my hand shook, too.

Mom looked at both of us. She didn't ask if we were sick from the raw steak. She didn't ask if it had started to rain. She didn't ask if I had teased J about getting homesick. She didn't ask if the bugs were too bad. Her silence was the most terrifying yet. Did she not even want to know?

My body felt cold. I rubbed my hands on my thighs. J and I were still in our shorts and T-shirts. That surprised me for a moment. I felt so fundamentally different that my blue flannel shorts, which I remembered putting on the previous morning and stripping down to before slipping into my sleeping bag, seemed traitorous. My hands were sticky along my bare thighs. My cheeks felt wet, and I realized I was crying.

We three sat there for some time. I felt a tightness and a closing-in: the moon-gleamed field pressed the pine trees closer to the house, holding us in its heart, hemming, handling. The flouncy kitchen curtains seemed ludicrous. My mother's eyes. J's near-silent chanting.

She spoke: "Two years." Another whisper, a whine.

No one had said a word out loud since we had woken. I wanted to scream to see if I still could.

"Two *years*."

I knew before I knew. My bones knew. J stopped his prayer. I felt him listening.

"Two *years*."

"What?" J said.

"Two years," my mother said, hands bone-tight on the unlit flashlight. "You've been gone for two years."

J leaned over and threw up on the floor.

"We had a funeral for you," she said. "We didn't know where you were. Thought you were dead."

I felt just as sick, and a moan leaked from my throat, filling the kitchen like the stink of J's vomit.

"Two *years*." My mother's voice was broken.

I looked at her face again, the face of this woman I knew so well, the person I knew the best. A new papery-ness was there, the same translucence from her hands crept up her neck and face. She looked weary and wary, and I didn't know if I was projecting or if she had new wrinkles, new lines around her mouth and under her nose. Her familiarity blurred at the edges as if she was almost the woman I knew but not quite. Seen through a lens. Or a fog.

I tried to touch her, reach across the table and take away the flashlight, hold her hand in mine, but she flinched away from me, drew farther into her robe, and I couldn't.

But then she exhaled, and her breath cleared the room.

I blinked, and my lids stuck together with grains of sleep and tears. Mom sighed again, and the room cleared more. I sat up and J coughed, the loudest noise so far.

The next few weeks were weird, let me tell you. We sat up until dawn that first night, figuring out what we were going to tell folks, and in the end, we decided that J and I had run into the woods to avoid school, been caught in a storm or whatever, got lost, got amnesia, and finally wandered back two years to the day from when we first disappeared. Our story was shaky as hell but weirdly corroborated by our total inability to tell it the same twice in a row.

Mom's parents were pissed. They had seen what our disappearance had done to her, and they were not inclined to entertain our "little trip." It took four visits to their cottage to convince them we didn't remember a thing. It felt horrible lying to them, sitting in their broad living room, listening to their anger, their confusion, their regret, their apologies, their tears.

It was a goddamn mess.

The whole entire thing.

Still is.

THEY CAME FROM OGIJIMA

S.L. Kerns

Takamatsu, Japan, is a nice quiet town for sixteen-year-old Arata. With no girlfriend and a recently separated family, he is a lonely boy. All he has to occupy himself is his love for music and baseball and his younger sister, Kaori—until the night the wild creatures from the island of Ogijima move into the city. With his family scattered and perhaps in danger, Arata pedals his way to them. Are they okay? Will he make it?

Arata, wearing earphones, sat on his bed. It was almost time to sleep. Posters hung on the wall of his favorite Japanese rock bands: Hi-Standard, Bump of Chicken, the Bawdies, the Blue Hearts, and Who What Who What. The latter's latest single vibrated in his ears, firing off neurons in a pulsating pattern.

At barely sixteen, Arata had grown tired of the K-pop trend sweeping across Asia. What good was his guitar for picking up girls if all they listened to was men in makeup singing over computer-generated beats? Without a girlfriend, he felt lonely, like a single dark cloud in clear blue skies.

The only girl who loved him was his younger sister, Kaori, and even she teased him, especially about his acne, but her comments didn't bother him. His skin was surprisingly clear compared to other members of his high school baseball team. The summer heat and sweat transformed the players into pizza-faced boys, and Arata only had to deal with the occasional blackhead on his nose and a few red pimples on his chin.

He looked pretty good in the team photo. His black hair, shaved on the sides and a little shaggy on the top, resembled a true rocker's style, a look he was happy with. He had the same sharp nose as his sister.

He missed living under the same roof with Kaori, but she had moved in with their mom after the divorce. They resided in Ota, and he lived with his dad in a townhouse five kilometers away near Sunport. His parents had become quite strict ever since they split up and stayed on his back about everything, from his black fingernails to his choice of words. He never received praise for being on the honor roll at school. Maybe they were bored without each other. Maybe they took out their frustrations on him.

Being a true rebel, he couldn't wait to graduate and get a few piercings, maybe even hide a couple of tattoos under his T-shirt. He would love to show off his piercings and tattoos when he got them, but the sleepy senior citizens of Takamatsu would accuse him of having joined the *Yakuza*. Why would he ever join a gang? For more rules? No thanks.

From his bed, with the next upbeat alternative-rock track playing, he turned out his light and stared out the window, watching the lighthouse shine on the harbor. Even in the night sky, the clouds appeared dark while they sped past the little island of Ogijima, rolling toward his window faster than Japanese boars could swim across to the island.

Arata had once encountered a white-mustached boar on Ogijima. He and Kaori had walked past a "Beware of Wild Boars" sign but shrugged it off while they marched down the shaded, narrow path encased by a canopy of green trees. The island was well-known for boars roaming between trees and in and out of small, damp caves.

Three minutes later, a branch had snapped to the left, and they stopped in their tracks when they saw the tail end of an ugly, brown boar dash into the thick of the forest. Though its back faced them, he still saw the long tusks curling out. It had to be well over sixty kilograms, nearly the same weight as Arata, and longer than Kaori.

His sister had screamed until he picked her up in one arm and grabbed a strong limb from the ground in the other. They kept their guard up for the remainder of the two-kilometer hike until they met back up with their parents, who were happily married at the time. Together and feeling safe, they sat and waited for the ferry back to Takamatsu, relieved to be rid of the boars for good.

So they had thought.

***

That night, while Arata lay snoring, snug in his bed with his unplugged smartphone beside him, a peculiar thing happened.

The waves of the sea splashed around as strong winds directed them like a musical conductor leading an intense symphony. The thunder ripped open the sky, sending the lightning free to strike whatever it pleased. A bolt shot down and tore through a ferry shipping wild boars from Ogijima to the mainland. Boars were sometimes shipped to the mainland when the islands became overcrowded with them, making it dangerous for people living there.

With the crew missing and the boars free, the animals frantically squealed and snorted their way to the nearest port, Takamatsu.

All through the night people dreamed happy thoughts of beautiful hikes, nice fishing where they reeled in the big one, large bowls of *Sanuki udon* shared with loved ones, and *hanami* parties under the beautiful cherry blossoms of Ritsurin park. They had no idea of the terror they were about to face.

As usual on Saturdays, Arata awoke late in the morning. With his eyes swollen from deep REM sleep, he scanned through the Facebook newsfeed on his smartphone, never noticing the low battery warning. Then he saw a shocking headline: "They came from Ogijima."

He jumped from bed and ran downstairs—in his maroon briefs—searching for his dad. The kitchen was empty, but his father had left a note saying he had to work at the electric company that weekend. He had obviously rushed off because his half-eaten breakfast was on the table.

Arata sat down for a bite while he read the rest of the news in his feed. He sweated and could barely stomach his meal. There had been so many attacks. He worried about Kaori and his mother. He tried to call his mother but got no answer. He checked every news source for names. He flopped back in the chair. It seemed his family was safe, but he couldn't be too sure.

He tossed the dirty plate in the sink, dressed in his previous day's clothes, and threw on his high school baseball cap to hide his bedhead. Riding his old black Fromage bike, he pedaled hard toward his mom's house. The rusty chain rattled like a snake and threatened to snap.

Saturdays were days for freedom, fun, shopping, eating out, sports games, and other outdoor activities, but the shopping arcades—the longest strip of them in Japan—were dead quiet. He rode past locked shops with gates down and blinds closed. He felt alone in the world.

At the first big crosswalk, he hit a red light and eased to a stop. The roads were empty, the usual parked taxis were missing, and the cute girls in short skirts weren't around for his viewing pleasure. Arata didn't see the point in waiting the ninety seconds for the light to turn green. He checked for police on patrol. Nothing. He kicked down on the pedals and sped through the red light.

Up ahead at the end of the next arcade, he saw it. His bike screeched to a halt. A brown boar turned its ugly head at him and snorted and squealed like a stuck pig. He had never heard such an awful sound.

The tusks extending from its face reminded him of devils he had seen in American films and on album covers of a fair share of metal bands from around the world.

He slowly turned his bike. There were several side roads he could take to his mom and sister. Before he had fully turned, the boar squealed again, and Arata heard the *clackety-clack* of hooves when it sprinted toward him. He quickly took off down the side street, past the one hundred-yen shop and his favorite record shop, ROOTS. He was out from under the shaded roof of Marugamemachi Arcade, but the boar gained on him, showing jagged teeth while its grunts grew nearer. Arata, soaked in sweat from the sweltering sun, had no idea how he would survive.

Then he saw something useful: a blue inter-city bus parked on the side of the street. Pedaling harder than he ever had in any race around the schoolyard with his friends, the chain snapped.

The boars were almost within reach. He tossed down his bike and dashed toward the front of the bus. He jumped, aiming for the flat section of the front end, and grabbed hold with his fingertips. His legs dangled while he tried to pull himself up, the challenge made greater with sweaty hands.

The boars had caught up to him. He looked down and saw four of them snapping at his heels and another seven or eight galloping toward him. He kicked his feet while straining to hoist himself. One of the boars caught the sole of his left shoe and ripped it from his foot.

He flopped on the roof and lay panting. He wiped the sweat from his brow and sat up. The heat on top of the bus was strong, and he was terribly thirsty.

An orchestra of grunts resonated from below. He peeked over the side. Over thirty boars butted the bus, trying to tip it over. While the bus rocked back and forth, Arata lay flat, gripping the sides, trying his best not to tumble off. He grunted under the pressure almost as loudly as the boars and turned his head, looking for an escape. To the left was a ladder on the side of a two-storey *sukiyaki* restaurant. It was a ten-foot leap, but with proper timing he was sure he could manage it and latch on to the railing.

He stood and balanced on the bus as he had learned a couple years previously when he surfed with his family in Okinawa. "Feel the waves," his dad had told him. "Feel them and go with it."

When the bus rocked left, he leaped. His ribs crashed into the railing and sent a terrible pain throughout his body. While pulling himself up, the bus toppled. He calmed down and prayed to the gods that someone was at the restaurant and would open the black door when he banged on it.

He tried and tried, but his knocks and cries went unanswered, and then he checked the knob. In a second, he was reminded why Takamatsu was such a beautiful city. Crime was almost non-existent, and doors were rarely locked. He entered the restaurant.

The lights were off. The place was silent except for faint cries of the maniacal boars. He made his way through the dark, feeling along the walls, looking for a light switch. Near the steps, he got his wish and flipped on the light.

The wooden stairs pointed the way to his escape. When he reached the bottom floor and looked around the red room, he spotted the kitchen and squinted. He felt poisoned by death when a foul odor gushed up his nose and into his lungs. He followed the putrid smell to the kitchen, gagging all the way. Life would have been easier if he had a gun like the Terminator, but if guns were available, the doors would most likely have been locked.

A sharp kitchen knife was better than nothing. He snatched one off the bloody cutting board, being careful not to touch the stale fish swarming with flies. With the knife in his hand, he headed toward the front door. Cracking it open, he peeped outside. All clear.

Quickly and quietly, he searched the empty arcade's rows of deserted bikes—each one tagged with a parking ticket for the alcoholics who had left them in the no-parking zone the previous night—until he found one with a cheap lock from Daiso, the one-coin shop. Using the kitchen knife, he sliced it off.

He hopped on the borrowed red bike—the pedal rough under his bare foot—and sped off toward his mom's. Closed shops whirred by, and his thoughts switched from the danger he had just escaped to worry for his family's safety. Panting through his dry mouth, he picked up the pace.

During the ride, he saw only one sign of life, from a cop car with sirens blaring, racing down Rainbow Dori. Finally, turning next to Yamada, his mother's little white house came into view. His eyes gleamed at the sight of the familiar yellow Honda N-WGN parked in the pebble driveway. He stopped in front of the black gate, unlocked it, and walked past the rocky path toward the door. He had always admired his mom's ability to turn a small front yard into a stunning Zen garden, but he ignored the beauty in his rush.

The downstairs was dark, but the light leading up the stairs was on. "Mom. It's me!"

Quick feet thumped on the stairs, and Kaori appeared. Arata welcomed the sight of her long black pigtails and blue Doraemon nightgown. Her eyes widened and welled with tears when she sprinted toward him. He caught her in his arms and squeezed her as if it was the last time he'd ever hold her. At the rate she grew, it might be true.

"Momma's upstairs," she said in a weak voice. "She has company."

Confused, he followed his sister up the stairs. The wooden treads creaked. At the top, they walked past the restroom on the left and straight toward their mother's bedroom on the right. The door was cracked open, and he heard the muffled voice of a man.

With his arm above his sister's head, Arata pushed open the door and nearly fell back with surprise. Sitting on the *tatami*, his mom leaned against his dad's shoulder. His dad's white-collared shirt was bloody. Kaori ran over to the mat and flopped between their parents.

"Dad?"

"Arata? How did—"

"I was worried about Mom and Sis. I thought you were at work."

"I passed along Rainbow Dori when I nearly hit one of those things. I crashed into a light pole. The car wouldn't start, so I hopped out and ran here. I wanted to go back and get you, but the radio said not to go. I figured you had checked the news on your Facebook and knew to stay home."

"Why didn't you call?" Arata asked.

"I did. Many times," his dad said.

Arata checked his phone. "Oh, crap! My battery died. I forgot to charge it last night."

His dad frowned.

"Sorry," Arata said.

His mother motioned for him to sit. He reached his parents, who gave him a big family hug.

The boars had done much damage to their quiet city, but it would be over soon. They'd wait it out as the news had instructed—but not alone.

They'd wait it out as a family.

UNINTENDED CONSEQUENCES

Kathy L. Price

Sometimes it pays to follow the crowd, as Carla and Jordie discover when they sneak off during an organized summer camp hike.

It seemed like hours had passed, but according to Carla's watch, less than twenty minutes had gone by since the last time she'd checked. The pain in her left leg was excruciating. The limb lay at odd angles and was obviously broken, the bone exposed and poking through the skin. Looking at it only made her feel worse. As she leaned back against the rock, she tried, once again, to get her mind under control, to focus on taking slow, deep breaths the way Jordie had shown her.

Don't panic. Stay calm. It'll be all right," she kept telling herself. At least the bleeding had stopped, although the T-shirt Jordie had used as a bandage was soaked with blood. The flies had found her and relentlessly buzzed around. They swarmed over her leg and bit her arms. Exhausted, she'd given up trying to swat them away. A sob escaped her lips when one crawled into her right ear and, out of desperation, she tried in vain to brush it out with her shoulder.

"Why?" she scolded herself for the millionth time. Why hadn't she been more careful? Why had this happened? It had been a perfect day—one about to get even better—and then this. She took a deep, ragged breath and wiped away tears. "Come on, Carla," she mumbled. "Be strong. Get it together."

She pushed up with her arms to try to shift her position against the rock without moving her leg, but no matter what she did, she couldn't get comfortable. She also couldn't keep her mind still. Her imagination ran wild with a million questions and dark, unthinkable answers.

How long will it take Jordie to return? What if something happens to him? Will he find the way back? What if he doesn't make it back?

"Oh God, don't go there, Carla. Don't think like that. He'll come through. He's got to."

That morning, the campers had been given the choice of working on lame arts and craft projects or going on a hike. The other kids were such nerds, and the camp counselors were stick-in-the-muds who didn't want to let the campers have any fun. Carla knew there wouldn't be much chance for privacy in the crafts room, so she was delighted when Jordie suggested they go on the hiking trip. Later, he had whispered it would be a cool idea for them to ditch the other hikers and head off on their own.

While the counselor had been announcing the "rules for hiking," Carla's heart skipped a beat when Jordie took her hand, gave it a squeeze, and winked. As the group started off, the two of them managed to place themselves at the rear. They lagged farther and farther behind and, at the first opportunity, slipped away and headed off in a different direction.

The mountain air had been brisk and fresh. The sun shone brightly, and the scent of pine was invigorating as they sauntered along the trail.

Jordie had helped Carla over a rotted log. He held her hand as she climbed over a huge rockfall and caught her by the waist when she jumped to the ground. The air between them crackled with tension, and the sexual attraction was strong.

After an hour or so, the thrill of sneaking off on their own and pulling one over on the counselors had worn off, especially once Carla realized they were lost—at least she was.

"I'm not. I know the way. Don't sweat it," Jordie had reassured her. "I've been coming to this stupid camp for years. I know these mountains like the back of my hand."

"So how come I've never met you, then? I've been coming here for years, too, and I've never seen you before. Trust me, I'd remember."

"I don't know. Maybe we've always come at different times. Camp's open the whole summer. Most years I've only stayed a week or two, and usually at the end of summer, just before school."

"Maybe that's why," Carla had replied. "I usually do this camp in late June or early July. Sure glad I came later this year."

While hiking, they had traded stories about past summers, life at their respective high schools, and their plans for the future. As it turned out, they had both applied at—and been accepted to—the same college. Was that fate or what? She saw it as a sign they were meant to be together. Maybe, if she was lucky, they'd have some of the same classes. Her innate insecurity made her wonder, though, if he'd still want to hang out with her once they were away from "this stupid camp."

After another half hour or so of climbing steadily uphill, they had come to a canyon with an inviting stream at the bottom. The heat of the day had become intense during their hike, so they were sweaty and dusty—the perfect excuse for a swim. The water beckoned as it danced over the rocks and sparkled in the sun.

"Let's go for a quick dip before we head back," Jordie had suggested.

"But I don't have my suit," Carla had said, feeling a bit shy.

Jordie had winked at her and grinned. "Then you'll just have to go without. Come on."

She had watched as he scampered down the steep hillside, whipping off his striped camp shirt and then his T-shirt. His body was incredible. Without doubt, he was the best-looking guy she'd ever seen: slim but muscular and athletic, with dark hair and amazing blue eyes.

Carla had never done anything like that in her entire life and felt a thrill of excitement. Her parents were old-fashioned and conservative. She hadn't even been allowed to date until the previous fall. In fact, this year she had tried to get out of going to camp by telling her folks she was too old. Was she ever glad she'd let them talk her into one last summer.

When she and Jordie had met that first day of camp, she had pegged him as a stuck-up jock who thought he was better than everyone else. He was so handsome and charismatic that she had written him off, figuring he'd never be interested in her. She had assumed he'd likely ignore her the way most of the boys in her school did. Though Carla had never been one of the popular girls, a boy she didn't particularly care for had asked her to the junior/senior prom that spring. Still, it had been a shock when Jordie started paying attention to her, and she had been even more surprised when they hit it off. Now he was asking her to get naked and go skinny-dipping with him. What would happen after that? Would she lose her virginity at summer church camp? Her girlfriends would never believe her.

Distracted by her thoughts, Carla had taken a careless step. A rock turned under her ankle, and she lost her balance and plunged down the steep incline at the edge of the trail. As she tried to slow her descent, rocks cut into her hands and cascaded along with her, tearing up her knees and elbows. She fell over a little cliff near the bottom, where she careened into a boulder. Her leg went *snap*, and she tumbled the rest of the way down.

That had been at least four hours previously, and the sun would be setting soon.

Carla sipped water from her canteen—at least she had water—and tried not to worry. No matter what she thought about, she couldn't stop the questions from swirling around in her head. How far back was it to the ranger station? Had Jordie gotten there yet? How long before someone came to her rescue?

Bruised and sore, cold and hungry, Carla leaned back against the rock. Her parents would be angry and upset when they found out she and Jordie had gone off by themselves. Despite that, she'd give anything to see them. Surely the counselor who'd led the hike would have missed them hours previously. Maybe they'd started a search long before she had even fallen down the cliff. Any minute they'd find her. Likely, too, they had dogs sniffing the trails. Or a helicopter.

She clung to shreds of hope, straining to hear the *whap whap whap* of rotor blades or someone shouting her name. Would she have the energy to yell back, to let them know where she was? Oh, what she would give to have one of the whistles the counselor and ranger had advised them to carry while hiking. Exhausted, she closed her eyes.

Carla jolted awake at a noise reminiscent of her leg breaking. She opened her eyes. Twilight had come to the forest, but enough light existed that she could make out her surroundings. She saw nothing amiss but listened intently. Had she heard a twig snap? Or had the sound been part of a dream?

Over the now-familiar gurgling of the stream, there was an extra splashing sound. Trying to remain as still as possible, she scanned the stream's bank without moving her head. The splash came from her right, beyond her view. Afraid of what she might see, yet desperate to know, she slowly twisted her head. Her eyes widened but sheer terror kept the scream in her throat.

A huge brown bear and two cubs were crossing the stream not twenty feet from where she sat propped against the rock. Part of her brain registered that the cubs were cute, but a female bear with cubs to protect and feed would be highly dangerous. Though she didn't know how to make herself invisible, she kept as still as she could, barely daring to breathe, and willed the bears to keep going. About mid-stream, though, the mother bear reared up on its hind legs and sniffed.

The blood, Carla thought. *Oh God, it smells blood.*

Before Carla and Jordie had veered off, the counselor had taken the group to the ranger station, where the ranger had given a brief talk about safety. Should they ever find themselves in a situation similar to Carla's, he had advised them to remain still and play dead. She prayed his advice would work, for she couldn't move even if she wanted to.

The bear waded up the creek and rose, once again, on its hind legs. The animal grunted and shook its head. Something dangled from the far corner of the bear's mouth. It looked like—no...no...no, it couldn't be.

Carla didn't need to pretend to be dead. She automatically froze when the bear ambled out of the stream and approached her. The beast looked even bigger up close, and the smell of wild animal, of blood and death, overwhelmed her.

Her breath caught in her throat. She couldn't swallow. Snippets of her life flashed before her, like she'd heard they did when death neared. She prayed the bear had already eaten and would be content to leave her alone. It sniffed around and pushed her left hip with its nose. Intense pain shot up her leg, and she bit her tongue to keep from screaming.

Please don't eat me...please don't eat me...please don't eat me....

The bear raked its giant paw against her shoulder and snuffled by her ear. She wanted to close her eyes, but wouldn't the bear see the motion?

What should she do? She couldn't fight the bear, but it was almost on top of her.

Any second she'd pass out.

She willed herself to pass out.

How could she remain calm?

Her parents' faces appeared before her for the second time.

I'm so sorry. I love you guys so much. I wish I could change things, to have another chance, to be a better daughter.

Suddenly, the animal turned. It paused, shook its head, and raised its right paw to its mouth.

Again, Carla glimpsed the material lodged between the bear's molars. At such close range, she even saw the button—a button attached to a scrap of cloth that looked exactly like Jordie's striped camp shirt.

THE FOURTH FLOOR

E.F. Schraeder

For the unlucky ones, sometimes the past finds a way to repeat itself. That's what five friends discover when they set out on a mission to blow off class. They explore a boarded-up part of the school and uncover an ugly chapter of their school's hidden history. When you're a kid in a class of troublemakers, sometimes there's no place to go but down.

"The video is about fifty minutes," Ms. Meier announced, tugging down the screen at the blackboard. Without turning around, she said, "It'll take up the rest of class time."

"Nap time," Jay yelled, yawning loudly. He flopped his head onto the desk.

"I heard that," Ms. Meier said. "Jay, you should learn how to throw your voice." Her expression leaned between a smile and a frown when she turned to face the class of misfits.

Lanelle raised her hand, waving it in the air as if a chance existed it'd be missed.

Ms. Meier sighed. "Yes, Lanelle?"

"Is there going to be a quiz after?"

"What do you think?" Ms. Meier smiled briefly. "Yes, there's going to be a quiz after. Then we're all going to go home. Just try to pay attention to the main points."

Christian scraped his chair on the floor as he edged closer to the window.

"Christian!" Ms. Meier snapped.

"The glare, Teach, I can't see," Christian replied.

Ms. Meier smirked. "Stand up and move, then. No need to torture us."

"Nope. That's your job," Christian mumbled. He picked up his notebook and moved quietly to a desk in the back.

Portia laughed, turning to the back of the classroom to wink at him. They'd been dating for almost a month, which in their world amounted to hanging out after school and sharing stolen cigarettes and beer. She sat in the third row of the classroom, refusing to pay attention to anything other than Christian and her two best friends, Kyla and Jasmine.

Ms. Meier clicked the video to play. "On that splendid note, I'll be right back. Watch yourselves." She spun on her heels and took a fast clip out of the room. She let the door slam behind her.

Christian walked over to Portia. "I love when she leaves us alone, don't you?" He planted a wet kiss on her neck.

Portia wiped it off, half pushing him away. "Stop! She'll be right back."

"Right," Jay said. "How long to smoke a cig? Three minutes? Eat a cookie. Add two. Take a shit? Five more—"

"She's right about one thing, Jay. You're nasty!" Cary slapped her notebook shut.

"We're all nasty," Jay said. "Nobody in this school gives a shit about us. We're the dumb class, stuck with the dumb teacher, in the dumb wing of the building."

"Speak for yourself," Lanelle chimed.

"I'm speaking for us all," Jay said.

A loud crash resonated from the hall.

Jay laughed. "Maybe she's dead."

Christian turned his attention to shooting spit balls. One landed on Kelly's desk.

"Shh! I'm trying to learn something," Kelly hissed.

Jay laughed again. "She told me to speak for myself, so I'm speaking."

"You fool!" Kelly shook her head and moved to the front of the class.

"I'm out," Jay yelled, pushing back a row of desks when he stood. He strolled into the hall and hung on the doorframe. "Anybody else coming?"

"Hells, yah." Christian followed him.

Portia took a few seconds but quickly whispered, "Come on," to Jasmine. Kyla stood, too. Once Portia gathered her flock of BFFs, it was easy to join them.

When they entered the hall, Kyla and Jasmine each pulled packs of cigarettes from their purses and lit up in unison.

Jay grabbed one, took a long drag, and handed it back to Jasmine. "Get my heart rate up." He sprinted down the empty hall.

Theirs was the only active class on that wing of the building. With Ms. Meier doing who-knew-what for who-knew-how-long, Jay was going to have at it. He pulled signs off the walls and busted into locked rooms.

Portia and Christian lagged behind, grabbing at each other while they walked until settling into holding hands. Jasmine and Kyla followed but stayed back.

"How long has this been the dummy wing?" Portia asked.

"Dunno," Christian said.

They lingered at a window, staring out at the bigger end of the school where the rest of classes were held.

"After the building is fixed—you know, the rehab—is our class getting moved?" Portia asked. She leaned into Christian just enough for him to smile.

"Dunno," Christian said again.

Kyla giggled. "You are a dummy."

Jasmine and Kyla approached the window, draping their arms around the couple.

"Where's Jay?" Jasmine asked, glancing around.

Portia poked Jasmine in the ribs. "I told you you liked him!"

"I mean it. I don't even hear him!" Jasmine said.

"Me, either," Kyla added. "And he's loud. You always hear Jay, you know?"

"Let's split up. Find him," Christian said. "I'll go down there." He pointed up the hall. "You go back toward class," he said to Kyla and Jasmine.

"Like he'd go back to class. Ever," Portia said.

"Seriously," Jasmine added. "You're just trying to get some. And our girl ain't doing that in some ugly school hallway." She wagged her finger at Christian.

"Fine. We go together then," he said.

Kyla nodded. "That's more like it."

Since their class was the only one on the floor, the hallways were kept mostly dark. Loose plastic sheets hung over the doors where the heaviest construction happened after hours.

"This shit gives me the creeps," Christian said, kicking back the plastic.

"You know Jay's messing with us, right?" Kyla forced a laugh.

"Jerk," Jasmine said.

Kyla smiled at Portia. "Told you she liked him."

"You in here?" They called into the doors and in the halls. "Jay? Where'd you go, man?" They kept yelling as they approached the corner and slowed down. Jay was still nowhere in eyeshot.

Christian pushed one of the doors. "Hey, look." He pulled back the thick plastic that covered what they thought was another doorframe.

"Is it an empty room or something?" Kyla leaned on the door.

"I think it leads to an elevator," Christian said.

"Is it locked?" Portia rattled the large metal handle and lock securing the opening.

"You're pulling the lock. You tell us," Christian said.

"Think so." She let the lock drop.

"Let's get it open!" Kyla said.

"What for?" Jasmine asked.

"What for?" Christian jogged to the custodial closet and pulled out a screwdriver and hammer. "To see if it works!"

Jasmine tugged on her friend's sweatshirt. "Portia, come on, let's go back to class."

"You go if you want. I want to see if it works," Portia said.

"Shit. I'm out." Jasmine headed back toward the classroom.

Kyla glanced from Jasmine to Portia, deciding whether to stay or go. She rolled her eyes at them both just when Christian bolted toward them, tools in hand.

"Gonna bust it open," Christian yelled, pounding on the lock.

"Don't have to bang it like that," Portia said.

Kyla giggled. "Banging is all he knows how to do."

"What I need to do is crack this open." Christian jammed the screwdriver into the lock and pried. Then he tapped it with the hammer a few times.

"Whack it," Portia coaxed. "That's it."

Jasmine stood at the end of the hallway, watching. She shook her head slowly at them, caught her breath. She looked around for Jay one last time and then yelled after them, "You're messed up, fooling with that." She waved and slid back toward her classroom.

The lock clicked open.

"You got it," Portia whispered.

"Nice. Let's see." Kyla pushed the blocking door aside and let it crash to the floor.

Portia gasped.

"Jeepers," Christian said.

"Oh, my God," Kyla mumbled. "It's empty."

They stared down the dark shaft.

Christian bit his lip, realizing he'd just opened access to a major hazard. "It's like straight down." His heart raced.

Portia smacked his arm. "Obvious much?" She paused. "Did you even know this school had an elevator?"

"No, but four flights of steps is a lot. Maybe they were trying to get it to code or something, you know? Accessibility?" Christian offered.

The three of them stared into the dark, empty shaft. Motionless. A waft of cold air drifted toward them. Then a strange, foul odor followed. The sight gripped them while they gaped down into the nothingness of the hole.

"Quite a construction zone, huh? No wonder they sealed it off." Kyla waved her hands in front of her face, trying to clear the funky smell.

Portia's voice was low. "I guess. Wonder if they'll finish it this year."

"Can you see the bottom?" Kyla asked.

Christian reached into his pocket and pulled out some coins, tossing them down. They clanked noisily after a few seconds. "See? Not like it's a pit to Hell or anything." He let out a long sigh, somehow relieved.

"What's up here?" Jay appeared, grabbing them.

"Oh!" Portia screamed.

"Dude!" Christian yelled. "You could scare the shit out of people sneaking up on 'em like that. Coulda' killed us." He motioned to the elevator shaft.

"Holy bat cave—" Jay broke off, his gaze following the deep chasm before them. "That's not right."

Portia stepped back. "Come on. We should get back."

"No way. Not after finding this." Jay's voice rose. His eyes lit up, excited by the mystery as much as by the challenge of the empty shaft. "You think it goes all the way down to the basement?"

"Probably." Christian smirked. "It's deep."

"Whoa," Jay added. "Are the cables broken?" He reached out, swatting them.

Christian and Portia shrugged.

Jay leaned over the gaping opening and grabbed the thick cables with one hand, tugging on them as he swayed over the abyss.

Portia stepped back. ""Be careful, moron."

"You're insane." Kyla laughed, goading him.

"You know it." Jay smiled at her. Keeping one hand on the cable, he swung himself into the opening. His legs flopped in the air for a moment until he grabbed the cable with his other hand. He slowly shimmied downward in the dark.

Christian peered down. "Dude, what the hell are you doing?"

In seconds, no one could see Jay, and then he yelled, "Go find a flashlight."

Kyla headed to the custodian closet. Portia grabbed Christian's arm when her friend walked away.

"Is that safe?" Portia asked.

"What do you think?" Christian slumped over the opening, about to follow Jay.

"Don't. I'm scared," Portia said.

"He's fine. Aren't you, Jay?" Christian called.

Portia held her breath while leaning into Christian, clasping his arm even tighter in the silence. "He's not. This is wrong." Her voice was breathy, fast, and tears welled. "No."

"Shit. Settle down. Don't go all emotionally disturbed on me now, girl. Hold tight." Christian straightened and grasped the frame of the doorway. "Jay, stop messing. What's going on?"

Kyla returned, shaking a flashlight and tapping it. "Found one, but the light's weak. Batteries are going out, I think. Who knows how long it's been since it was used." She stared at Portia. "What's wrong?"

Portia stammered, "J-jay." She shifted from side-to-side, trying to form the next words. Sweat beaded on her forehead.

Kyla touched Portia's arm. "It's okay. Take your time. Breathe."

"Portia, come on—" Christian said.

"Let her tell me. You don't know what she's like when this happens. She's got to get it out on her own," Kyla said.

Christian nodded.

Portia's small frame trembled for a few moments, and when she finally responded, her voice shook and words came in gasps. "He's," she paused, "not," she swallowed, "answering."

"He's fooling with us," Christian added impatiently. "Little shit."

"We'll see, okay?" Kyla pointed the light into the shaft. "Jay?"

Portia grabbed her friend. "N-not t-too c-close!"

"Just breathe. Don't freak on me." Kyla smiled and handed her friend the flashlight. "Here, you look."

Portia took a small step forward and held the light, her hand wobbling. "Oh!" she screamed, jumping back. "S-something in there." She stared into the hole. "Something m-moving."

"Yah, Jay. The jerk." Christian huffed. He stared into the darkness. A hollow thumping sound came from what looked like nowhere. "Jay, knock it off now, okay? Jay!"

A sleek white cat suddenly sprang from the shaft, landing silently on the floor.

"Jeepers!" Christian yelled, jumping back.

"Oh, my God!" Kyla screeched.

The cat swirled around Portia's legs, rubbing affectionately, and then sat down abruptly and stared at them, blinking its pale pink eyes.

Portia remained motionless, staring at the little creature. "You don't belong here, do you?" Her voice turned to a whisper. "You don't want to stay here alone?"

"Is that what you saw?" Christian asked.

"Where'd it come from?" Kyla asked.

Portia gazed warmly at the slender cat. She knelt to touch it.

"You okay?" Kyla asked her.

"He's sweet, isn't he?" Portia slowly said, ignoring the question.

"Uh huh," Kyla replied.

"You think he was stuck down there?" Christian asked.

"I don't know. Cats are funny. They can get in and out of things people can't imagine, you know? Probably he sleeps in there somewhere. The shaft must be warmer than outside." Portia spoke with such authority that her words had to be true.

Kyla smiled at her friend. It was the most Portia had said without stammering or gasping. Either the anxiety was passing or the cat helped soothe her. "What a great cat."

"Hey, you know, if he's in and out of the shaft, maybe Jay's on another floor and like, can't hear us. You know?"

"Good thinking," Kyla said.

"I'll stay here with him," Portia said, pointing to the cat. "You go look, okay?"

Kyla shot Christian a worried glance and said to Portia, "How about I stay with you?"

"I'll go. Be right back." Christian ran toward the stairs. He clasped the handrails with both hands and took the steps two or more at a time, leaping down each flight as fast as he could. The whole way down, he yelled, "The ass. He has to be somewhere."

"You should go, too. He may be at the other end of the hall," Portia said. She sat on the floor petting the cat. "Look at his big pink eyes. I've never seen anything like him."

"Why don't you go back to class?" Kyla asked.

"It's a curse," Portia said, her voice a whisper. "He's gone."

"What?" Kyla asked. "I mean it, you should go."

"I'm not going anywhere without him, Kyla. I'm staying put." Portia stretched out her legs and patted them, inviting the cat to sit on her lap.

"Promise?" Kyla asked tentatively.

Portia nodded.

***

Christian decided on a last-resort effort and headed to the regular kids' class wing on the first floor. Someone must have seen Jay. It was just like Jay to run off and not think he'd freak everyone out.

When Christian reached the entrance linking the two buildings, the bell rang. He ran through the halls asking about Jay. He asked at least twenty kids. Nothing.

"You from the upstairs class, huh?" a bony kid asked.

Lockers clanked around them, and an endless row of kids rushed through the halls, shoving and talking. The kid pulled Christian to the side of the hallway, clinging to his shirtsleeve.

Christian was impatient. "Yah, I am. Why? You got something to say?"

"No, I'm not judging. I'm not like that. My brother went there. Before. He's older. From when they first brought over the other school and merged them. Ten years ago."

The kid's fingers dug into his arm. How could a scrawny little runt have such a death grip?

Christian stared at the kid's pale face. "All right. And?"

"It's not right what they did then."

"What?"

"You don't know, probably. Hardly anyone does unless they had kids here then. The school district hushed it. Lied."

"Look, man, I've got to find my friend. If you can't make sense, I've got to go."

"There was a big fight about merging the special ed school."

"Shocking." Christian rolled his eyes. "Of course parents don't want a precious baby like you mixing with my kind."

"That's why they made the addition. All like, 'separate but equal,' you know?"

Christian nodded. He tapped the floor, impatient.

"And it was supposed to be a big win. Mainstreaming education. New protocols. Joint lunch hours. Improved opportunities for crossover classes. That kind of thing. But the district ran out of money. Fell short on the levy—"

"Levy? Jesus. Can you get to the frigging point?" Christian punched a locker behind the kid's head.

"Chill, man. I'm just the messenger. That's what I'm saying. This isn't the first time. Two kids went missing then, when they blocked it off."

"Blocked what off?"

"The elevator."

"You're not saying—"

"That's exactly what I'm saying. They said it was a mass runaway, but kids like them don't run away. He was in the special class. Didn't talk. No friends. A funny looking, skinny albino kid and his little brother, my age. Where were they going to run to?"

"Shit." Christian's eyes narrowed. Did he say albino? He felt his face contracting with a question.

"The parents didn't have any money. Didn't have any way to prove they were lost. The older kid was sixteen and just—poof." The kid snapped his fingers. "Vanished."

"What'd they do?"

"Nothing. Moved away. Some kids for a long time said the kids had cursed the school. But you know, can't prove that either. Ever since, they just cut it off. Treat it like two schools basically."

"What do you think? I mean about the curse?"

The kid shrugged. "I bet they tried. I mean, weird stuff happens everywhere, right?"

"Right." Christian looked around the empty hallway. "Don't you have a class to get to?" His heart pounded. The kid freaked him out.

"No. Last period. Study hall. No rush."

Christian rubbed his face and mumbled. "Like red eyes, white hair, right?" he asked, knowing the answer. "Weird, there's this cat up there like that. What are the odds?"

"Right. Weird. What are the odds?" The kid's voice was soft as a breeze.

"Hey, any luck? Did you find him?"

Christian turned at the unexpected interruption. "Kyla, what the hell are you doing here? I thought you were staying with Portia?" Then he waved to the kid behind them. "Bye."

"Who you talking to?" Kyla asked.

"That kid," Christian pointed toward the hall leading to the cafeteria.

Kyla stared up the hall. "Okay, freakazoid. Empty hallway."

Christian looked confused. His eyes widened. "Whatever." He ignored the shiver of unease and the clench in his stomach. "I don't have time to find him for you. We got to get back to her. Come on."

"She promised she'd stay where she was. She was like, transfixed by that cat, you know?"

"Hurry!" Christian yelled, dragging Kyla by the hand, racing up the steps twice as fast as he'd come down. "Come on." He glanced back to the hall. What happened to the weird kid?

"God, what? I'm trying." Kyla huffed, lagging behind him.

When they arrived at the fourth floor, they tore up the hallway toward the elevator shaft. Their class had been long dismissed, and the hall was empty and still.

"Portia," Christian called as they approached the shaft.

No answer came. The hallway was as empty as a tomb. The flashlight lay on the floor where Portia sat just minutes previously. Then its light flickered and dimmed.

"Portia!" Kyla yelled, looking around. "Where is she? Where'd she go?"

Christian looked into the darkness of the shaft, half expecting to see Portia. Half expecting to hear a meow. Neither came. His heart sank. He felt it in his bones. Vanished.

"That wasn't just a cat," Christian said. He knew they were both gone.

NO DEEPER

Chantal Boudreau

Shawna and her younger brother, Milo, venture into the desert to capture tarantulas for extra pocket money. When they stumble upon a mysterious cave, Milo can't resist exploring it, and Shawna is forced to follow. Neither expects the dangers lurking within its depths.

The air was so dry Shawna tasted the metallic tang of dust with each breath even though no wind disturbed the eroded soil. The sun had baked the dirt beneath her feet into a brittle crust. Sweating didn't help much either. It clung to her skin, a hot, sticky layer that attracted the dust and occasionally rolled off her forehead into her eyes. She disliked the salty sting.

Milo, her younger brother, skittered ahead of her in the withering sunshine. He always found the energy to move that way, no matter what his environment. Shawna wasn't that much older and typically tolerated the heat, but that day it felt particularly draining.

She paused to secure her dark brown hair more firmly into its ponytail and cleared her throat at the same time. "Do you see any yet?"

The siblings weren't in the desert terrain for fun and games. The stroll through nature's dirt griddle was purely financial. Shawna needed money for the new boots she had her eye on, and the best way to make money was to trap tarantulas for the pet store in the city. The store owners paid a pretty penny for the giant spiders Shawna and Milo brought to them.

There were nicer ways to earn a buck in their part of Texas, like farming or ranch-handing, but Shawna's father worked the oil fields, so his kids didn't have an "in" on the farms or ranches. That, and Shawna liked being her own boss.

"I've been checking the shady spots, but so far, nothin'," Milo replied, shaking his head. He was fairer than Shawna, with a crooked nose and a freckled face. He was lankier than her, too, driven by nervous energy.

Shawna's temperament tended to be far cooler and collected than her brother's, though one thing scared her that didn't bother him nearly as much, which was the only reason she took him with her on the outings.

"What about snakes?" she asked with a shiver.

He glanced up at her, squinting into the sun, and grinned in a mocking way. "Nope. Ain't seen any of them, neither. I told ya—I'll tell ya if I do."

In a couple of years, it would be a matter of Milo choosing to accompany her rather than her letting him come along. That was why Shawna tried to be nice to him. But for the moment, their mother had deemed him too young to go hunting for tarantulas on his own.

The pair had decided to scope out a new area, having hunted down the population in their favourite spots. While Milo, his nose practically to the ground, continued to explore various cracks and crevices surrounding them, Shawna picked up on something in the distance—an inconsistency along the horizon.

She pointed. "What's that?"

Milo froze and then stood straight, following her finger with his greenish-brown eyes. "I dunno. A rock outcropping maybe. Might be a good place to look. Lotsa holes and shady spots."

Shawna hesitated. Those same features might also appeal to snakes; they might even harbour nests of them. At a young age, she'd had a bad run-in with a nest, which had made her phobic.

"Well?" Milo looked impatient.

"Yeah, let's go. But you're going to have to scout it out before I get too close."

He shrugged. "Whatever. And if I find any spiders while you're playing scaredy cat, the money for them is mine."

Shawna begrudgingly agreed. If it was a matter of risking a run-in with snakes, the boots would have to wait.

The closer they trudged to the outcropping, the larger it seemed. By the time they were within spitting distance of the rocks, they saw that what had appeared to be shadows from far away were more than simply shadows.

"It's a cave!" Milo dashed ahead with his usual enthusiasm.

Shawna hung back. She didn't like the look of it at all. "Be careful, Milo. We don't know how far down it goes or how stable it is."

He stopped at its mouth and peered in. "It don't look so bad. The way in ain't that steep, and I don't see a lot of loose rock. The walls are pretty smooth, actually, like someone carved it out." He threw a taunting glance over his shoulder. "I'm going in."

"Milo, you don't know if it's safe. Milo…. Milo!"

Shawna's brother chose to ignore her. He ducked out of sight, laughing at her as he went. Maybe he doubted she would follow, well aware of her fears.

"This is dumb, Milo. You know you're supposed to listen to me. Mom'll have your hide."

Harsh words didn't help. Like it or not, Shawna was forced to follow.

It took her less time to catch up to her brother than she would have expected because he had stopped partway down the decline. Perched on all fours, he was examining something close to the ground. In fact, Milo had pulled his flashlight from his rucksack, both to better see whatever writhed in the dirt and to prod at his discovery.

The unidentified moving thing looked serpentine enough that Shawna squealed and prepared to flee. But Milo stopped her.

"Shush, you chicken. It's not a snake. It's not even an entire critter. Looks like an arm off one of the octopus thingies at the aquarium, only it's moving on its own."

Despite her panic, Milo's description had Shawna far too curious to run. She gradually found the nerve to join him, squatting to get a better look.

He was right. As snake-like as it had appeared at first, upon closer examination the fleshy bit on the cave floor looked more like a single tentacle, with small white suckers. The mass wasn't solid either, simply a wriggly, gummy limb moving independently from its body—wherever that was.

Shawna wrinkled her nose. "Ugh, that's disgusting." It was almost as bad as a snake but not quite. At least it couldn't bite her. It had no mouth or teeth. "How is it even moving, and where the hell did it come from?"

"It couldn't have come from the canyon Badlands. There must be an underground lake farther down. I'm going in deeper." Milo stood, resettling the rucksack on his back and adjusting his grip on the flashlight.

"Deeper? No way. We're not going any deeper. Stick this thing in one of our jars if you want. We can show it off when we get back home and figure out what and where it came from then. We're here to get spiders, remember. We won't find any farther down. It's too cool and damp."

"Put it in a jar? That's not a bad idea." Milo withdrew one of his tarantula jars and lowered himself to the tentacle again. With no better means of moving it, he picked up the disembodied limb with his bare hand and shovelled it in the jar.

Shawna cringed and resisted the urge to vomit when he peeled suction cups off his palm and fingers. While the tentacle did go into the jar, it was a tight squeeze, and the cover refused to go on. Milo shrugged and slid it back into his sack as it was.

"You can't put it in there like that. It could get loose and wriggle around," Shawna said.

"So?" Milo stepped farther into the cave.

"What—hey! I said no deeper. Where do you think you're going?" She didn't follow right away. "Damn it, Milo!"

"Stop your cussing, Shawna. I'm going to find this thing. It could make us famous. You said you wanted money? This could make us rich." He disappeared into the shadows, the beam from his flashlight visible.

Angry at his belligerence and lack of caution, Shawna forced herself to follow. She pulled out her own flashlight when the natural light grew dimmer and the footing became more treacherous with the dampening of the rock. At one point, she slipped and put out her hand to catch herself. She quickly retracted it, wiping her fingers against her shorts. The cavern walls were slimy, coated in mildewed sweat.

She called out to Milo a few times, but he didn't reply. In fact, she heard nothing other than the slow *drip drip* of pooling water until she reached the bottom of the incline. At that point, her sneakers splashed into cold wet where the narrow cavern widened into a chamber. It was some sort of underground lake, the darkness within eerily aglow with patches of violet and yellow luminescence.

Along with the echoing drips, Shawna heard whispering farther in the chamber. The sounds weren't from Milo, though. The indiscernible words carried a soft but adult feminine lilt. A woman.

"Milo?"

He didn't answer, so Shawna sloshed forward into the chamber. The cool water leeched through her sneakers and made her shiver— or, at least, she chose to blame the tremors on that. While she edged along, something sleek and spongy brushed against her leg, startling her to screams. Her flashlight beam revealed the culprit to be another disembodied tentacle, squirming in the water by her foot. She gave it a solid kick, sending it splashing out of sight.

"Milo?"

She made out her brother's mumbling although she couldn't decipher his words, but they ran in sync with the woman's words, which intensified. It sounded like a chant or even a prayer. Eventually, the words made sense, a few of them differing depending on the speaker, for Milo replied with pronouns in the first person.

"You will follow me. You will worship the great Ayi'ig, daughter of Yig and Yidhra. You will attend to me in my underground lair, servicing me and bringing me offerings befitting a Great One. I will provide you with power and knowledge, and in exchange you will be my devoted slave, bowing to my will. You will love me, and you will kill for me. You are mine. Mine."

Shawna advanced, searching ahead with her light. She caught a glint she hoped might be Milo and focused the beam on that spot while she continued to move forward. She picked up his face, lips moving and expression devoid of emotion as he stared straight ahead. Then she realized that where he stood, frozen waist-deep in the dank water, he wasn't alone.

At first, Shawna thought a tall woman stood next to him, embracing him. The body beside her brother's undulated with a beckoning femininity, seductive, alluring. Upon closer inspection, Shawna saw that, rather than arms looped around her brother, fondling him and caressing his hair, monstrous tentacles similar to the one that had been writhing its way up to the mouth of the cavern wrapped around him. Unlike that errant tentacle that had drawn Milo into the cave, these were attached to a beast thoroughly foul and frightening—not the beguiling woman Shawna would have expected to match the voice.

Shawna retched and gagged with revulsion at the sight of the otherworldly creature entwined around her brother, mesmerizing him with its words and blinding him to its true form. It didn't help that the abomination reminded her of snakes, the way its limbs coiled and tensed. Tearing her attention away from her brother, she directed the flashlight's beam upward to get an idea of exactly what she faced. Its sinewy torso and flailing arms extended high above their heads within the underground chamber.

Shawna regretted looking. Had she made a surprise grab for her brother and tried to pull him free, they might have escaped its clutches. But once aware of the size of the monster that had ensnared him, fear paralyzed her, and she couldn't bring herself to take another step forward.

And that wasn't the worst of it.

Even though the beast horrified and disgusted her, she couldn't stop her upward examination of it. Had she done so, she might have been able to make a quiet retreat to seek help, with the meagre hope that upon returning, her brother could be rescued. But that was not how events played out. Her flashlight's beam continued climbing until it reached the summit of the monster. The giant octopus-like head staring down at her wasn't what made her finally break. Rather, it was those eyes—massive, looming serpentine eyes. It was clearly part snake.

Shawna's scream echoed loudly through the chamber. In the face of an outrageous example of her greatest phobia, all sanity abandoned her and left nothing behind but pure instinct and panic.

She ran.

She ran without any recognition of where she was going, how fast, or how far. All she was aware of was the need to put as much distance as she could between her and whatever that terrible thing was. She didn't think about Milo. She didn't even notice how badly she scraped and bruised her knees while scrabbling out of the cavern, and she barely felt the sting of the hot sun and gritty winds when she emerged into the desert heat.

She ran as though her life depended on it.

Her senses and sanity did not return to her completely even when the light of day dimmed and the air cooled. She was hopelessly lost, but none of that mattered. The image of those serpentine eyes had burned into her brain. Even though it was far away, that monster, that Ay'yig, was still with her, haunting her every waking moment and then following her into sleep.

***

Fortunately, or perhaps not so fortunately, Shawna was found a couple of days later, far from home and almost dead from exposure and dehydration. Her parents and the authorities tried to question her as to what had happened to Milo, but she wouldn't answer, at least not in any coherent way.

In fact, the only thing Shawna did other than stare at the wall or out the window was to cover her head while obviously trying to avoid looking at the ceiling.

The only clear words the nursing staff could decipher from the poor girl, her face etched with unadulterated terror, were: "It's looking at me...make it stop looking at me," and "No deeper, Milo. I said no deeper...."

TIM AND THE TERRIBLE, HORRIBLE, NO GOOD, VERY BAD REANIMATED ANIMAL ATTACKS

Katherine Sanger

Tim wants to spend an evening with Ivy, his girlfriend. Instead, he's stuck driving a truckload of dead pets to his father's pet cemetery. Then things go wrong.

Tim eased his father's truck through the sunbaked traffic jam. Cars had been backed up for hours. When darkness fell, they moved again, and he glanced at the empty passenger seat. He couldn't blame Ivy for not being there. Dropping off dead animals at his father's pet cemetery didn't qualify as a date to him either. But traffic was slowly moving. Maybe the rest of the evening could be salvaged.

He ran his hand through his curly brown hair. An abandoned car sat on the side of the road. Was that what had slowed them? An empty car?

Tim sighed and flipped through the radio presets. He hated driving his father's truck. Country songs on every station. He went through the stations, trying to find something worth listening to. One station caught his attention.

When he had first tuned in, he heard a scream and assumed it was a rebroadcast of a morning talk show. The host came on, laughing a bit. "There's another one—the vampires are attacking everywhere, huh?" The DJ laughed again, and Concrete Blonde's "Bloodletting" filled the truck's cab.

Not too shabby, Tim thought. *At least it's from the 90s.*

It was dark when he arrived at the pet cemetery. He hated being there so late; the spot creeped him out. The big empty field with little grave markers sticking up from the neatly cut grass looked nice during the day, but once the light disappeared, the area turned sinister. He pulled into the drive in front of the outbuilding and tin shed. He honked.

He had never liked his father's business, and nights like this re-affirmed his decision to finish college and obtain employment with a large corporation instead of following in the family business.

No one came out from the building. Tim honked again. Where were the guys? Even if they were out back smoking, they should have heard the honk. He turned off the radio, rolled down the window, and shouted, "C'mon, Louis. C'mon, José. I haven't got all night."

He didn't hear any answering smart-ass remarks. He stepped out of the cab, leaving the truck running. If he had to, he'd unload the dead animals and stow them in the shed. He'd done that previously when he'd arrived too late.

Gravel crunched underfoot as he circled the truck. It was darker around the side, and he hurried to reach the back of the truck where the lights of the outbuilding were visible.

He turned the key in the lock, grabbed the handle, and with a heave, pushed it skyward. "What the hell." Boxes had been ripped apart and animals littered the floor. A poodle leapt from the mess, and Tim screamed and backpedaled.

The poodle jumped too high and sailed over Tim's head. Its nails scraped through his curls when he fell backward. He regained his balance. Cats and a German shepherd followed. To his right, he glimpsed the poodle, which was advancing toward him, growling. On his left stood the cats, hissing and spitting. He'd lost track of the German shepherd. Noises came from behind him, and he was afraid it was the shepherd. What did the animals want? He didn't wait to find out.

He raced toward the shed. He reached the door and fumbled with the handle. A cat sank a claw into the back of his leg. He kicked it free and jerked open the door, almost falling into the darkness. The door barely shut before the first of the animals thumped against it. He slapped the shed wall to his right, searching for the light switch while he kept the door closed with his weight. The cold of the tin door seeped through his T-shirt. His hand finally found the switch, and he was grateful for the light from the single bulb in the ceiling.

He scanned the shed and, seeing no animals lurking in its four corners, relaxed. It was time to take stock. The shed had items that would be good in a fight—shovels and picks and plenty of blank grave markers.

Tim piled a few of the markers in front of the door so he could safely move away from it. They would be strong enough to hold the door as long as the animals didn't organize, which he hoped wouldn't happen anytime soon. He heard them outside, scratching at the door. The sound of claws on tin bothered him more than fingers on a chalkboard.

Chalkboard...school...Ivy! Tim's hand flew to his hip, only to realize his cell phone remained on the dashboard in the truck's cab. He paced the small confines of the shed, cursing his dumb luck and trying to think. Where was Ivy? Was she okay?

Nails had stopped clicking on the tin. He leaned closer to the door, hoping the moment wouldn't morph into a movie scene when bad guys suddenly crashed through and killed the victim.

Nothing happened. Where had the dogs gone?

He almost shoved the grave markers out of the way so he could open the door and run, but he held back, wishing there was a window in the shed. It would help to know what was happening outside.

Then he heard it. A low, muffled noise. The sound of dirt shifting.

He looked down. He'd had plenty of dogs dig under fences to get out, but these animals were digging in!

Tim had to move. He grabbed a pick from the corner and held it low. He kicked the concrete markers in front of the door, using his leg to shift the weight so they toppled to the side. He felt a twinge where the cat had drawn blood. He burst through the door, fear burning in his chest.

The dogs weren't in front of the building. As he'd thought, they were digging their way in around the side. But the cats stood before him. The minute he appeared, they hissed at him. Using the pick like a crowbar, he swung, knocking them aside rather than impaling them. He didn't want to end up with a pick of semi-dead animals.

He raced to the right, past the locked passenger door of the vehicle, and around to the front of the truck. The dogs gained behind him, their paws skidding in the gravel, raspy noises emanating from their throats.

The cab door was open. His feet slid in the gravel when he stopped to peer into the cab. He didn't want to waste time, but he also didn't want to find himself trapped in the truck with a Doberman.

Nothing.

Tim sank into the seat. A dog caught his dirty grey sneaker. He shook his foot. Shaking didn't help, so he brought the pick down on the dog's head. The dog yelped and dropped, taking Tim's shoe with it. He slammed the door and rolled up the window.

He was alive.

He had made it.

He reached for his cell phone. From deep in the recesses of the windshield dash, a gerbil flew at him. It caught him between the thumb and finger, grabbing the fleshy bit and sinking its teeth.

Tim screamed at the intense pain. He thrashed his arm back and forth, trying to dislodge the little furry creature, but it stayed, biting deeper and harder. A thin line of blood ran down his wrist and up his arm. He grabbed the gerbil with his left hand and tugged, but it wouldn't come loose. It bit even harder, and he felt a sucking sensation where the gerbil had latched. He punched at the window, putting the gerbil between the glass and the rest of his hand.

After three blows, the gerbil slipped off. Tim stomped it with his sneaker. He rolled down the window, grabbed one of the gerbil's legs, and threw it to the other animals. He rolled up the window and looked at his hand.

The wound was puffy and bleeding. There were two distinct marks. He felt dizzy looking at it.

Could you bleed to death from a gerbil bite?

Was that thing even a gerbil?

He shook his head and picked his phone off the dash, bracing himself in case another gerbil came out of nowhere, but none appeared. He flicked open the phone and called Ivy.

A fast busy. No voicemail. No chance to leave a message. He hung up and called home. His dad would still be at his meeting, but what about his mom? Again, fast busy. His father didn't believe in cell phones, so he couldn't reach him.

Tim tried Ivy and his home again. Still no answer. He needed to find them. He headed out of the cemetery.

On the road from the cemetery to the highway, he didn't notice anything out of the ordinary although it was dark, quiet, and empty.

But the highway was a different matter. Dead animals covered the pavement.

Tim breathed deeply, trying to make sense of it. The situation was roadkill taken to an extreme: squirrels, turtles, cats, dogs, and other animals no longer recognizable littered the highway. The unknown carcasses concerned him the most.

Cold sweat formed on his forehead while he stared into the night. He kept his foot on the accelerator and drove through the mangled animals. He winced when animals crunched under the wheels but felt less guilty when, from the rearview mirror, he saw creatures rise from the asphalt.

He shuddered and rounded the curve, passing the same stalled car on the shoulder. A blue Buick sat in the middle lane. Tim slowed to pass. In the circle of light from the Buick's interior dome, he saw a man slumped across the front bench seat. A number of squirrels surrounded him. The man didn't move.

The man in the car wasn't the only human casualty on the road. Tim saw a few fender-benders—or so it appeared in the feeble glow from the streetlights. Large mounds of dead animals with human arms and legs sticking out, covered in a dark fluid he guessed was blood, lay beside the vehicles.

A raccoon approached a bloody female body on the road. It sniffed, holding its head at a peculiar angle. Was its neck broken? The animal nuzzled her with its snout before moving to the next body.

Mesmerized and terrified at the same time, Tim couldn't avert his face. The sight was worse than watching a traffic accident. Much worse. This wasn't a hit and run but an attack and slaughter.

It was war.

Without taking his gaze off the road, Tim voice-dialed Ivy again. Still no answer. No voicemail, just that same fast busy signal.

He kept driving, passing more devastation. "Gotta get to Ivy," he mumbled, his voice echoing in the empty cab. "Gotta get to Ivy."

Within twenty minutes, Tim headed down Ivy's street, repeating his mantra. It didn't seem strange to say it out loud. It was focus. He could say the words, think of Ivy, and hold onto hope.

Ivy's beat-up red Ford Escort was parked in front of her building. He pulled up next to it and rolled down his window. The Escort's engine hummed, the car surrounded by dozens of cats in various stages of decomposition. The animals clawed at the doors, scratching the paint. They cried and mewed, and Tim's hair stood on end. The noise wasn't what he expected and sounded more like wolves howling to announce Dracula's presence in a horror movie.

"Ivy!"

The cats' volume dropped when a few turned and focused on him. What was wrong with their faces? The light! No light reflected from their eyes.

"Ivy!"

The sunroof on Ivy's car creaked open an inch. "Tim?"

Tim leaned out the window, not caring that the cats were suddenly riveted to his movements. "Ivy, I'm here. I have my father's truck."

He heard laughter from the crack in the sunroof. "Perfect."

It became quiet in the car, and the cats scratched again.

"What are we going to do, Tim? I can't get out of the car. The cats won't go away."

"What's your gas situation?"

"What? Just under half a tank."

Tim thought for a minute. "Your car won't do any damage if you hit anything big, but this truck can take on almost anything. Let's get away from these cats and then you can get in here. We'll figure it out from there."

"You won. We're going out in your father's truck tonight."

Tim smiled when he heard her loud, unmistakable sigh. How like Ivy to retain her sense of humor.

He pulled into the middle lane. No traffic moved around him. Ivy's car eased from its spot, smushing a cat's head into the road. As Ivy drove behind him, the other cats rushed the limp form.

Tim drove toward his house. With Ivy accounted for, he concentrated on his parents. His father would still be away, hopefully somewhere safe, but his mother should be home. Their house would be safer than Ivy's apartment—maybe. Fewer animals.

A better defensible position. And, of course, his mother. Even if they couldn't stay there, they could at least get his mother while Ivy jumped into the truck.

They drove through messy roads and turned at the exit. Tim crossed his fingers and drove down the street toward his house, watching Ivy's headlights follow. Nothing moved in the shadows as they passed the few scattered, darkened houses set back from the road.

Light shone from the upstairs front window—his parents' bedroom. He pulled into the driveway and stopped. Light pooled on the empty porch, revealing the open front door. Blood smeared down the otherwise immaculate white paint. He itched to rush in.

The passenger door creaked open. Tim reached for the pickaxe and then saw it was Ivy. She jumped in, slamming the door behind her. Her long black hair was tousled, and her eyes were wide. She looked out the window, following his gaze. "Oh, my God."

He stared at the door. "My mother was home alone. My father, well...that's why we weren't seeing each other tonight. But she was here."

"Tim...I'm sorry. But you can't go in there. You won't come out. I'm sure of it. Look, I'm worried, too. My sister is camping in the woods this weekend, and my parents are out of town."

Tim's eyes were still locked on the bloodstain.

"I don't guess you've been listening to the radio, have you?"

He shook his head.

"It's like this everywhere. They're saying to stay home. It's not affecting living animals, but once an animal dies, it...changes. They're lying in wait, waiting to smell someone still alive. Sometimes they cry at the door. I'm sorry, Tim. I only met her a few times, and she seemed so sweet and—"

His voice was flat. "Sweet enough to have opened the door if she heard an animal crying."

Ivy nodded. "We need to find someplace safe."

Tim didn't respond. He needed to breathe, to suck in air, but he couldn't figure out how to make his body do it. He exhaled fine, but not enough oxygen came back in. He rested his forehead on the steering wheel and closed his eyes. "What if she's in there?" He felt like he was suffocating.

"She probably is. But there's nothing you can do for her."

He digested Ivy's words and looked at the house again. The bloodstain started at about his mother's height. Part of him wanted to fight, but deep down, he knew Ivy was right. He waited another minute, hoping to see or hear a sign of life.

Then a shadow appeared in the doorway. A possum, its muzzle bloody and its eyes black and flat, crawled out from the house, moving slowly and laboriously as though its back were broken.

Tim bit his lip and reached for the car door.

Finally, he dropped his arm. "Okay, where do we go?"

Ivy leaned across and flicked on the radio. They listened to voices, trying to figure out what to do. Every station broadcast the same information but in various tones of panic. There were places to go, but the animals possessed a good sense of smell and gathered wherever people existed. With a strong enough barrier, one could be safe. For a while.

No one had determined how long the animals would last, much less what they were. Some reports claimed they were vampires, others said they were zombies, and others called them reanimated. Whatever they were, they were everywhere.

"How about McAdam's Base?" Ivy suggested. "That was in the list the guy mentioned, and it's not too far from here."

Tim shrugged. "Sure. McAdam's."

He reversed out the driveway and headed back to the highway.

***

"There it is." With the truck idling in neutral, Tim gestured through the windshield to the inside of the heavily fenced and gated army base. The central guard post was deserted, and the arm of the gate was raised. Lights shone in the surrounding parking lots, making it brighter than high noon in a western.

Cats, dogs, gophers, badgers, and other unrecognizable creatures that had once been normal surrounded the fence and the gate. The light seemed to keep the animals at bay.

"I guess we should drive in, huh?" Ivy's eyes were glued to a section of fence two and three deep with enormous dogs.

"Greyhounds." Tim gestured to the left. "The track was that way."

"Oh. I thought greyhounds were skinny."

"Me, too." He didn't speculate why the dogs' stomachs were as large as they were.

He shifted the truck into gear. The animals swiveled around to the source of the noise. Dead eyes squinted into the gloom of the truck's cab. Tim repressed a shiver.

He depressed the gas and let up on the clutch. The truck jumped and stalled.

The animals advanced on the truck. He cranked it again, and the truck moved forward without problem. A few animals neared, and

Tim ran over them. Others backed down and waited at the gate. He blew through the gate and into the parking lot. He drove as close as he could to the path that led to the buildings, slamming the truck into a spot.

"The animals seem to be keeping back. We need to make a break for it now," Tim said.

Ivy nodded, her chin set and determined. "Let's go." She leaned into him, quickly kissed him hard on the lips, cracked open her door, and sprinted across the pavement toward the brick building before he had a chance to open his door.

Tim popped the door and dropped, racing behind her, trying to keep up. The girl could run! He was impressed.

He heard guttural growls and pathetic mewing behind him. He didn't look back. He rasped out breaths. His heart pounded. His run was nearly a limp thanks to his missing shoe.

Ivy reached the door before he did. She pulled it open just when he caught up. They looked back. The animals were still at the fence.

"Look!" Tim pointed toward the mass of bloody and broken animals.

Ivy peered over her shoulder when one of the smaller dogs placed a paw on the parking lot. It yipped and jumped back.

She shook her head. "Why'd we run?"

"Because they might overcome that fear of light."

A voice made him jump, and he faced the door. A tall uniformed man stood before him. Tim reached the man's chest; he'd never felt short previously.

Ivy stepped backward, forcing Tim to move. The man yanked them inside, and the door slammed shut.

Tim got his bearings. The hallway was dark compared to the blinding light of the parking lot. Shadows lurked in the corners, and patterns from the wire-reinforced windows marked the floor.

"Thanks," Ivy said.

"Glad to have you here on base. It's a bit crowded, but there's room this way." The officer turned and led them down the hall.

Ivy slipped her hand into Tim's, and they followed. Tim wasn't sure of the man's uniform. Had they been addressed by a major? A lieutenant? He'd never been involved with the military. He knew the base existed, of course, but had only a vague impression of its presence in town.

"What's it like out there?" the man asked.

"Bloody," Tim said, the only word that came to mind.

The officer nodded. "That's what we've heard. How'd you make it here?"

Tim narrated, stopping every few sentences to remember the details. It had been a matter of hours, but his entire life had stopped and then restarted in the nightmare of happenings. Before he had finished the tale, they reached the mess hall and huddled until he finished.

"Did you say you'd been bitten by one of those things?"

Tim held up his hand. "Yeah, but it was just a gerbil." He pointed to little red marks in the triangle of flesh between his thumb and forefinger.

The officer shook his head. "If you've been bit, you need to go there." He pointed to the left, to a set of double doors.

"What's that?" Tim asked.

"Infirmary. Everyone who's been bitten needs to be quarantined."

Tim shrugged. Did he have a choice? He and Ivy followed the officer.

Two people, with wounds far more serious than Tim's, lay in cots. A male, with both legs in bandages up to his knees, seemed to be in a drug-induced stupor. His eyes were open but unfocused, and every few minutes, he gurgled.

A woman lay in a cot beside the man. The top of her head was covered in bandages soaked red in spots, but she breathed deeply and evenly. An IV was attached to one arm. Just looking at her made Tim queasy.

The officer cleared his throat, and the man behind the desk looked up, snapped to his feet, and saluted. The officer nodded his head at Tim and Ivy before leaving. The man came out from behind the desk. His uniform was rumpled but spotless.

"Who was bit?"

Tim raised his hand. "I was. But it's really small." He held out his injured hand.

The man, obviously a doctor, squinted. "There's a bite there?"

"Yeah, it was a gerbil."

He shook his head. "Better safe than sorry, I guess." He took Tim's hand and probed the red marks.

Tim grimaced. It was sore to the touch.

The doctor applied ointment. "We'll keep you here for observation. Grab a bed." He gestured to the cots that lined the wall and turned to Ivy. "What about you?"

"I'm just here for moral support," she said. "Those gerbils are vicious."

Tim couldn't tell if she kidded or was serious.

The doctor nodded. "Okay. You can stay with him."

Ivy led Tim to a cot at the far end of the room, away from the other injured individuals. The cot against the wall was narrow, with a small vertical window on the wall above it. Tim fell to the cot, feeling bars dig into his thighs. Ivy joined him.

"How do they sleep on these things?" he asked her.

"Drugs?" She smiled, and he couldn't help but smile back. She unfolded the blanket at their feet and spread it over their legs. She snuggled into him, her head on his shoulder, and he leaned his head against hers.

Despite best intentions, Tim couldn't help but want to sleep. He fought it, waking himself every few seconds. He felt Ivy doing the same.

Stress followed by a bit of comfort would automatically lead to sleep, wouldn't it? But he had been bitten by one of those creatures. What if he was changing? What if they were right to quarantine him?

He fretted until he heard a sound that he recognized as a death rattle. The man behind the desk was up before Tim realized where the noise had come from. The doctor rushed to the woman's side, and Tim held his breath.

The rattle stopped, and the room went silent. Not even the injured man's gurgles broke the stillness. The doctor stood next to the woman, careful not to stand too close, watching. Tim worried that, if this was anything like the movies, the woman would come back to life and eat them.

Ivy had given in and slept on Tim's chest. He didn't want to wake her. If they were about to die, he didn't want her final minutes full of panic and horror. If they weren't about to die, it didn't matter if she slept through the woman's death. With his justification firmly in mind, Tim found he couldn't look away.

The doctor and the dead woman were almost equally still, but injured man still breathed. After a few minutes, Tim exhaled when the doctor returned to the desk and the man with the bandaged legs gurgled.

The next thing Tim knew, Ivy was shaking him and whispering in his ear. "Tim."

He forced his eyes open. "What?"

And then he heard it. A loud, deep rumble.

Ivy giggled and whispered, "The doctor is asleep. He's been fighting it. He gave up a few minutes ago and closed his eyes. Look."

Tim peered at the man snoring behind the desk. He had slumped forward, his chin resting on his chest.

Ivy giggled again.

Tim kissed her. "Go back to sleep."

She nodded, still giggling.

"Really," he whispered again. "This isn't some teenage girls' slumber party."

She giggled louder and tickled him under the blanket.

"You're going to wake him up. Then we'll be in real trouble."

"Oh no, we don't want to make him mad, do we?"

Tim rolled his eyes and shook his head. "Go to sleep."

She nodded and relaxed beside him. The doctor continued to snore. Tim felt himself slipping back into sleep but took one last glance at the dead woman. The sheet had been pulled over her head. Shouldn't she have been moved? Or were they afraid to do that?

***

Sunlight filtered in through the windows high in the walls. Tim felt the glare on his eyelids even before he opened them, and he knew the long night was over.

He gently shook Ivy. She resisted, mumbling. "Five more minutes, okay?"

He shook her again. "Ivy."

Her eyes popped open. "Tim? We're really here?"

"Yeah."

"Oh. I hoped it was all a dream."

They still leaned against each other but had slumped down a bit in the night. Tim looked around the room. The woman's body was gone. No one was behind the desk.

He threw off the blankets. "C'mon." He held out his non-bitten hand to Ivy. He stood and pulled her to her feet. "Let's take a look."

They stood on the cot and peered out the window. No animals could be seen. The field beyond the base was empty.

THE STONE FOUNTAIN

Matthew D. Laing

Two teenagers head into mysterious Stanley Park Estate, searching for ghosts and the unexplained. As the evening progresses, Jen and Valerie, an inseparable pair of entirely different character, are unsure what they discover. The reality is either paranormal or something entirely different.

In front of Stanley Park's cast-iron gate, Jen MacIntyre waited for the arrival of her childhood friend Valerie Hansen. Both girls were seventeen and seniors at Centennial High School.

The sun was quickly fading from the once-pale blue sky, and marvelous shades of magenta and marigold filled the horizon. From behind the park's large gate, a harsh and powerful wind moaned and rustled through the mass of trees.

Jen shivered. Goose bumps crept like a rash up and down her body. Although dressed warmly in a heavy fall jacket and a woolen scarf, she hated being alone—especially when the surroundings would darken even more.

Unlike other preserved turn-of-the-century estates, Stanley Park was sparsely visited except for picnickers during the summer months and the few volunteers who maintained its trails. The park sat at the far end of Millwood, across from an old, abandoned farm whose mammoth wooden barn stood in complete disrepair, falling apart like a jumble of wooden toothpicks. That night, not one car came down Jenkins Lane—not even Val's old Honda Civic.

According to Jen's severely drained iPhone, it was 8:45 p.m., and Val was fifteen minutes late. The plan had been simple, Jen thought: meet at Stanley Park at 8:30 p.m. and head home at ten before her mother had a fit.

Val believed in all that otherworldly rubbish; Jen was there as a friend and for protection. Wandering alone in the dark could be dangerous, and heck, she'd seen every *CSI* episode and knew all too well the type of people who roamed around at night. In case some old man staggered out of the bushes, she carried a plastic whistle.

Despite Val's fear of the supernatural, she was an avid practical joker, and Jen wouldn't put it past her to hide in the bushes and wait for an opportune time for a scare. Perhaps she was inside the wooded section of the park, near the old stone fountain.

Jen finally decided to call Val's cell, but a black screen greeted her. The battery was dead.

The wind continued to gust and twirl her dark brown hair into a messy tangle, and for the second time that evening, she shivered violently. On her right and across Jenkins Lane, she could still make out the farm, the grounds dark and shadowed with the bright sunset offering an intense contrast. The mess of the barn grew more sinister while the light slowly faded. Perhaps strange white eyes peered out from abscesses and shadows—eyes waiting to creep out when darkness reigned supreme.

She determined her chances were better if she headed into Maple Park and waited for Val by the Victorian fountain, away from the road. Even if Val hadn't made it inside, the stone fountain stood just past the entrance, sort of a way station—a checkpoint all had to pass when heading into the park.

Jen took out a small pad of paper from her pink pocketbook and scribbled a message: "At the fountain, Val. J."

She folded the paper in half and lodged it in the driver's window of her maroon Toyota Camry. If her intuition was correct, Val would be inside the park, perhaps thinking of a childish way to frighten her. But it wouldn't work.

Ever since they were children, Val loved to watch *Ghost Hunters* re-runs and ancient, crappy horror films that made Jen belt out with laughter. Even while Val's living room grew dark and the heating system clanged and clanked, Jen would smile and glance at her friend cowering under a blanket. Jen had never seen a ghost or a monster and couldn't see reason in the supernatural and the unknown.

Every time Val spoke of her father's home out in Barnsfield, Jen brushed it off. The strange noises were the heating or the creak of the stairs—just how old homes were prone to be—nothing sinister. It was all a trick of the mind, an illusion of light, a manipulation of sound, and the booming and thrashing of a vintage heating system.

Sometimes Jen felt guilty for her quick and dismissive demeanour. Val was genuinely frightened of her father's cellar and the dark shadows that allegedly moved whenever she headed down to the cold storage. She once told Jen she saw the figure of a bearded man behind a cardboard box next to the furnace. His body was a dense black mist, and she swore his piercing eyes were white and fully conscious. When she retreated and dropped a basket of apples on the cellar floor, *it* followed her back through the winding basement and up the stairs. She had whispered to Jen that she had never been so afraid in her life: that feeling of being chased by the unknown; that little voice in your head telling you not to stop.

After another few minutes, Jen swung open the gate to Stanley Park, which was closed but not locked. When the great cast-iron door with intricate swirls and circles pushed inward, squeals and squeaks rifled through the air like the hunting cries of a barn owl. She jumped back and then, realizing the sounds were the gate's old hinges, proceeded to follow the dirt trail into the park. She crossed a small grassy field littered with small bushes and weeds before reaching the start of the forest, a few hundred metres from the gate.

She stopped, reached into her backpack, and pulled out a large red flashlight. A muted click echoed when she pushed the power button, and she cast the strong white beam straight ahead, hitting the wall of foliage that loomed on an almost ninety-degree angle. Enormous tree trunks extended like stone pillars into a multi-coloured forest canopy bright with shades of gold and scarlet still visible against the fading sky.

Ahead was the entrance: a gap cut straight into the thicket like a door, dark and absent of detail.

Then she saw a faint yellow light, glowing like a strange orb, coming from inside the thicket. It moved to and fro until it abruptly disappeared like a great and enormous firefly trapped within the park's wooden walls.

Val! Just as Jen had figured, her friend waited near the fountain. Her old and cumbersome hand-me-down flashlight cast more of a yellow beam of light in comparison with Jen's recently purchased white LED light. Val must have found a good spot to hide. She knew Jen would take the hint and go on without her.

Flashlight in hand, Jen stepped into the forest. At first, she was a little spooked by the dark and dense thicket, but then, remembering the all-too-familiar trail, she felt more at ease. She was no stranger to Stanley Park and the old trails that cut through trees and wound like a serpent around at least a dozen stone statues and once-elegant fountains.

In its heyday, the park must have been fantastic: an incredible array of walkways and gardens amidst the cluster of trees. The large home on the Maple Park Estate had long ago been demolished and its property converted into farmland, but the wooded park had never been tampered with. Millwood acquired the rights in the fifties and designated the land historically protected but open to the public.

While following the path under the guidance of her flashlight, an occasional branch reached in from the sides of the trail and tugged at her jacket. Her breath steamed. Except for her footsteps, it was almost dead quiet. In the distance, a bird beat its wings fast and heavy, almost crashing against the breeze. A small grey mouse crossed the path and scurried into the brush so quickly Jen wondered whether she had imagined it. Looking back up, she still saw the yellow light ahead.

Then the light vanished.

Jen continued around the bend and into a small circular clearing, which was at least a hundred feet wide. Several weathered park benches hugged its edges. The white stone fountain's pale and shiny exterior reflected the bright beam of her flashlight, and she soon reached its large, round base.

The fountain was turned off for the winter. The murky, brown water inside the basin brimmed with rotting maple and oak leaves. On the top of the basin posed two embracing figures, with the young male holding an umbrella for protection from potential storms. During the summer, the water sprayed from the umbrella, and Jen loved to watch. In the hot summer months, she dipped her hands into the cool water.

Jen aimed her flashlight on the fountain. Dark fungus or moss spread over the statue in small fuzzy patches and covered the couple's eyes. Had the statue always been like that? She remembered the figures' eyes as grey, smooth, and round. Then reason set in; the night played tricks on her. Despite that, the figures looked strange and creepy, reminding her of horror movies, where a possessed girl's eyes turned black and demonic and otherworldly.

She shrugged and broke off her curious inspection of the fountain. Thanks to Val, she was becoming paranoid. Heck, ghosts didn't exist, but that didn't mean a murderous and deranged psychopath wasn't hiding in the shadows.

Jen tired of waiting in the silence for Val's charade to be carried out and spun around with her flashlight. "Val, I know you're out here. I saw your flashlight. Come out!"

Silence prevailed. Val didn't emerge, but the yellow light Jen had seen previously, which she'd assumed had been Val's flashlight, suddenly reappeared. To her right, the yellow glow glimmered and seeped out from behind the dark and dense trees.

Suddenly she knew where Val was—at one of her favourite spots, the lion statue.

Jen continued her brisk pace farther into the thicket, following a path that twisted around foliage, a few rusted metal garbage cans, and two park benches.

How different the park felt at night. During the day, birds chirped. In the summer, squirrels and chipmunks scurried, gathering needed supplies for the long winter ahead; and cheerful voices of children echoed throughout the park.

While she did not believe in the ghosts or other tales about the park that children often whispered about, Jen pondered the changes after the sun set and understood why kids could be afraid.

The silence and the darkness made people jump.

The stories were always told after dark, with childish dares to wander alone through the park while others remained patiently in the parking lot. A few of the town's kids swore to have seen a bizarre light from behind the trees, a light that moved farther inward when approached—drawing the walker toward the edge of the park's trails and into the deep and untouched forest at the back of the former estate. According to the tales, however, not one kid had ever made it all the way to the source of the light. Jen figured the light had been one of the park's maintenance crew cleaning up rubbish or emptying trash cans.

Leaving her train of thought, Jen realized, once again, that the yellow light had disappeared. For sure, Val hid near the lion statue, and Jen was reassured of that when the white beam of her flashlight revealed the stone head of a familiar grinning lion.

Moments later, Jen stepped into another circular clearing, smaller than the first, with wooden benches hugging the sides and the giant lion statue in the middle, contained within a ring of round flagstones. The sitting lion, about four feet off the ground, faced forward toward the trail head. Another bird, one she could not place, croaked a few short calls.

She approached the statue and shined her light on the lion's sculpted face. A thick green moss or fungus covered the top of the lion and had crept down the head and over the body, similar to the fountain with the embraced lovers. Hadn't the statue been smooth and well-preserved? The lion's eyes were black and cold, and the stone appeared decayed and rotting.

"Val!" Jen's voice echoed in the clearing. "Valerie! Where are you? This isn't funny anymore."

No response.

Jen's heart thumped. Val liked to play occasional pranks, but this went too far, even for her. Val knew Jen hated being alone at night.

"Val, if you're out there, I'm heading back to my car." Her voice broke. The light might not be her friend's flashlight. *The stories of Stanley Park....*

Just when she turned to head back down the trail, she heard an odd, childlike voice behind her.

"I'm over heeeerrrre!" The voice wavered, cutting through the silence, reminding Jen of dolls with strings that, when pulled, emitted a high-pitched girl's voice.

Then a bright and intense yellowish light appeared directly behind her, lighting up the clearing and the sides of her face. Jen did not turn her head. Her heart fluttered.

Fight or flight. She sprinted back toward the trail, with her flashlight grasped tightly in her right hand. Her scarf flew off her neck and hovered in the air before it hit the ground. She figured she was a good five minutes away from the fountain.

"Jen! Jen, stop," a familiar nasally voice echoed. The voice was not as strange as the first shout, and she stopped and turned.

Val, smiling sheepishly, her green eyes full of life, brandished a bulky flashlight. Her curly orange hair shone under the white beam from Jen's flashlight.

Jen's heart slowed. "Val, seriously that wasn't cool. You scared me half to death!" Though annoyed, she was relieved to see Val and embarrassed she'd been frightened by children's stories.

Val responded with her typical wide smile and a chuckle. "Sorry, Jen. I was only kidding. Dale dropped me off early, so I went to the lion statue and decided to scare you. I tried calling you at least a dozen times. Then I saw your flashlight."

"My phone died. I guessed you were in here, waiting to scare me. And then I saw your crappy old flashlight."

Val replaced her playful look with one of subtle confusion. "I know you don't believe in ghosts or anything weird, but these statues have *changed* since the summer. They're all creepy now and covered in some gross moss."

"I saw that, too, but there must be a plausible explanation. Maybe it gets like that every year around this time?" Jen said before heading back down the trail a few paces to retrieve her scarf. She brushed off a few dead leaves. "That damn tale about the park popped into my head back there."

"The one about the mysterious light?"

"Yeah, the one Billy Biggs told us in front of Oswell's Convenience Store."

"Don't worry, Jen. It's dark is all. You're too cynical to believe in this shit anyway." Val walked over and wrapped her left arm around Jen's shoulder. "I was a little afraid, too. As soon as it got dark, I kept hoping you would arrive. And you know how I get, but I figured it would be worth it."

"Thought you were taking your car? I left you a note in my window in case you were late."

"Dale thinks there's some problem with my battery. Ma forced him to get his fat ass off of the couch and bring me down here. I said you'd give me a lift home." She paused. "That cool?"

"Yep. And let's get out of here. I've had enough of a scare tonight. You got me this time, Val."

Val nodded and smiled.

***

Jen and Val followed the winding trail back toward the entrance. The darkness eased under both beams of light, and they made good time.

Val jabbered about her date with Brian Carson and how he was the starting quarterback for the Millwood Ravens. Jen stopped listening to her friend when a twig snapped behind them, near the entrance to the circular lion clearing. Jen's heart once again fluttered. Her skin prickled. Was someone—or something—watching and following them?

She glanced at Val, who continued talking about the movie she had seen the previous night. Apparently she hadn't heard the sound, for she gave no indication anything was wrong.

Cutting Val off mid-sentence, Jen asked: "Didn't you hear that noise back there?"

A smile crept across Val's face. "Jen, you're being paranoid. I didn't hear a thing." She pointed with her left hand. "Look, there's the fountain, and we'll be out in five." Val continued her story: "So Brian and I had to catch a later showing at the Otterfield Theatre...."

Val's voice faded in and out while Jen's fear increased. An intense pressure filled her lungs. She jumped when another crash, louder and more profound, echoed from the brush behind them. Thrashing, like footsteps stomping through fallen wood and dead leaves, broke the silence. Then the noise stopped.

Val's smile left her face and her eyes widened. "Jen, I heard that one, but maybe it was only a raccoon or a squirrel or something." Her hands shook.

"I don't care what it was. Let's get out of here," Jen whispered.

She jogged down the trail and around the giant stone fountain. She didn't look behind while they raced out of the thicket and to the park's cast iron gate. For a moment, the doors would not budge but then gave way.

Jen glanced back toward the tree line. All remained still and dark. "It was probably nothing," she muttered in between deep exhales. "Let's get out of here. I'm freezing."

They headed toward the car.

"Didn't you say you left me a note?" Val asked, looking at the Camry's barren windows. "'Cause there's nothing here."

"I put it in the driver's window," Jen walked to the car. "Strange. Maybe the wind took it. There were some pretty strong gusts tonight." She tried not to think of the possibility that someone else had found it.

"You're probably right. Let's get going."

Jen reversed the Toyota Camry out of the gravel parking spot and headed down the short road to Jenkins Lane.

"Impossible," Val whispered, looking out the back window.

"What?" Jen peered into the rearview mirror. A yellow glow moved behind the tree line. The light zigzagged, disappeared, and then emerged as if being carried from the edge of the thicket to the front gates. "What's that light from?"

"I don't know," Val mumbled.

Jen stepped on the gas and revved the car forward. When she reached Jenkins Lane, she glanced to the right and glimpsed the mangled barn on the other side of the road.

She looked back at the entrance but was greeted by darkness and no sign of the light they had witnessed moments previously.

MEASURED IN MINUTES

Jeff C. Stevenson

It's a week before KISS's 1975 landmark album Alive! *is released. Twelve-year-old Sam finds an unlabeled cassette tape that soon replaces his obsession with his favorite band.*

How nice to tromp home after a boring day at school, make a little noise, do a little damage to the leaves and remind them who was boss.

It was Thursday afternoon, September 4, 1975, and Sam Reynolds would have his copy of KISS *Alive!* in only six days. His parents hated the band and the music and what the name KISS stood for: Knights in Satan's Service. Sam explained to them that the last part was totally wrong and promised to only listen to the music with his headphones on so they would not be exposed to the lyrics.

His Koss headphones. Koss for KISS. They were so pricey, they were actually called stereophones. The sound was incredible and worth the effort to own. He'd mowed lawns, did every chore his dad told him to, and kept his room as neat as he could. Then, at the end of three months, he had enough money to purchase them. One hundred and thirty-five dollars and they were his.

He was just days away from the release of the new KISS album, and he had the money saved to purchase it. Koss for KISS. Life was good.

Sam kicked leaves and thought about KISS that early September afternoon when a cassette tape, minus its case holder, skirted in front of him like a stray ice cube on a kitchen floor. Had he booted it out from under a settled pile of leaves? Or had it waited for him deep in the grass of Mrs. Gaworski's yard and scooted itself out onto the sidewalk?

He would have kept walking since the tape was probably unplayable, but he noticed the odd leathery exterior. It was sort of shiny, and for some reason, he thought it would be warm to the touch and soft, too. Which was crazy since it was a piece of plastic.

But he had to see what it felt like. In less than two seconds, he had processed all that, and the next thing he knew, he had scooped it up, never missing a beat kicking up the next mound of leaves.

The cushiony feel reminded him of his little sister Amy's coin purse, the one he always snatched quarters from. The cassette felt good in his hand, like it belonged there in the same way the right grip on a bat feels. Snug and secure and ready to rock.

Other than the letter A on one side and B on the other, no further information was on the cassette. No band name or song titles and no manufacturing logos, not even little tick marks that indicated how much tape was wound on the spools. Tape length was measured in minutes of total playing time, and most of the cassettes Sam had were C46, which meant twenty-three minutes per side. He had no idea how much time was on that cassette or the content, but how cool if it were a demo tape from a hot new band. That would be very, very cool.

He had mercy on the last few piles of leaves. Instead of crunching and kicking them, he bypassed them and ran the remaining three blocks home to listen to the tape.

***

Sam slammed the door to his room after saying "hi, ya" to his mom in the kitchen and smacking Amy's hair when he hurried by. He popped open his Craig tape recorder, removed the Foghat cassette, and put it back in its case.

After examining the mystery tape to confirm it wasn't loose (which would cause the wheels in the Craig machine to eat it) or wrinkled (which the wheels would cause further damage to), he snapped the cassette into the machine to play side A first. He closed the lid and pressed rewind.

The motor engaged, and after a moment, the machine clicked off. Typically that meant the tape was fully rewound. But Sam had seen a lot of tape silhouetted on the right side. It needed to be rewound, and all that tape should be rushing to the left so the tape could play from the beginning, pulling left to right.

He popped it out and examined it. Side A was more than halfway played, so he tapped the cassette gently on his desk to free up the tape in case it was stuck. Back in the Craig, he hit rewind again, but the machine clicked off.

"Okay, have it your way," he muttered and pushed the play button. He watched through the rectangular peephole as the tape pulled left to right. A tiny squeal of the motor sounded but nothing else. He inched up the volume.

After a few more seconds of silence, a male voice, sounding like a math or science or social studies teacher, said: "Today is Thursday, September 4, 1975. The next word is Sacramento."

Then the tape recorder clicked off.

Had Sam heard correctly? When he tried to rewind the tape, it refused. He pushed the forward button, too, but the tape had moved all it was going to. He removed the cassette and tried to gently advance the tape using a pencil inserted in the wheel sprocket but no movement. He didn't want to force it since it might break the tape. Unsure what to do next, he set it on his desk.

He couldn't believe what he had heard. The voice on the tape had said today's date. Which was impossible unless it was a big joke, but why would anyone bother? And he'd been alone when he found the tape; no one had been around to plant it for him to find. And the next word being Sacramento. What did that mean? He'd been to his state's capital many times since it was less than ten miles away. Why would that be "the next word," and what did that even mean?

Sam examined the cassette but discovered nothing new. It still had a warm, comfortable feel to it and an ever-so-slight give to the plastic, almost pliable like it had gently melted. He had a desire to taste it, give it a lick, but that was gross. As to the contents of the tape, it had spoken, and that was that. He tried again to get the machine to advance the tape, but it was a no go.

And then his mom called him for dinner. Her timing was perfect, for he was suddenly starving and didn't want to be alone in his room anymore.

***

After dinner, Sam rushed to finish his homework and have it checked by his parents so he could watch *Welcome Back, Kotter*, his favorite show and the funniest one broadcast on Thursday nights. They were lucky to have two TVs since his parents loved *The Waltons*, which was on at the same time.

When *Kotter* was over, he turned off the TV and made a point of stomping up the stairs to annoy his dad.

"Don't run up the stairs!" his father shouted from the den. "How many times do I have to tell you?"

When Sam passed Amy's room, he grabbed the door handle and pulled it closed with a loud slam to startle her. She was only eight and screamed and cried whenever he tortured her; it was so easy.

"Mom!" she shrieked from behind the door.

Once Sam was in his room, he sat down in front of the tape recorder. With side A set, Sam pushed the play button. The machine clicked off. He sighed and swore. Since the cassette wouldn't play, he removed it from the machine. He held it with one hand on top and one on the bottom. By cupping it, he could more intensely experience the strange warmth. And he also found the leathery exterior pleasing to his touch. The desire to taste it, to put it into his mouth again overwhelmed him, but he shooed it away. That wouldn't be right. Not yet.

He sat until he heard his dad's heavy footsteps on the stairs.

"Past your bedtime, Sam."

It was close to 11 p.m. Startled, Sam quickly yelled out okay, trying to keep his voice casual. His chest had filled up with a nest of busy squirrels.

More than two hours had passed.

Have I just been sitting here? Sam, though frightened, was also strangely thrilled by the idea. Perhaps he had dozed off for a couple hours, but that would have been weird since he'd never fallen asleep in his desk chair.

His hands remained clasped around the cassette tape the entire time. He examined his palms, expecting them to be embedded with the image of what he had been holding, but they looked the same as always. He was tempted to lick his hands. He felt woozy like he was surfacing from a dream, struggling to rejoin the wakened world.

He placed the cassette on his desk. When he stopped holding it, his senses snapped back into place. Touching the tape made him light-headed and slightly drunk like when he'd been at his buddy

Darrell's pool party the previous summer and had rapidly finished off three beers.

Later in bed, the thought came to him that the tape had probably been created to help someone learn English. Basic phrases were said, such as the month and day of the week and certain words to help with pronunciation. He wasn't fully sold on the idea, but he needed to sleep and that solution worked like a round peg that slipped neatly into its corresponding hole.

For the last minutes of Thursday, September 4, the fragile answer was solid enough to allow him to fall asleep.

***

It happened in Sacramento the next morning, Friday, September 5, but Sam didn't hear about it until lunchtime.

He and his buddies gathered on the front lawn of school, trading the contents of lunch bags their mothers had packed and debating which KISS album was better, *Hotter than Hell* or *Dressed to Kill*. In the midst of the heated discussion, Mr. Waxman strode past them, stone-faced, with his secretary looking shaken and hurrying to keep pace. Everyone on the front lawn watched with great puzzlement and curiosity. Mr. Waxman was a beloved principal and went out of his way to joke and interact with the students. The idea that he would walk past so many of them—more than fifty—without acknowledging anyone was out of character.

"I wonder what's up," Darrell said before taking a huge bite of an apple.

"He looks really upset," Ted added, tearing into a two-pack of Twinkies.

Sam hadn't told anyone about the cassette tape. He didn't know what to say about it, and no one would understand why he was so drawn to it. It was like being the only one who knew a great event was about to happen: if you told, it wouldn't be quite so majestic. That morning when he woke up, his first thought was a compulsion to hold the cassette for as long as he could before his mom called him for breakfast. Cuddling it in those quiet morning minutes was like sharing a powerful secret with your best friend.

After lunch, when they were back in class, Miss Anderson told them about the assassination attempt on President Gerald Ford. One of the teachers had heard about it on the radio, and Mr. Simmons, the art teacher and audiovisual instructor, had a TV in his classroom, so he passed along updates to the teaching staff.

175

"What we know is that the President is all right," Miss Anderson said. "It happened this morning around 10 a.m. in Sacramento. A former follower of Charles Manson tried to shoot the President while he was in Capitol Park. They caught the woman, and the President is fine."

While everyone in the class asked questions and talked about Charles Manson, the only thing Sam thought was that it had happened in Sacramento.

The next word is Sacramento.

***

The TV was on when Sam got home that Friday afternoon, turned to a special report on CBS about the assassination attempt. His mom watched it intently and barely noticed he was home. But when he tried to slip by and hurry upstairs, she grabbed him for an especially long and intense hug. Then she kissed him on the cheek and warned him not to torment his sister.

Amy was on the floor, playing with her dolls, and ignoring his mother's request, he grabbed one by the hair, swung it into the air, and watched it drop. "Look! She can fly! Oh, wait. No, she can't."

Amy screamed, "Mom!"

"Both of you be quiet," Sam's mother said.

Once in his room, Sam closed the door. He had those squirrels in his chest again, and they were having a dance party. Had Sacramento been a coincidence? Or had the voice on the tape really predicted it?

He looked at the tape machine, and as casually as possible, walked over and pushed the play button.

"Today is Friday, September 5, 1975. The next word is yellow."

It clicked off.

The voice was the same person, a professional actor or teacher who talked clearly and distinctly. And once again, he had said the current date and announced the next word.

Yellow.

Sam knew better, but he had to try. He pushed the rewind and play and fast-forward buttons, but the tape refused to budge. The same happened when he flipped it over to side B.

If side A told the future, would side B tell the past? But since the tape seemed to be done for the day, he wouldn't know until the next time it chose to be activated. And when would that be? Since the voice was very specific about the date, maybe it would only do it once a day?

176

"Which means it won't play again until after midnight," Sam mumbled as he fondled the cassette.

He didn't remember taking it from the machine, but it felt so good to hold and gently squeeze and allow its warmth to soothe and relax him. He licked it, and he savored the texture and taste, like lapping sugar off a piece of Bazooka bubblegum before chewing it.

"Sam! Are you up there? It's time to set the table for dinner." His mother hollered as if he were deaf.

"I'll be down in a minute." It was after 6 p.m. Once again, he'd lost track of time, had simply drifted away. He always set the table at six, his dad was home by six-fifteen, and dinner was at six-thirty. House rules. Sam knew that. Where had the last ninety minutes disappeared?

He put the cassette into the tape recorder and pushed play. Nothing. He took it out and turned it over to side B. Again, nothing happened after he pushed the play button, but he left side B in place, ready to play. He wanted to test his theory to hear what the voice said, whether side B was about the past and side A the future.

Sam set his alarm for midnight and hurried downstairs to set the table.

***

The alarm barely rang before Sam silenced it. He had had a hard time falling asleep, too excited to see if his hypothesis was true. He turned on his desk lamp and pushed play. The B side did not move, and the machine clicked off. He flipped over the cassette and pushed play.

"Today is Saturday, September 6, 1975. The next word is kite."

The machine clicked off.

"Yes!" Sam hissed. He had been right, or at least, half-right. The tape only played the message once a day, and the new message couldn't be accessed until after midnight. And the B side didn't play at all. The cassette was only about the future—one day at a time and one word for each day.

The next word is kite.

Sam climbed back into bed. It was 12:07 a.m. The day was Saturday, and the word for that day was yellow. The following day would be Sunday, and that day's word would be kite.

Something with yellow will occur on Saturday, he thought as he dropped like a stone into a deep sleep.

He woke two hours later, having difficulty breathing, his tongue thick and his throat blocked. He gasped, unable to inhale. He was choking on something. He reached into his mouth and found the cassette tape. Its smooth, supple exterior hadn't scratched his mouth or lips since it had a comfortable flexibility about it. As Sam felt around its contours, he realized it had become formfitting, like the retainer his friend Ted wore or his grandpa's dentures.

Once Sam realized the cause of his breathing difficulty, he stopped gagging and struggling. He relaxed and fell back to sleep, his breathing adapted to the foreign object that filled the space between his teeth.

***

"Sam, we have some bad news," his mom told him Saturday morning at breakfast. "Mrs. Gaworski is dead."

"What?" Sam had passed her house ever since he had been old enough to walk around the neighborhood alone. She had let him use her bathroom once when he was in dire need, could be counted on to hand out full-size candy bars at Halloween, and was always friendly to him and his friends when they saw her around town.

"It happened early this morning," his dad said.

The best breakfast of the week was on Saturdays, when the family sat at the table in relaxed mode. His mother made pancakes or waffles along with bacon and eggs. Sundays were rushed because of church at ten o'clock. During the week, his dad left early due to his commute, and breakfast was a free-for-all with Cap'n Crunch or another cartoon cereal and a banana when the weather was warm, and Malt-O-Meal and toast during colder weather.

"When I got the paper this morning, Murphy next door had just heard the news and told me," his dad continued.

"What happened to her?" Sam asked.

"She was up early and dragging her trash cans to the curb. A car came out of nowhere and jumped the curb and ran over her and then sped off."

"They don't know who did it?" For some reason, Sam pictured a rolling pin passing back and forth over Mrs. Gaworski, ensuring she was dead. But that couldn't be right.

"Nope. Murphy told me all he heard was that it was a yellow Mustang. The police are out now trying to find it."

"She was a sweet lady," Sam's mom said sadly, refilling hers and her husband's coffee cups.

"You know, she only lived a few blocks away," his dad said, "so you be careful when you're out there screwing around, okay? You never know when some crazy driver will lose control. Hear me?"

Sam nodded, thinking only of the yellow Mustang that he doubted the police would ever find.

***

Back in his room, he sat on the bed. What should he do? If he told anyone about the tape, they wouldn't believe him. No evidence existed; he couldn't play the messages back after they had been heard once. And they changed every day.

Yellow was Saturday. Tomorrow is kite.

If the words weren't so common or vague, maybe he could do something or warn someone. Why did the cassette do what it did? Why had he found it, and what was he supposed to do about events the voice foretold?

"Sam? What are you doing up there? It's a nice day. Why don't you call your friends and go out?"

His mom's voice startled him. He had been sucking on the cassette tape, and when he looked at the clock, he saw it was 11:37 a.m. When had they finished breakfast? His dad had left to do errands, and Sam had gone up to his room. Maybe it had been around 10 a.m. Another ninety minutes had been lost. He couldn't speak with the tape in his mouth, and it was too delicious to remove.

After a few seconds, his mom called out again. "Sam?"

Reluctantly, he removed the cassette from his mouth and replied, "Yeah, I heard you."

***

Sam spent the afternoon at Florin Mall, kicking around with the guys. Before he left home, he had slipped the cassette into his pocket. He didn't know why. It seemed like the right thing to do, and no one noticed it was there. All afternoon, he took great comfort at having it with him. Of course, he'd rather have it in his mouth, but no one would understand that.

He went to bed around eleven-thirty. He didn't set the alarm for midnight. He didn't want to hear the voice state tomorrow's date or announce the next word.

***

Sunday morning Sam woke with a strange taste in his mouth. He had been sucking and gnawing and licking at the cassette as if it were an all-day sucker, but it never changed shape or diminished in size. While in his mouth, it was flavorless, but he did have an overall

179

sense of wellbeing, an assurance that everything would be all right. But an hour or so later, after he had removed it, his mouth had a sickly sour aftertaste that no brushing, flossing, or mouthwash could expel. The only way to remove the taste was to suck on the cassette again.

After church, he hurried upstairs to change clothes. He took the cassette from his pocket and placed it back in his mouth. It had turned into a baby's pacifier and made him feel calm and secure.

He glanced out the open window at the busy cul-de-sac. People washed cars and mowed lawns. Children ran about, playing tag, walking dogs.

The kite was such a familiar shape that Sam's reaction to it surprised him. He didn't recall ever gasping at one previously, but when the flying toy tapped at his window, he did just that.

The instant the kite hit his window, he realized it was new. The material was clean and retained its bold colors—blue and white with a cobalt tail—and the string looked solid.

Looking down, he saw a young girl, about Amy's age, pulling the string. The kite bounced and soared and dipped, but the girl had solid control and ran backward to keep it aloft. Adults and children watched the aerodynamics. Dogs barked, obviously wanting to join in the fun.

Maxine, a two-foot tall Airedale, bounded toward the girl and the kite. The girl had just stepped off the Jackson's lawn and on the pavement when she tripped over Maxine and cracked her head on the concrete.

The entire street froze.

Blood exploded from the back of the girl's head and gushed onto the sidewalk. The river of blood pumped to the curb and down the rivet drain. The kite, released from its anchor—the little girl— soared, gathering the string the child had once held, slurping it up into its tail like a vacuum cleaner cord recoiling into the machine. And then the kite rose higher and higher into the bright blue sky and almost immediately vanished.

Just like the yellow Mustang, Sam thought.

Suddenly, the street came alive from every side, and people rushed to surround the dead girl. Sam turned away from the window. In his hand, the cassette gave him solace. He placed it in his mouth and lay down on his bed.

Sacramento. Ten miles away.

Yellow. Three blocks away.

Kite. Outside his window.

Whatever it was, it was getting closer.

***

Sunday night, Sam set the alarm for midnight. He wanted to hear Monday's word. If it was getting closer to him, maybe he could figure out how to prevent the next tragedy. Perhaps the word wouldn't be so vague.

Sam didn't need the alarm; he couldn't sleep. When the clock showed midnight and that Monday morning had arrived, he took the cassette out of his mouth. It was never soggy or slimy with saliva; it was as if it sucked and extracted moisture out of him.

He inserted side A into the machine, closed the lid, and pushed play.

"Today is Monday, September 8. The next word is—"

The machine clicked off.

Sam turned on his desk lamp and popped out the tape. It was at the end of side A. Though he had never been able to rewind it, it had worked its way to the end. He turned it over and put side B facing up into the machine. He pushed play.

The machine hesitated and then clicked off.

It was pointless to keep trying. Both sides of the tape would be stubbornly silent.

There wouldn't be another word for twenty-four hours.

He climbed back into bed. He opened his mouth, and the cassette filled it.

***

Monday night Sam set the alarm again. When he awoke at midnight and played side B of the tape, nothing happened. No voice announced the date or the next word. No amount of tapping the cassette or twisting the sprockets advanced the tape.

For some reason, the cassette had gone silent.

***

On Wednesday morning September 10, 1975, Sam opened his eyes, awake before his mother called him, which was a first. He had slept well.

Something nagged at him about the importance of September 10, but he couldn't recall the source of the anticipation. It couldn't be that crucial or he would have remembered. He felt warm, calm, serene. Everything would be fine.

Then he remembered why September 10 was important. The KISS album was available, and his friends would head to the Music Plus record store after school to buy it. He'd tag along, but it didn't matter to him anymore.

He was preoccupied with choosing the next word. It had to be the right one for the occasion.

Maybe the next word would be kiss.

Sam smiled and hurried down the stairs for breakfast.

MIDNIGHT MAN

Kevin M. Folliard

*On an oppressively hot evening,
thirteen-year-old José is desperate
for a wink of sleep, but he'll fight to stay awake once the sinister
Sandman arrives to deliver gray smoke-filled nightmares.*

José couldn't sleep. He seldom could on smoldering nights in July with no air conditioning. The Nevada heat was worse than Chicago. Like everything in Sun Valley.

After his parents announced they were moving, José's mother had promised: "You'll love Nevada. It's hot, but it's *dry* heat, so it's not *that* bad." José still waited for the part that wasn't *that* bad.

His father had secured a job managing a casino buffet in Reno. Every night, he came home reeking of shrimp and collapsed on the couch with a beer. After dinner, he passed out listening to talk radio.

His mother cleaned rooms at the same hotel. She was up at 4:00 a.m. every day and down for the count by 9:00 p.m.

When José couldn't sleep, he watched movies since they had no cable or internet. His mom told him it would be a while before they caught up enough to afford those things. But his dad had a collection of DVDs. In the few weeks they'd been in Nevada, José had watched all of them. He'd watched *Terminator, Scream,* and *Back to the Future* several times. He could recite them.

He also borrowed novels and comic book collections from the Sun Valley Library. But after a certain hour, his mind grew frustrated with printed words, and all he could do was sit and sweat. His eight-by-ten-foot bedroom was practically a closet. Even those nights when it cooled down, the tiny space stored heat like an oven.

For the first few weeks, José tried not to complain. He had nothing to wake up for anyway. But seventh grade started soon. He would be the new kid at a new school. He didn't want to be the kid passing out at his desk from exhaustion.

The day before school started, he nodded off in a chair by the library reference desk. A pleasant chill swirled down from the air conditioning vent above. He closed his eyes, and his body relaxed for the first time since they'd arrived in Sun Valley.

"Hey!" A surly librarian roused him by the shoulder. She narrowed her eyes. "This is a library, not a motel. Out with you!"

José stewed all the way home. He was sick of not sleeping. Sick of Sun Valley. The next day, he would be in a classroom full of strangers while all his friends back home started junior high together. The Nevada sun blazed and scorched his skin. *Is it too much to ask to cool off? Just for one night?*

When his parents got home, he pleaded with them. "Everyone has air out here. It's normal. You need it."

José's father collapsed on the couch. "We need food, clothes, and a roof. That's it." He stretched and reached for his portable radio.

"Every window on every unit on every building down our street has an air conditioner," José insisted. "It's survival. We can get a used one online. It won't be that much."

"We'll get one," his mother assured him, "once we catch up."

"We never catch up," he muttered.

"Moving is expensive. We're building a new life."

"I can't sleep at night."

At José's words, his father pried himself off the couch. "Work harder. Get a job. Work all day long and you'll sleep." He tuned the radio to the evening news, lay back, and within a minute, he snored.

José couldn't argue. Regardless of temperatures in the upper 90s, his parents always slept. They were always exhausted.

That night, before his mother went to bed, she came into José's room and sat with him. "Are you ready for school tomorrow?"

He shrugged.

"You're friendly and handsome. Just be yourself." She smiled.

He forced a smile.

"Here." She placed a cold gray coin in his hand. A nickel.

"What am I supposed to buy with five cents?"

"Whenever my sisters and I were restless, Abuela would place a nickel for each of us on the windowsill. She said the Sandman would put us to sleep and collect the money. The next morning, the money would be gone."

"Of course," José said. "She put it back in her purse after you fell asleep."

His mother laughed. "Perhaps. But whatever happened, we always fell asleep." On the way out, she tapped the windowsill. "A little change can't hurt you. Buenas noches, mi hijo."

After his mother shut the door, he got up and stuck his head out the window. The sun had set hours previously, and it still hadn't cooled off. Not even one degree.

He set the nickel on the windowsill. "If you can make me sleep, Mr. Sandman, I'll give you more than five cents."

As the night wore on, the tiny room grew hotter. Sweat trickled down José's forehead. He set his *Ghost Rider* comic book on the cardboard box that served as his nightstand and flapped his shirt.

He wiped his forehead with crumpled bed sheets. *It shouldn't be this hot this late at night!* Back home, summers were hot and muggy. Chicago heat didn't last this long. It cooled off. It rained.

Across the room, his black backpack hung on the closet knob. The digital clock burned 11:59.

He crossed to the second-storey window and stuck his head through. Hot air hugged the building, but if he stretched his neck out, he felt the faintest chill. Only enough to tease him. Not enough to cool off. His bedroom faced the alley and the drab stucco exterior of the next building.

He glared down at the open dumpster, bloated with trash bags and a torn armchair. *There is nothing to see from this window when I can't sleep, when it's ninety-nine freakin' degrees. Nothing but garbage.*

"Nevada is beautiful," his mother had promised as they drove though endless gray cornfields of the Midwest. "There are lakes and deserts, and stars at night."

José imagined what had to be beyond the building and all the ones after it. Mountains, lakes, desert, and a dark sea of twinkling white stars. All the stuff he couldn't touch or see. He glared at the nickel on the windowsill, pinched his fingers together, and flicked it into the alley. The coin banked off the other building and hit the concrete below with a faint *clink*.

"You can keep your nickel, Mr. Sandman. Nothing could help me sleep in this dump anyway."

A distant sound caught José's ears: music.

He poked his head farther out the window. Someone whistled a happy tune. He watched the sidewalk at the end of the alley. The music sharpened, and José's heart jumped when he recognized it. The 1950s song from *Back to the Future*: "Mr. Sandman."

A tall, gray figure in a long coat and fedora strode past the alley between the buildings.

How can anyone wear a coat in this weather? José wondered. His stomach tensed when the man stopped whistling and turned in his direction.

The light across the street silhouetted the man's coat and hat, but José saw an orange dot the man brought to his lips. He puffed a cigarette.

José pulled his head back inside. He had the distinct feeling he'd been noticed. But so what? It wasn't a crime to stick your head out a window and look around. *But who walks around in ninety-degree weather, in the middle of the night, wearing a coat? Nobody good. Nothing good.*

He stared down at the alley for a moment. Everything was silent again.

Then the whistling started back up. Louder.

He clutched the windowsill. His heart pounded in anticipation of that moment when the shadowy figure would enter into view, holding his fiery dot.

The man's ashen figure slipped past the window. The glowing dot hovered at his side. He continued to whistle. High sharp notes echoed between the buildings.

José inched forward to get a better look.

The man stooped and picked up something. He tilted his head back, stared at José, and held the discarded nickel between his thumb and pointer finger.

They locked eyes. José's bones chilled. He knew immediately it was bad to be seen by that man.

It wasn't that the man was a stranger creeping around in the middle of the night. Or the fact he might be concealing something dangerous beneath his inappropriately long coat. It was those sickly tones of gray. The man looked like a character who had walked out of one of his dad's old black and white movies. His hands and face had a strange smoky quality as if the man wasn't flesh, just a mass of dust that could be swept away by the breeze.

The man's smile accommodated too many teeth for a normal person's mouth, and the irises of his eyes burned like rings of lava.

The Sandman whistled the tune of "Mr. Sandman" and then took a long drag of his cigarette. He didn't exhale, but smoke seeped from his pores. Without breaking eye contact, he flicked the butt behind him into the overstuffed dumpster. Orange sparks bounced against the old green armchair.

The man whistled again.

José broke away. He backed against the bed and shuddered. His heart pounded. *That wasn't real. I'm just tired. Wait five minutes, look again, and he'll be gone.*

José waited on edge for the red digits to flick from 12:04 to 12:05 to 12:06, 7, and 8, and finally 12:09. He crawled back to the window, slowly raised his head, and inched his gaze past the ledge.

The man's eyes burned back. His toothy smile widened. He raised an ashy hand and waved. Gray vapors seeped between his fingers.

"Go away," José whispered.

The man laughed in response. A scratchy, smoke-filled laugh. Dust puffed from his hat. He clenched his fist and raised it above his head. Then he pantomimed a pounding motion. His fist collided with an invisible barrier, and José's bedroom door banged.

José spun in surprise. "Who's there?" But he knew who it was. He glanced back out the window.

The man pounded the air three times. José's door thudded: *Bang! Bang! Bang!*

"Please go away."

The man pounded: *Bang! Bang! Bang!*

"Go away!" José shouted.

Bang! Bang! Bang! On the third bang, the man exploded into a cloud of dust and vanished from the alley.

The doorknob jiggled. José rushed to the door and locked it. *Bang!* The door held, but the walls rattled.

Bang! Dust puffed beneath the crack under the door. *Bang!* Gray vapors seeped through the sides with each impact. *Bang! Bang! Bang!*

José yelled for help.

Bang! Bang! Bang!

The gray vapors reeked of gasoline fumes and stale tobacco. He screamed for his parents again. How could they not be hearing this? *Because the Sandman had already put them to sleep.*

Bang! Bang! Bang! More dust seeped beneath the door.

José tore the sheets off his bed and dove for the floor. He stuffed the sheets into the openings. *Bang! Bang! Bang!* He folded the bedding up the sides of the doorframe, too, filling as much space as he could with fabric. *Bang!* The dust stopped seeping through. *Bang!* Only a few speckles of gray vapor wafted over the top of the door. *Bang!*

Everything was silent. He caught his breath. He stared long and hard at the door and had a sudden and terrifying thought: *The window is open!*

He scrambled to his feet and raced to the wall. He yanked the brass handles, but the window stuck in the warped frame. He jerked and wiggled the window side-to-side until it moved. Inch-by-inch the window lurched until it sealed with a thud. He locked it and sighed with relief.

José turned his attention back to the door, in time to find a steady stream of smoky dust pouring from the vent in the ceiling. It spilled onto the floor, piling higher and higher. The dust crackled and hardened into legs and the billowing flaps of a crusty, gray coat. Ashy hands and arms caked upward. The man's torso filled out. His head formed like smoke in an upside-down jar. Plumes of dust arose from his feet and twisted into his hat.

The man's toothy smile widened into place. Rings of fire lit his eyes. He whistled the tune of "Mr. Sandman" again.

"Please," José whispered. "Please go away." He backed against the wall.

The man crossed the room in three strides. He didn't walk around José's bed; he ghosted through it. His legs clouded under the mattress and rejoined his torso on the other side.

"Leave me alone," José begged. "Please."

The Sandman loomed over José and laughed, low and dark. His eyes burned.

"What do you want from me?"

He tipped his hat. "You know what I want." His voice rumbled like a volcano. He laughed harder. Smoke snaked between his pointy teeth. "Go to sleep, kid."

He removed his fedora and produced the nickel in his right hand. He dropped the coin in his hat, and a pillar of smoke fired into the air. The Sandman blew the thick, gray cloud into José's face.

José's lungs filled with burning sulfur. He coughed, gagged, and wheezed.

The Sandman's laugh echoed. His eyes burned away. His body dissipated into smoke.

The room wasn't hot anymore. It was ice cold. And gray.

Everything was gray.

***

The next morning, José awoke on the floor. His sheets were shoved under the door. He couldn't remember why exactly he had shut the window, and his room smoldered like a furnace.

But even though his shirt was drenched in sweat, deep inside he had a strange icy sensation. He struggled to remember a deep, cold nightmare. But he had no idea what it had been about.

His father, on his way to work, dropped José off at his new school. The front doors were locked, so he waited on the steps. It was hours before the other kids would arrive, too early for teachers even. And though the rising sun blazed over distant orange cliffs, the chill from his nightmare still hadn't left his bones.

Eventually, the doors opened from the inside. A janitor in a gray jumpsuit motioned for José to come in. "Bright and early, huh?"

José huffed up the stairs. Sunlight seared his vision, blocking the man's face. But when José reached the door, he froze.

The janitor's hair hung past his eyes in gray clumps. His skin was pallid. Colorless. Beyond him, the hallways swelled with shadows.

"If I had a nickel for every kid waiting on these steps, I could quit my night job." The janitor smiled, showing small pointy teeth. His irises burned crimson.

ABOUT THE AUTHORS

Chantal Boudreau

Chantal, an accountant by day and an author/illustrator during evenings and weekends, lives by the ocean in beautiful Nova Scotia, Canada, with her husband and two children. She writes and illustrates horror, sci-fi, steampunk, and fantasy and has had several of her stories published in a variety of anthologies, online journals, and magazines. Her novels have included *Fervor*, a dystopian series, and *Masters & Renegades*, a fantasy series.
http://chantellyb.wordpress.com

Chiara De Giorgi

Chiara was born in Italy and has been living in Germany for the past ten years. She is a reader, a writer, and a story-teller. She loves reading any kinds of books in any of the languages she knows and has an inclination toward novels. She has two children: a great deal of her experience in smart storytelling is thanks to them. Writing is a lifetime hobby. She prefers short stories but would like to attempt something longer in the future. She has published many short stories on the internet and three books for children in Italy. She also leads readings and workshops based on her books, both in Italy and in Germany. Basically, she loves stories to read, invent, write, tell, or talk about!
http://chiaradegiorgi.blogspot.de/

Kevin M. Folliard

Kevin is a Chicagoland fiction writer with a degree in English and creative writing from the University of Illinois in Urbana Champaign. His published fiction includes scary story collections *Christmas Terror Tales* and *Valentine Terror Tales*, and adventure novels for twelve and up, such as *Jake Carter & the Nightmare Gallery, Violet Black & the Curse of Camp Coldwater, and Jimmy Chimaera & the Temple of Champions*. Folliard's work has been collected in *Sanitarium Magazine*, as well as anthologies by Nosetouch Press and Black Bed Sheet Books.

He has also developed films and web series for the Champaign based studio Neon Harbor, including the acclaimed videogame parody "Press Start" series.
www.KevinFolliard.com.

Heron Greenesmith

Heron lives in Somerville, MA, with her family and their cat. She is a policy attorney for LGBT people by day and loves to read and write spooky stories.

Alan Kemister

Alan Kemister is the pen name of a retired scientist living in Halifax, Nova Scotia, who is experimenting with writing fiction. Alan has a keen interest in environmental science and dabbled in yachting and golf before turning to creative writing. He is interested in both science fiction/dystopia and mystery genres. He is the author of seven published short stories and one poem. Alan is currently working on a mystery novel about a detective in a fictional town on Nova Scotia's South Shore.
alkemi47.blogspot.com.

S.L. Kerns

S.L. Kerns may have southern roots grounded in Kentucky, but he's branched out to a life in Asia. He spent nearly six years lost in Bangkok before moving to his current home in Japan. He loves soaking in words of wisdom from being an avid reader and a good listener. He also loves bodybuilding and likes to think of himself as one of the physically strongest prose writers since Yukio Mishima. He teaches English and has recently begun writing, using his surplus of wild experiences to fuel his stories. His work has been published or is forthcoming online in *Flash Fiction Magazine, 101 Words, Silver Birch Press, Visual Verse, Degenerate Literature, Funny in Five Hundred,* and *Eastlit,* and in paperback in *Kill Those Damn Cats: Lovecraftian Anthology, Anonymous Anthology,* and *47-16: A Collection of Poetry and Fiction Inspired by David Bowie Volume I and II*. He also blogs for Muay Thai Lab.
www.slkerns.wordpress.com

Matthew D. Laing

Matthew writes from Ottawa, Canada. So far he has had two short stories published with the *Corvus Review* and *Danse Macabre* and poetry published with *The Literary Yard, Bewildering Stories,* and *Three Drops from a Cauldron.*

Rod Martinez

Rod was born and raised in Tampa, Florida, and was attracted to words at an early age. His first book, *The Boy Who Liked to Read,* was created in grade school. His teacher kept it. Eventually he discovered comic books, but his high school English teacher told him to try short story writing. He wrote a middle grade adventure *The Juniors* that was picked up by a publisher, and the rest, as they say, is history.
http://rodmartinez.us
http://qire24.wix.com/the-juniors

Stephen Millard

Stephen Millard is a writer of prose, poetry, and music who was born in the heartland and now lives in the San Bernardino mountains of California.

Val Muller

Val Muller is the author of the young adult novel *The Scarred Letter* and the kidlit mystery series *Corgi Capers*. When she isn't writing or chasing her two- and four-legged kids, she's busy teaching and editing. She grew up in haunted New England and has been working her way south ever since.
www.ValMuller.com
www.CorgiCapers.com.

A.W. Powers

A.W. Powers is a fan of all things mysterious and crawly. A careful observer and listener, he writes mystery and horror fiction while safely entrenched in his suburban Minneapolis, Minnesota, home. Someday soon he'll do something he considers insanely scary—open a website and join social media.

Kathy Price

Born and raised in a conservative, small town in western Pennsylvania, Kathy happily adjusted to the culture shock of her family's move to Southern California when she was fourteen. After graduating in 1975 from California State Polytechnic University, Pomona campus, Kathy married her landlord, and they returned to the East Coast. With the exception of a five-year stint in Ohio, she spent most of her working career as a histotechnologist at the Smithsonian Institution in Washington, D.C. Kathy considers herself fortunate to have had the opportunity to travel extensively over the years and to have met some of the most interesting people in the world. Now widowed and retired, she is currently living with her two Scottish terriers just off the beach in Southern Baja California, Mexico.

Kristin Roahrig

Kristin's short stories and poetry have appeared in various publications. She is also the author of several plays and lives in Indiana.

Tom Robson

Tom started to write in his forties when his target audiences were the elementary students he taught. Flushed with two successes in Atlantic writing contests, he continued this into retirement. Writing was a hobby until he had three ghost stories published in *Out of the Mist*, an anthology compiled by the Evergreen Writers Group. His adaptation into a performance piece of Catherine Scholes' book *Peace Begins with You* is in *The Peaceful School: Models That Work*, by Hetty Van Gurp.

A collection of his stories and poems written over a thirty-year period have been assembled into *Written While I Still Remember, A Patchwork Memoir*, published in 2014 by Mackenzie Publishing.

Tom enjoys writing short stories and journals of his travels. He occasionally tries to be poetic. He wants to gather his poems from his computer for publication, which will wait until he proves it is possible for a man in his eightieth year to write a romantic novel. *We'll Have to Wait and See* is in the works. A lifelong tendency toward procrastination must be overcome before this book can reach a publisher. Tom was born a proud Yorkshireman and enjoyed youth in the New Forest where he first became a teacher. He came to Canada in 1971. He now lives with his wife in Dartmouth, Nova Scotia.

https://robsonswritings.wordpress.com/

Katherine Sanger

Katherine was a Jersey Girl before getting smart and moving to Texas. She's been published in various e-zines and print, including *Baen's Universe, Black Chaos, Wandering Weeds, Spacesports & Spidersilk, Black Petals, Star*Line, Anotherealm, Lost in the Dark, Bewildering Stories, Aphelion,* and *RevolutionSF,* and edited *From the Asylum,* an e-zine of fiction and poetry, and *Serial Flasher,* a flash fiction e-zine. She's a member of HWA and SFWA. She taught

English for over ten years at various online and local community and technical colleges.
http://www.fromtheasylum.com
https://www.facebook.com/katherine.sanger.5
twitter @KatherineSanger.

A.P. Sessler

A resident of North Carolina's Outer Banks, A.P. Sessler frequents an alternate universe not too different from your own, where he searches for that unique element that twists the everyday commonplace into the weird. When he's not writing fiction, he composes music, dabbles in animation, and muses about theology and mind-hacking, all while watching way too many online movies.
His short stories have appeared in audio podcasts such as Manor House and Human Echoes as well as print anthologies such as *Now Playing in Theater B, Ain't Superstitious*, and *Hides the Dark Tower*. His short, "Beneath the Bell Bay Light," was recently nominated for the Pushcart Prize.
https://www.goodreads.com/author/show/6917738.A_P_
Sessler
https://twitter.com/APSessler
https://www.facebook.com/AP-Sessler-
259899174205799/timeline/

E.F. Schraeder

Schraeder's creative work has appeared in *Dark Moon Digest, Carnival of the Damned, Voluted Tales, Between the Cracks, Flashes in the Dark, Haz Mat Review, Animalia, Four Chambers*, and other journals and anthologies. Author of a poetry chapbook, *The Hunger Tree*, new work is also forthcoming at *Slink Chunk Press, Far Horizons*, and elsewhere.
www.efschraeder.com.

Paul Stansbury

Paul is a lifelong native of Kentucky. Now retired, he lives in Danville, Kentucky. He frequently reads his work in public. His poetry has appeared in *Kentucky Monthly*. His stories have appeared in the anthologies, *Brief Grislys*, published by Apocryphile Press; *Neo-Legends to Last a Deathtime,* published by KY Story; and *Frightening,* published by SEZ Publishing. His work has also appeared in a variety of on-line publications.

Jeff C. Stevenson

Jeff is an active member of the Horror Writers Association and a professional member of Pen America. His articles, flash fiction, short stories, and novelettes have appeared in *Prism* Magazine (editor's choice), *Classic Rock, Freedom Fiction Journal, 9 Tales Told in the Dark, Flash Fiction Press, Urban Temples of Cthulhu Mythos, Tales at the World's End, Detectives of the Fantastic, Reaping, and Hypnos Magazine.*

His first book, *FORTNEY ROAD: The True Story of Life, Death, and Deception in a Christian Cult,* was published in June 2015 by Freethought House.

"Fortney Road is a unique and compelling true story."—Dean Koontz

"Fascinating and disturbing."—Jonathan Kellerman

"Strongly recommended. Exceptionally well written, organized, and presented." —The Midwest Book Review

Visit *Fortney Road*: https://fortneyroad.com
Purchase *Fortney Road*: http://goo.gl/TU74lw
Author Profile: *http://goo.gl/dWEA8N*

Randy Whittaker

Randy is a guy who writes for fun but is desperately trying to become rich by doing it.

Cassandra Williams

Cassandra, hoping to not be discovered, lives her dream somewhere in a modern cabin in dense woods, where she writes fiction and ponders a different and better world. Six cats, computer, and internet keep her sane.

ABOUT STEVE VERNON

Steve Vernon, Nova Scotia's hardest-working horror writer, has been writing scary stories for over forty years. He writes for kids, for grown-ups, and for every age in between. You might want to try some of his local books published by Nimbus Publishing including *Haunted Harbours: Ghost Stories from Old Nova Scotia* or his young adult novel *Sinking Deeper: Or My Questionable (Possibly Heroic) Decision to Invent a Sea Monster* or his children's picture book *Maritime Monsters.*

Or else you might want to look for his fifty independently released e-books and paperbacks on Amazon including *Sudden Death Overtime—A Tale of Hockey and Vampires* or his fat full-length novel of scarecrow terror *Tatterdemon.*

You can find out more about Steve Vernon at his blog YOURS IN STORYTELLING.

https://stevevernonstoryteller.wordpress.com/

Or you can follow him at Twitter.

https://twitter.com/StephenVernon

***

I've always LOVED flash-fiction. There is something super-cool about telling an entire story in less than two hundred words. It's the same kind of super-cool feeling that gets a fellow into building doll-house furniture or constructing ships in a bottle.

The following story came to me back when I was employed at Swedwood—a long-closed furniture factory once located in the Burnside Industrial Park in Dartmouth, Nova Scotia—working on a factory table saw while I was pushing my four thousandth board of the morning through the whirling blades. I use the story all the time in my high school writing workshops to demonstrate the use of multiple voices in a story.

BEAT WELL

by Steve Vernon

Let's play a trick...
DONTCALLME...
...on old punkinhead.
...THAT!
nyah nyah punkinhead
YOU BROKE IT. YOU BROKE IT.
nyah nyah pun...
I GOT YOU NOW.
Letgoletgoletgo
I'LL SHOW YOU A TRICK, I'll SHOW YOU

***

(I remember poppy, he showed me how, he showed me first. First you slice opent the top. Dig out the pulp, thank god no seeds. Gouge out eyes, nose, and mouth. There. Oh. One more thing. There. Jack o' lanterns.)

***

Old John lived way up on Carpenter's Hill, so it wasn't until morning when they found them propped against old John's freshly whitewashed fence, staring sightlessly down upon the town below. The town where they had lived. The three boys still wore the costumes their folks bought at the five and dime. Shattered upon the ground was the remains of a broken jack-o-lantern. The boys were dead. Hidden within the skull of each boy was a tiny candle, flickering quietly, where once only childish dreams burned. They found old John in the kitchen, making pumpkin pie.

198

SOCIAL MEDIA LINKS

MacKenzie Publishing

MacKenzie Publishing website—
https://mackenziepublishing.wordpress.com/

TWO EYES OPEN Facebook page—
https://www.facebook.com/twoeyesopen/

OUT OF THE CAVE Facebook page—
https://www.facebook.com/Out-of-the-Cave-1668695366743672/

***

If you are in need of editing, formatting, and/or publishing, contact MacKenzie Publishing at writingwicket@gmail.com.

***

If you enjoyed *OUT OF THE CAVE*, please leave a review. Thank you!